LIEUTENANT

RICK SHELLEY

ACE BOOKS, NEW YORK

This is a work of fiction. Names, characters, places, and incidents are either the product of the author's imagination or are used fictitiously, and any resemblance to actual persons, living or dead, business establishments, events, or locales is entirely coincidental.

LIEUTENANT

An Ace Book / published by arrangement with
the author

PRINTING HISTORY
Ace edition / October 1998

The Penguin Putnam Inc. World Wide Web site address is
http://www.penguinputnam.com

Check out the Ace Science Fiction/Fantasy
newsletter, and much more, at Club PPI!

ISBN: 0-441-00568-3

ACE®
Ace Books are published by The Berkley Publishing Group,
a division of Penguin Putnam Inc.,
375 Hudson Street, New York, NY 10014.
ACE and the "A" design are trademarks
belonging to Penguin Putnam Inc.

PRINTED IN THE UNITED STATES OF AMERICA

10 9 8 7 6 5 4

1

The temperature had finally fallen below one hundred degrees Fahrenheit, but the humidity remained near one hundred percent. There was not the slightest breath of wind to bring even modest relief. Lieutenant Lon Nolan had been perspiring heavily, but the sweat could not evaporate to cool him. All it did was soak his clothing and add to his discomfort. Just remaining motionless, resting, was tiring. The stagnant jungle air of New Bali was so thick with moisture that breathing was work. It was almost three o'clock in the morning. Company A, 2nd Battalion, 7th Regiment of the Dirigent Mercenary Corps was ready for action.

Lon lifted the faceplate of his helmet to get a little air. He felt as if he were near suffocation with the visor down—and little better with it raised. After a moment he took the helmet off, then wiped sweat from his face with his sleeve. The action did little good. His sleeve was already damp.

"This is ridiculous, Ivar," he whispered. "You'd think that after two months of this sauna, a man would get used to it."

Platoon Sergeant Ivar Dendrow grunted. "Some things you never get used to, Lieutenant. You just bear it as best you can." He paused, then added, "I'll bet there's not an ounce of body fat left on any of the men." Not that there had been much fat on any of them before they arrived on New Bali—fitness was a way of life for the mercenaries of Dirigent.

"At least we're near the end," Lon said. "If nothing goes wrong in the next few hours, we should be back aboard ship by this time tomorrow." He knew that he was talking more than he should, even though the next few hours should be as simple as a training exercise on Dirigent. The only casualties in his two platoons on New Bali had been heat-related, and all three of those had happened in the first week. Now, although everyone was still uncomfortable, they were sufficiently acclimated to avoid further problems of that nature. The only positive thoughts Lon had of New Bali were that there were no stinging or biting creatures with a taste for human blood. The insects left them alone. There were, apparently, no snakes, and the lizards stuck to native prey—even the large lizard that seemed to be a near relation to Earth's Komodo dragon.

"If nothing goes wrong in the next few hours," Dendrow echoed. He lowered his faceplate just long enough to look at the time on its head-up display. "It's about that time, sir."

Lon suppressed the sigh that wanted to force its way out. It would have been inappropriate. He wiped his face again, using the other sleeve this time, then put his helmet back on. When he spoke to third platoon's sergeant again, it was over the radio channel that connected him with both Dendrow and fourth Platoon Sergeant Weil Jorgen. "Get the men up and ready to go."

New Bali was a relatively old colony world, but it had grown very slowly. After four hundred years, the total population was only three million, widely dispersed among two dozen cities and hundreds of smaller settlements. The impetus for early settlement had been the pharmacological promise of the world. The discovery of thousands of medically useful organic compounds in New Bali's tropical ecosystem had justified the initial colonization. Discovery of accessible lodes of platinum and gold had led to a boom just at the time when medical applications of nanotechnology had reduced, then virtually eliminated, the need for medical drug therapies.

Alpha Company, 2nd Battalion, 7th Regiment, Dirigent Mercenary Corps, was about to find out whether two hundred professional soldiers could stage a successful coup and capture the world's central government and communications facilities.

Singaraja, New Bali's capital and largest city, boasted a hundred thousand inhabitants. Originally a small enclave on the northern edge of the Utan delta from which researchers could stage forays into the jungle, the city had grown mostly northward along the seacoast in a thin strip. Proximity to the ocean mitigated climatic conditions. There could be a twenty-degree difference in temperatures between the coast and a mile inland during the day—and sometimes as much as thirty degrees at night, when the breeze generally came from the southwest.

"Third and fourth platoons ready, Captain," Lon reported as soon as his platoon sergeants had confirmed that fact.

"Right. It'll be a few minutes yet," Matt Orlis, the company commander, replied. "Just keep cool, Nolan. Everything by the numbers."

"Yes, sir." Lon did not worry about the admonition. He was the junior officer not only in Company A, but in the entire regiment. He was used to having officers spell things out in detail, as if they were afraid that he could scarcely put his trousers on right without specific instruction. The New Bali mission was his first contract since receiving his commission.

"You've got the easy half of the job, Government House and the communications center," Orlis said.

"Yes, sir, I remember," Lon said, interrupting before the captain could go on to explain in more detail. *I know the mission,* he thought. *I know what we should be facing.* The targets for the company's other two platoons were the central police station and the capital's militia barracks.

"The revised strike time is oh-four-thirteen," Orlis said. "We hit all four targets at the same time."

"We'll be on time," Lon promised, glancing at the timeline on his head-up display. He switched channels on his radio to tell his platoon sergeants and squad leaders that there would be a short delay. It *was* short. Only three minutes passed before Captain Orlis gave the order to move out.

"Let's go," Lon told his platoon sergeants.

Every man in the two platoons knew the details of the operation. The DMC believed in sharing information as fully as practical. No matter how badly the chain of command might be fragmented by casualties in battle, the unit would be expected to continue its mission, even if a junior noncom ended up in command of a platoon. Or a company.

Third and fourth platoons moved along separate tracks a hundred yards apart. Lon hiked with third. He had been assigned to it as a cadet, before earning his commission. He felt more comfortable with that group.

Moving silently through the jungle was not difficult, or particularly dangerous, even at night. The floor of the tropical rain forest was mostly clear, except along streams and treefall gaps, where sunlight could reach the ground and stimulate the growth of new trees and undergrowth. And the night-vision systems built into the helmets of the mercenaries gave them almost full vision.

The two columns of soldiers moved in almost perfect silence, watching their flanks, alert for anything. Their course had been mapped and scouted ahead of time, so there were no surprises in the terrain. No alarms to send them diving for cover.

We'll have as near total surprise as we could ever hope to achieve, Lon thought. *It won't be until we leave the jungle and get into the city that there'll be any real danger of discovery.* He was grateful for activity, for the increased tension of moving toward the target. That let him quit wallowing in the discomfort of the climate. He kept as close a watch on the men of third platoon as their platoon sergeant or squad leaders did. Fourth was too far away for direct observation, but Lon had his radio set to monitor fourth platoon's noncoms' channel.

The staging area had been less than a half mile from the border of the jungle. There was a clear line marking the edge of Singaraja—city on one side and untamed jungle on the other. Looking out from the city, the rain forest appeared as a solid green wall, up to 130 feet high. The border was like a treefall gap, miles long and filled by young trees and the adventitious vines and shrubs that took advantage of any opening to the sun. The human residents had to maintain constant vigilance against the forest to keep it from reclaiming land they had "stolen." There were always interlopers, seedlings trying to establish themselves in the open.

"The point has reached the edge of the forest, Lieutenant," Corporal Tebba Girana of third platoon's second squad reported after the two platoons had been on the move for twenty minutes. "They're holding just this side."

"Okay, Tebba. We'll take five here. Put two men through the tangle to observe." Lon switched to talk to the point squad for fourth platoon, which was just reaching the same line, and gave them the same instructions. Then it was time for a final talk with the platoon sergeants.

"This is where the fun starts," Weil Jorgen commented.

"It shouldn't be too bad," Lon replied. "The local militia's geared to looking for trouble from inside the city, not coming out of the jungle. As long as we don't make mistakes, there shouldn't be much danger of them spotting us until we're within a block or two of our objective, if then." *As long as we don't set off a thousand dogs barking,* he thought. One of the tidbits of information they had about Singaraja was that there were twelve thousand dogs in the city. The original colonists, the ones who had come to find medicinal plants in the jungle, had brought dogs to help sniff out the plants that were most valuable, and the canine population had increased since.

"I wouldn't count on any of that, Lieutenant," Ivar said. "These local lads have had good training, and they know that *something* is coming."

"Let's just do our job," Lon said. "We'll cross into the city the way we planned. One squad from each platoon across the open space first. Then two squads. Then the rear guard. Once we're all on the city side, we move toward the objectives. And even though the timing is critical, I want the same care we'd take anywhere. If we run into trouble before we reach our objectives, it could throw the timing too far out to recover.''

"We're ready," Ivar said. Weil grunted his agreement.

"Okay, let's go," Lon said.

The strip of dense growth at the edge of the rain forest was nowhere thicker than thirty yards. Within that narrow belt, conditions could be chaotic, and difficult for anything larger than a rodent to find a way through. But there *were* a few spots. Alpha Company had scouted the verge carefully. Beyond that thicket was a hundred yards of flat, cleared land. Automated equipment tended the barrier, mowing the grasses that had been planted to serve as the first obstacle to the jungle. Beyond that, a plascrete roadway served as a more solid barricade. And, finally, there were the gardens and yards of private homes, then several commercial buildings before the area where Government House and the communications hub for Singaraja and all of New Bali stood.

When his platoons were ready to move through the border of the rain forest, Lon went forward to join third platoon's point squad to have a look for himself. He switched his faceplate to full magnification and slowly scanned the open area from left to right. After two minutes, he was certain that there was nothing moving within visual range. Singaraja was quiet. There was some light. The capital of New Bali boasted streetlights and a scattering of neon signs in the business district. Along the edge of the city, some of the houses showed outside lights.

"Move it," Lon said over the radio channel that connected him to all of the squad leaders and both platoon sergeants.

As two point squads started to cross the open field, two more squads from each platoon moved through the dense border of the jungle to cover them. The last squads remained on the forest side of the dense growth, against the minimal chance of attack from the rear. The point squads spread out into broad skirmish lines, jogging across the open fields, bent low. In the dark, against the backdrop of the rain forest and the green wall of its border, they would be virtually invisible to any watcher without the assistance of night-vision helmets or goggles.

As soon as the squad leaders reported that they were in position and had seen no indication of defenders, Lon ordered the next squads across, and the rearguard squads moved through the tangle to the city side, ready to follow. Lon and Weil moved with the middle squads. Ivar stayed behind to move with the rear guard.

Normally, running a hundred yards in full battle kit would have been only moderately taxing for Lon. In training, back on Dirigent, the men of the DMC— including all officers—regularly ran carrying the forty to sixty pounds of equipment they would have in a combat situation. But the temperature and humidity, added to the tension of going into action, made the crossing almost difficult for Lon. He felt himself gasping for breath before he reached the strip of black plascrete that marked the halfway point between jungle and the first houses.

Lon gave himself one short stop by moving to the side and watching as the rest of his men moved past. Then he started jogging again, staying close. There was no real chance to rest even when he flopped on the ground behind the skirmish line his men formed when they completed the crossing. He had to watch for the rearguard squads to cross, and get point squads moving through the residential strip that stood between them and the commercial and governmental district of Singaraja.

He conferred with his noncoms on the radio. No alarms had been sounded. Not even a single dog had started barking at their proximity. *Two minutes,* Lon told himself. *We all need that much of a break to catch our breath.* He glanced at the timeline on his helmet display, knowing that he could not afford more than two minutes. He could not be certain that there would be no delays later. Lon went over the routes that his men were to take to their targets. Although the two buildings were close together, his platoons would remain separated throughout the rest of the journey—a safety measure, to minimize the chance of total disaster if they were discovered. Two routes—one squad in front of each platoon and another trailing behind—would also minimize the few slight sounds that might be unavoidable.

"Move out," he told the platoon sergeants when the two minutes were over.

For a few minutes, they would still have the cover of full darkness, following back lanes, separated from the nearest houses by gardens and back yards, far from porch lights, and farther from the first streetlights. There was no running now. The men moved at a slow walk, five yards between each of them. Everyone kept eyes open and weapons at the ready. An ambush by the New Bali militia was not out of the question. And if first and second platoons ran into trouble, the locals might quickly move to block Lon's platoons as well.

Lon had the external audio pickups on his helmet at maximum gain, and he strained to hear any possible threat—as if intense concentration might extend the reach of his hearing. One dog started barking in the distance, too far away for the baying to be the result of Lon's men moving. Almost at once, several other dogs started to answer the call of the first. Most of the ruckus seemed to be off to the north, away from any of the Dirigenters.

"Halt!" Lon ordered over his all-hands channel. "Let's give the mutts a chance to settle down before any of them close by start yowling." Lon listened to the scattering of dogs barking against the silence of the night. Gradually, over a period of several minutes, they quieted down.

"Okay, let's get going again," Lon said once he thought that the remaining disturbance was far enough away that it was unlikely to be picked up by dogs closer in.

Five minutes later, he had a call from Tebba Girana, whose squad had the point for third platoon. "We're at the first checkpoint, Lieutenant," Girana reported. "The food warehouse is across the street from us. Lights half a block on either side. The alley next to the building is dark."

"Wait where you are until fourth is in position. I want both point squads to cross at the same time," Lon said.

With an entire world available, the people of New Bali

had chosen to make their citics almost as crowded as they would have been back on Earth. Although streets and alleys were broad, buildings pressed in against them. Where the New Balinese could have allowed acres of open space around each commercial or governmental building, they had instead lined them up next to each other along the streets. Instead of dozens—or even scores—of small green oases in the commercial zone of the city, there were only two large parks set aside, at opposite ends, nearly a mile apart. Government House and the central communications building bordered one of those parks.

It was 0349 hours when fourth platoon's point squad reported that they were in position—two blocks from Tebba facing the same street. Lon acknowledged the report, then switched channels to talk to his platoon sergeants.

"We've got twenty-four minutes, and there's still a fair distance to travel. Barring trouble, we start moving and keep going until we're in position around our objectives." As soon as Dendrow and Jorgen responded to that, Lon said, "Move 'em out."

Awareness of the heat and humidity had slipped away from Lon. Once he was moving again, inside the city, closing on the two buildings that his platoons were to take, he was too tightly focused on the mission to worry about anything so trivial as personal discomfort. He was still new enough as an officer that he found it difficult not to try to do everything himself, keep track of every single man and watch every degree of the terrain around them. He could, at need, check on the vital signs of all of his men—pulse, respiration, and body temperature. He could monitor all radio traffic within the platoons. The temptation was there, but there was no way that one man could do everything—not with even moderate success. He did keep his eyes moving, scanning ahead and behind as well as to both sides, and he tried to listen to the environment rather than to intrasquad talk.

He had a mild adrenaline rush as he crossed the strect into the alley next to the food warehouse with half of third platoon. But there were no alarms, and in seconds the men were across, split into two columns to walk down the sides of the alley.

At the next intersection, the point squad was waiting. That was the second checkpoint. From the shadows at the mouth of the alley, Lon could see Government House.

It was not particularly large, barely half the size of the analogous building on Dirigent—a structure that served both as the seat of government for the world and also as headquarters for the Dirigent Mercenary Corps. New Bali's Government House was only two stories high, shaped like a letter E. The long side faced the mercenaries, and the smaller strokes were wings aimed toward the park beyond. The building was two hundred feet long across the front. The width was eighty feet. There were streetlights at each corner, lights over each of the three entrances that Lon could see, and lights on in several windows.

No police or militiamen were posted outside the building. There would be, at a minimum, guards inside each entrance, although only one of those doors was left unlocked at night, and there might be two or three roving guards inside—a total of no more than eight security officers. *If* the intelligence was right and the New Balinese had made no changes.

The number of workers in the building at night was uncertain. It should be small—New Bali was not large enough to require extensive round-the-clock staffing of Government House—consisting of one mid-level official, perhaps a few clerks, and the maintenance and cleaning staff. The estimate was between six and twenty.

The communications building would be an even simpler affair. Two people ran the operation at night, and there would be one guard, and perhaps one person to run the cleaning machines.

"Oh-four-oh-five," Lon whispered on his connection to his platoon sergeants. "You both know the drill here. Get the men in position."

Lon would go into Government House seconds behind the squad that was assigned the main entrance, along with one other squad. Fire teams, each half a squad, would force the other entrances to Government House and neutralize the guards there. Once the doors were secured, the rest of the building would be searched quickly to find the rest of the people on duty. If everything went perfectly, there would be no need for shooting. *If . . .*

All that Lon could do for the next few minutes was watch, his tension increasing almost with every second. This was when the chance of discovery was greatest. A civilian driving through might spot armed men scurrying toward the objectives and raise the alarm. A police patrol might happen by. A guard might step outside for a breath of air. *Anything.*

If surprise was lost, the operation might be lost as well. *No screw-ups, please!* Lon thought. He wanted everything to go perfectly. Two hundred men attempting to usurp control of an entire world seemed almost insanely audacious, but Lon had put worries about the sanity of the exercise behind him. It *was* possible. It had been done on other worlds.

One by one, the fire teams reported that they were in position, close to the objectives. By 0410 hours, everyone was set. Lon moved closer with the last squad, crossing two streets and moving into the shadows on the lawn in front of Government House. The men went prone, half of them facing the building, the others facing the streets. Lon reported to Captain Orlis that third and fourth platoons were ready to move in, and that there was no sign that they had been detected.

"Good job, Nolan," Orlis replied. "Wait for my command. Everyone moves at once."

"Yes, sir."

Time showed its own insanity for Lon then. The seconds dragged like hours, waiting for the order, but when Orlis's order did come, it felt as if no time at all had passed.

"Go" was all the captain said. Lon repeated the order on a channel that connected him to all his sergeants and corporals. Then he got to his feet with the men of the final squad, and they moved toward the main entrance to Government House as third platoon's first squad burst through the doorway to take the guard there by surprise.

For the first six seconds, Lon thought that luck would hold and that the two buildings would be taken silently, but before he reached the main entrance, he heard several gunshots off to his left, apparently from the door near that end of the building.

"What was that?" he demanded on the channel that connected him to third squad's leader, Ben Frehr.

"The guard here spotted us coming in," Corporal Frehr reported. "It's okay, Lieutenant. We've got the situation under control now. No casualties."

"What about the guard?" Lon demanded.

There seemed to be restrained amusement in Frehr's voice. "He'll live."

Gunshots meant that the element of surprise ended a few seconds two soon. Two roaming guards within the building had time to report the sounds, and they were ready when third platoon found them. They did not resist, but they had had time to spread the warning.

"We've got Government House and the communications center secure, Captain," Lon reported at 0420. "The guards inside here had time to raise the alarm, though."

"We expected that, Nolan," Orlis replied. "No matter. We've got the militia barracks and police headquarters surrounded. We're negotiating for their surrender. They're in no position to resist, and they know it."

"Then we contact the governor?"

"Or he contacts us," Orlis replied. "It shouldn't be long. I expect we'll have a final resolution within an hour or so. Set your defensive positions and wait."

Wait, Lon thought with distaste after he had given his orders and moved up to the second floor of the building. He had sentries posted there, high enough to have a wider view of the area surrounding Government House. *Ninety-nine percent of what we do is wait.*

At 0447, Captain Orlis told Lon that the militia were stalling, refusing to capitulate. The police station had surrendered, but there had been only six officers inside—not the twenty to thirty that the Dirigenters had expected.

"Sounds like something might be up," Lon suggested.

"If so, we'll find out soon enough," Orlis said. "I've given the militia a deadline—oh-five-hundred. I told them if they haven't surrendered by then, we destroy the barracks with them inside."

"I want everyone alert," Lon told his noncoms. "The locals might have something up their sleeves. Except for the men watching the prisoners, I want every eye looking for activity outside. And keep the men down. I don't want anybody where a sniper could take them out."

Wait!

At 0501, Lon heard the dull *crump-thump* of two explosive charges going off in the distance. *The militia didn't surrender,* he thought. He felt a tightening in his stomach. There might have been as many as three hundred men in the barracks compound, twenty percent of the world's entire militia force.

"Foolish heroics," he muttered, shaking his head. "Stupid way to waste people."

Five minutes later, Captain Orlis had news. "We went in. There was only a single platoon of militia in the barracks—thirty-five men. Watch for trouble. The rest must be somewhere in the city."

Lon's stomach growled nervously. Most of the militia missing from where they were supposed to be. The same for the police. *They knew something was up,* he thought. *Then. Where are they?*

He alerted his noncoms. And sweated. Government House was efficiently air-conditioned, but sweat came to Lon anyway. He prowled the second floor, going from room to room, standing in the dark at the side of windows, looking out, searching for any hint of approaching soldiers. *They'll come, sooner or later,* he thought—he *knew.*

It did not take much for his thoughts to move to *We can't hold. Surprise was all we had going. We had to take all of the local forces available in the city at once. We didn't do it.*

The waiting was different now. He knew what had to come. When a loudspeaker came to life outside, just minutes after five-thirty, as the sun was beginning to brighten the eastern horizon, Lon was not surprised. He had been expecting it.

"You, in Government House," a metallic-tinged voice said, amplified far beyond necessity. "Lay down your weapons and come out. We have you surrounded and out-numbered."

Lon immediately called Captain Orlis and reported. "What do we do?" he asked.

Orlis did not hesitate. He had just received a similar message. "Surrender, Nolan. It's all we can do."

2

The three mercenary officers were brought before the governor of New Bali together. Lieutenants Lon Nolan and Carl Hoper, platoon leader for the company's first and second platoons, flanked Captain Orlis as they were returned to Government House and taken to the second-floor office of Governor Pranj Nuwel. The three ranking officers from the Singaraja militia barracks were also present.

Governor Nuwel stood behind his desk and stared at the Dirigenters for a moment. Then he smiled and nodded shallowly before coming out to the center of his office, coming face to face with the outworlders.

"Captain Orlis," Nuwel said with a broader smile. "I think we can consider the contract fulfilled." He extended his hand and the two men shook. "You and your men have done an admirable job of training our militia. The, ah, final examination you staged this morning was most impressive."

"Thank you, Governor," Matt Orlis replied. "The demonstration has to be as real as possible, or it doesn't prove anything. Your men have been excellent students."

"The people of New Bali will be able to sleep more soundly in future," Nuwel said. "We survived the first coup attempt by the grace of God. If our dissident minority tries a repeat, they shall find us far more prepared, thanks to you and your men."

"I hope it never comes to that, Governor, but if it does, I'm sure that your men will be able to cope with any situation that does arise."

Governor Nuwel shook hands with the lieutenants, offering each a smile and a few words of gratitude. Then he returned to Orlis.

"Captain, I know that you're in something of a hurry to return home, but I do hope that you and your men can see yourselves free to give us a few more hours. My government and the city of Singaraja have prepared a small celebratory party—a luncheon, if you prefer—for late this morning."

"Thank you, Governor. We would be honored," Orlis replied.

Huge pavilions of green and yellow fabric had been erected along the beach. Insulated tarps covered the sand under the canopies. Fans and dehumidifiers struggled to make the pavilions comfortable. In the governor's pavilion, several long tables had been set. All of the mercenaries were there, officers at the head table that was perpendicular to the rest, sitting with Governor Nuwel and his chief civilian and militia officials, as well as the mayor and council president of Singaraja.

The festivities started two hours before noon, with the mercenary officers being presented to scores of local notables. Cameras and microphones were present for the inevitable speeches that preceded, followed, and interrupted the eating, and were broadcast to the people in the other pavilions and via the public complink net to the rest of New Bali.

Lon and his companion officers wore off-dress white uniforms. The enlisted men wore clean fatigue uniforms. None of them had brought anything fancier along on a contract.

"I'd just as soon use the time to take a nap in a refrigerator," Lon had said earlier, when the three officers were alone together for a few minutes after their meeting with Governor Nuwel. "Get some sleep. Get away from the heat."

Captain Orlis had laughed. "You'll get your chance soon enough, Nolan. This is part of the business. We've got to leave a good impression. Maybe a reference from the people here will bring another job or two for the Corps in the future."

By the time they were escorted to the beach for the luncheon, Lon was feeling very sluggish. There had been no sleep for the mercenaries the night before, and he had not slept well for several previous nights, basically since the Dirigenters had moved into the jungle, away from the relatively comfortable accommodations they had enjoyed while they were training the local militia. "We need to get in a little refresher training of our own" was the cover story that Captain Orlis had given the local militia commander. "You've got a sort of terrain that we don't have back home." Only the governor had known the actual reason: the training was a cover for some sort of final exercise to test the militia. And even he had not known exactly what the mercenaries were going to do or when, just that they were going to put the militia to the test.

In the governor's pavilion, drinks were served early and often. The enlisted men had beer and wine. At the head table, the drink was a lemon-flavored liqueur of a yellow tint, served over ice. It was deceptively innocuous, sweet and mild in the mouth. But, as Lon quickly discovered, it seemed to erupt about halfway to the stomach, providing an inner heat that chased away any awareness of the outside temperature.

"Whew, that's really something," Lon said, turning to the militia lieutenant at his right after his first taste of it.

The New Balinese officer grinned. "This is but ice water, my friend. The yellow djorja is less than sixty percent alcohol, and watered down slightly in the mix. And this is on ice, diluting it further. The green djorja we drink in the evening—neat—now *that* is a real drink."

"I'll take your word for it," Lon said, daring a second cautious sip of his drink.

The djorja lost its bite after a few more sips. Lon found himself taking more each time. It provided a pleasant sensation once the shock of introduction had passed. *It's a good thing I came prepared,* Lon thought while a waiter refilled his glass for the third time—before the first course of the luncheon had been cleared away, *I'm going to need a killjoy-patch before dessert.* The patch, applied to neck or arm, would provide molecular agents to metabolize the alcohol quickly and remove any alcohol-related toxins from his system. A killjoy-patch could take a man from unconscious-drunk to duty-sober in twenty minutes.

Lon glanced along the table. Captain Orlis was also drinking freely and appeared to be showing no ill effects from the djorja. *I'll bet he stuck a killjoy on before we came,* Lon thought. *I wish I'd thought of that.* He looked around, then tried to put on a patch of his own without being obvious about it. He applied the patch to his wrist, under the cuff of his shirt, then looked to see if anyone had noticed. No one was pointing and laughing. Satisfied, Lon rewarded himself with another drink.

By the time the formal festivities ended, it was past two in the afternoon. Lon had lost track of the amount of djorja he had consumed. Even with the killjoy-patch on his arm, he was feeling a slight buzz. He recognized the familiar euphoria of moderate intoxication, the feeling of reduced weight, a touch of light-headedness, the pleasant sense of satisfaction. All was well with the world. It felt eminently comfortable in the pavilion. Not even the assault of the sun and unconditioned air when he emerged from the pavilion could disrupt his feeling of well-being and comfort.

Captain Orlis showed no impatience. He conversed with a group of notables from Singaraja. The governor had said a few final thank-yous to the mercenary officers, then left to return to Government House. The four Dirigenter platoon sergeants were assembling their men (and making certain that everyone who needed killjoy-patches had them) for the march to the spaceport and the trip up to their ship for the journey back to Dirigent.

Lon stood on the periphery of the group surrounding Captain Orlis, trying not to look bored or impatient. He was almost startled by the touch of a hand on his arm.

"A small present for you," said the lieutenant who had

been seated next to Lon, proffering a box. "This is the real stuff—green djorja."

Lon grinned as he accepted the gift. "Thank you." He nodded. "I hope I have the nerve to try it some evening soon."

The shuttles were waiting at the spaceport. Lon had scarcely noticed the two-mile march from the beach. The formation had been remarkably lax for Dirigenters, but all Captain Orlis had to say was "For God's sake, make sure we don't leave anyone behind." The men were counted before the company left the beach. Noncoms watched along the way to make certain that no one dropped out of formation. The men were counted again when they reached the spaceport, with assurances being passed up the chain of command that everyone was present. Even after that, Lon stood where he could watch both troop entrances to the shuttle his platoons would ride and counted heads again. And when the men were all inside, he ordered a final roll call.

Two attack shuttles could carry the entire company. The men's gear, weapons, helmets, and packs, and the rest of the company's equipment, had already been taken up to the ship by transport shuttles while the men of Alpha Company were being feted by the New Balinese.

"Make sure everyone gets strapped in tight," Lon told his platoon sergeants. "I don't want any drunk soldiers floating around the cabin when we hit zero-g."

"I've already told my squad leaders and their assistants to do that," Weil Jorgen said.

Ivar Dendrow nodded, then added, "I just hope nobody starts puking when their stomachs don't know which way is down."

That goes for me too, Lon thought. *If one starts, we might have a dozen others toss their cookies.* Most especially, he did not want to be the one to start the parade. It would be too embarrassing.

There was no rush about this trip. The shuttles remained on the ground for ten minutes after the doors had been sealed and the roll taken once more. The Dirigenters waited for a local shuttle flight coming into Singaraja to land before their shuttles were given clearance to take off. The shuttles taxied to the end of the runway and took off no more than ten seconds apart.

The pilots made an "economical" boost, keeping the shuttles subsonic until they were at fifty thousand feet and out over the ocean, thirty miles from the nearest settlement on the ground. The shuttles went to rocket power then, but the acceleration remained moderate—for attack shuttles. Even at peak, the men aboard the two boats never experienced more than two and a half gees.

Video monitors spaced around the troop cabin offered views of New Bali and then—once the shuttles were in space—also one view of their ship. *Piranha* was a *Scorpion*-class transport, large enough to carry slightly more than two companies of soldiers along with supplies for two months. The *Scorpion*-class vessels were the smallest dedicated troop carriers in the Dirigenter military fleet. With only Alpha Company aboard, *Piranha* seemed more spacious than a civilian liner.

Lon felt a moment of queasiness when the shuttle's rockets shut down and robbed the passengers of any feeling of weight. He rebounded against the straps of his safety harness, looking around for any signs of men who might get spacesick. If it was going to happen, it would likely happen in the first couple of minutes of zero gravity. He did not *quite* hold his breath.

So far, so good, Lon told himself when the most critical period had elapsed. *Booze or not, they look okay.* He took stock of his own physical feeling. His stomach felt uneasy, but did not seem ready to reject any of the food or djorja. Then he remembered the package he had been given, the stronger green djorja now stowed safely beneath his seat, and managed a smile. *I will have to try that,* he thought, *after we get home.*

Without helmets, there was no radio communication among the soldiers. It felt strange being in a shuttle and not wearing full field gear. But the only practical limitation this time was that Lon could not confer with his noncoms or with Captain Orlis. The captain was in the other shuttle. Lon *could* talk with his platoon sergeants, but only by shouting. Neither was seated especially close.

One of the pilots increased the magnification on the video of *Piranha*. Lon could make out the open hangar doors waiting for the two troop shuttles to rendezvous, rectangles of bluish light against the matte black of the ship's hull.

Soon, Lon thought. But it could hardly be soon enough. He was looking forward to sleeping between sheets again; to good, freshly prepared food rather than battle rations; and—most of all—to comfortable temperature and humidity levels. He closed his eyes. Even in zero gravity, he felt that he could drift off to sleep. If he permitted himself to. That was something else he was looking forward to—plenty of sleep, interrupted only by meals and the barest of other necessities. *Piranha* would offer that luxury. During the two weeks that the trip back to Dirigent would take, Lon would have only minimal calls upon his time. There would be little work for anyone in the company. Coming home from a contract was a time for rest and recuperation.

Lon did not completely allow himself to fall asleep on the shuttle. He dozed, but his eyes came open every minute or so to assure him that all was well. It was not very restful. He kept thinking of things he needed to remember to do or say once they got aboard ship. He did have responsibilities.

An announcement over the loudspeaker that the shuttle was about to dock with *Piranha* finally brought Lon out of his torpor. He blinked several times and did his best to disguise the gaping yawn that forced its way through his mouth. He stretched as best he could within the confines of his safety harness, and looked around to see that many of his men were going through similar routines. A few men appeared to be asleep. He had no problem with that, save envy. They could sleep until they docked, if they could manage it.

Sergeant Dendrow spoiled it, though. "Look lively," he

called out loudly. "Wake those men up. We're not about to carry anyone aboard."

There were groans and a few good-natured complaints from the men. Someone said, "Carry me, carry me!" in a falsetto that effectively concealed the speaker's identity. It was not the first time that Lon had heard that voice make a wise cracking comment in the past few months. Lon kept a straight face despite the way that Dendrow spun his head trying to see who the joker was. *Ease up, Ivar,* Lon thought, just a second before Dendrow's face relaxed and he managed a smile and a slow shake of his head.

"One of these days!" the platoon sergeant said with mock seriousness. "I'm going to find out who our female impersonator is, and then we'll see who has the last laugh."

At least they're in good spirits, Lon thought. He had worried that the oppressive climate of New Bali might cause morale problems, as bad as a combat contract could when things went wrong. *Maybe the party the New Balinese threw for us helped.* Lon smiled. The party and the thought of the contract-completion bonus that the men would receive as soon as they got home to Dirigent.

The feeling of weight returning was a relief, even though it came quickly as the shuttle was hauled into its hangar and secured to the deck. Lon unfastened his safety harness before the pilot gave clearance. Lon did remain seated until the message came over the loudspeaker. Then he was on his feet, springing up as if he were rebounding from a trampoline.

"Okay," he called out. "Let's get aboard and get squared away. I want weapons and field gear cleaned before anyone gets the idea of sacking out for the next two weeks." Humid conditions were rough on rifles and pistols, even without the insult of the putty bullets that had been used in the final examination for the New Balinese militia.

The responding groans were softer this time. The order had been inevitable, and everyone in the two platoons knew it, even the sprinkling of rookies—men who had never been on contract before. The men were, after all, professionals. They depended heavily on their weapons and other gear—

often for their very lives. And if anyone did forget, even momentarily, the sergeants and corporals would be certain to remind them.

Both exits opened. The hangar door had been sealed. The chamber had been pressurized. Lon moved to one of the exits and stood there while third platoon went through the doorway, with Ivar Dendrow standing across from him. Fourth platoon used the other door. Platoon Sergeant Jorgen monitored his men.

The platoons moved out of the shuttle in good order. There was little congestion as the men hurried to get back to their shipboard accommodations. Spartan though those might be, they would seem luxurious after the tropical rain forest of New Bali. For a time, perhaps only a few days, everything would seem better than the men had ever realized before. It was not that the colony world had been so primitive, just a reflection of how stressful the climate was.

"Sometimes it astounds me," Sergeant Dendrow said, almost under his breath, after the last of the men had left.

"What?" Lon asked, a little startled at the way Ivar's statement seemed to reflect his own thoughts.

"Some of the lads have already forgotten the misery. By the time we get home it'll just be something to brag about in the bars, how rough conditions were on New Bali."

Lon shook his head. "Be thankful for small favors," he said, stepping through the hatchway to the hangar deck. "I'd hate to see them coming out with their chins in their socks."

Dendrow chuckled softly as he followed the lieutenant out. "Aye, sir. That's always rougher."

The inspection, before dinner that evening, was relatively informal but thorough. Corporals inspected the rifles and other field gear of their squads. Platoon sergeants inspected at random, checking the equipment of two or three men in each squad—and the squad leaders. Finally, Lon did his own random sampling, knowing full well that he would not find anything to complain about in weapons or anything else that the corporals and sergeants had passed. But he did not slough off his duties. He also had Sergeant Dendrow check *his* gear, while he inspected the weapons of his platoon sergeants. Even Captain Orlis would have his rifle, pistol, and field kit inspected by other eyes. No one wanted to have anything wrong with his professional tools.

During the trip home, the armorer would inspect each weapon more closely, to make certain that it had not suffered damage, and repair any wear and tear he found. An electronics technician would run diagnostics on battle helmets, mapboards, and every other piece of electronic gear that had gone down to the surface of New Bali. Faulty units or components would be repaired or replaced before *Piranha* got home. Alpha Company would land on Dirigent as prepared for action as it had been when it reached New Bali.

Piranha was boosting away from New Bali by the time the inspection was over and the men were sent off to dinner. Captain Orlis had assured everyone that there would be no unnecessary fatigue details during the trip. The only chores would be the daily routine of keeping the barracks cabins clean and the hour of physical conditioning each morning to make certain that the troops were as fit for action when they got home as their equipment would be.

The trip home would take fourteen or fifteen days. Any interstellar journey required that long, whether the distance traveled was three light-years or three hundred. The ship would make three "jumps" through Q-space. *Piranha* would be five days out from New Bali before its first Q-space transit. The other two jumps would be spaced three days apart—three days of traveling in normal space—and they would emerge from the final transit three days out from Dirigent.

"Two weeks after we get home, a few of the men will start wondering when we'll be shipping out again, when the next contract might come our way," Captain Orlis told his two lieutenants after dinner. The three officers were together in the captain's stateroom, sharing a bottle of wine from home.

"Well, this wasn't a combat contract," Carl Hoper said.

"It takes longer after a hard one, when men have died and others have been wounded." He spoke softly. All three of them had been on contracts like that. Lon Nolan's predecessor as leader for the company's third and fourth platoons had been killed in action the last time out.

Lon thought about Arlan Taiters, and about the other men he had known who had been killed. He did not intend to say anything, but a thought forced its way past his lips almost without his realizing that it was coming. "Two weeks after we get home, they'll be back from their after-contract leaves. Most of the men will have drunk up their bonuses. All they've got to look forward to on Dirigent then is training routine and a stint with the planetary defense command." He shrugged and glanced at the other two self-consciously. Rather to Lon's surprise, both Orlis and Hoper considered his facetious comment seriously.

"That's only part of the answer, Lon," Orlis said after a moment's reflection. "True for some of the men, some of the time, but there's more to it."

"Some of the men, especially those who've been in the Corps longest, get to feeling as if they're not . . . fulfilling their purpose in life in garrison. They're in the profession of fighting, and when they're not doing that, they get to feeling as if they're not earning their keep, or doing their duty."

"And some would just rather be doing something different than what they're doing at the moment, no matter what the alternatives are," Orlis said. "Enough shop talk. We've still got half a bottle of this wine to finish tonight. Let's save the philosophy until we get home and have plenty of time for it."

3

Lon could not make up his mind whether he agreed with the decision or not—but he tended toward *not*. The news could have been relayed to Alpha Company as soon as *Piranha* emerged from its last Q-space transit in Dirigent's solar system. That would have given him, and all the men in the company, an extra three days to get used to the idea, to get their initial . . . resentment of it out of the way. As it was, they were not told until they were back on base, after the bus parade through the capital city from the spaceport to base. The men had collected their duffel bags and were moving them from the trucks into the barracks shortly after midnight on a Tuesday morning when Captain Orlis and his two lieutenants were called to battalion headquarters.

"Don't get too comfortable," Lieutenant Colonel Medwin Flowers said after Alpha Company's officers had been shown into his office.

There was a brief silence before Captain Orlis spoke. "You might as well drop the other shoe, sir."

"I know it doesn't happen like this often," Flowers said, "but you'll be heading back out in"—he glanced at the clock—"about sixty hours. This is a big one, the entire regiment."

Orlis blinked and nodded. "What's the contract, sir?"

"We've been hired to defend the people and government of Calypso against invasion from Belletiene—or liberating them if, as we expect, the invasion takes place before we arrive and they have been unable to repulse it alone."

"Neither name rings a bell, sir," Orlis said.

"Officers' call tomorrow morning at oh-nine-hundred," Flowers said. "I held off the briefing since I knew you'd be back today. There's a brief summary on your office complink. That won't take you more than five minutes to work through."

"Yes, sir."

"Get your men squared away, get them out on the streets. They've got until oh-three-hundred Thursday free, no duty. The same goes for the three of you. Except for the officers' call tomorrow, you're on your own until reveille Thursday."

As if on command, Alpha Company's three officers came to a halt just after they left battalion headquarters. "One thing at least," Carl Hoper said. "Two weeks from now we won't have anyone wondering how long it will be before our next contract."

"I don't know whether to feel disappointed or relieved—or upset," Lon said. "I know I haven't been here all that long, but I've never heard of anyone going back out this quickly."

Orlis shrugged. "It happens, but not often. Different rotas." The Corps went to great lengths to insure that every unit got its fair share of contracts. Separate lists were maintained for regiments, battalions, companies, and smaller units. Contracts came in different sizes. "We might as well get back to the barracks and break the news that there won't be any furloughs."

"I know one man who's not going to be happy about that," Lon said. "Belzer was planning to get married and take a honeymoon." Janno Belzer was a private in third platoon, one of the men Lon had become friends with during his stint as a cadet, before earning his commission.

"Tell him the General sends his apologies," Orlis said with a chuckle. There was only one general at a time in the DMC, head of the Council of Regiments, elected by the colonels who commanded the fourteen regiments, from among their own number. The General was also Dirigent's head of government.

"It'll take more than apologies to appease his fiancée, I think," Lon said, shaking his head and smiling. "She worked hard to get him to finally set a date."

Lon slept on the second floor of the barracks, between the bays where his men were quartered. His room was sixteen feet square. As an officer, he also rated a private bathroom. His office adjoined the bedroom, with a connecting doorway between them. Both rooms were rather spartan in appearance. The one extravagance that Lon had accumulated in his time on Dirigent was a deluxe entertainment console that gave him connections to the public complink net, with its enormous libraries of books, videos, and music as well as live programming and communications.

He had already decided that he would have to unpack his duffel bag, even though it would have to be repacked in two days. He would want to check each item and replace any that might not survive another contract. He was sitting on the edge of his bed, wondering if he should bother to check the latest news feed, when there was a knock on his door.

"Come in," Lon said, turning toward the door. He was not at all surprised to see Janno Belzer. "Come on in and have a seat," Lon invited, gesturing to the one chair in the room. "I expect you're a bit disturbed about the news."

"Yes, sir, I guess you could say that," Janno said as he moved toward the chair. There were delicate matters of DMC protocol involved in the relationship between the two. On duty, they were lieutenant and private, with no special allowances permitted. Off duty, especially away from base, their friendship continued, as little changed by circumstances as possible. It was a situation that came up frequently among the mercenaries. The official rules were few. In each case, the men involved had to feel their way through the possible traps.

"We went off duty when you closed the door, Janno," Lon said, speaking softly. Belzer's reply was a gesture that combined both shrug and nod. "I don't choose what units to send out on contract," Lon added.

"I know," Janno said. "I'm trying to look on the bright side. This way, there'll be more money for our honeymoon. It's just . . . well, Mary's not going to be very happy. She must know we're back. That kind of news spreads fast."

"Mary will be waiting when you get back. You know that," Lon said.

"I'm not worried about *that*," Janno said quickly. "It's just that . . . could I ask you a favor?"

"Sure, I'll do what I can."

"Will you come along with me when I tell her?" There was earnest pleading in Janno's voice, as if he were a child begging his father for something special.

"When she gets mad, you'd rather she had me to be mad at instead of just you?"

For just an instant, a look of utter shock affixed itself to Janno's face. When it faded, he almost blushed. "Well, there *is* that too," he admitted, "but that isn't what I was thinking about. It's just that she'll believe you right off, and if it's just me, she might wonder for a time if maybe I was trying to back out of the marriage. I don't want her to think that, not even for a second."

"Sure, I'll come along," Lon said, suppressing the urge to laugh. "When are you going to tell her?"

"I already checked. She's working tonight. I figured I'd tell her there, at the Dragon Lady. She's planning on quitting before the wedding, but she wouldn't quit until she saw me—saw that I got home safe and sound. Just in case." There was no need to explain any farther, and Janno was clearly uneasy with that much.

"Give me an hour," Lon said. "I need to shower and change into civilian clothes, and I do need to hang around a bit in case anyone else has special . . . circumstances."

No one else came to Lon with problems. He had not expected anyone else. As much as possible, Lon Nolan knew his men—not just their abilities and their attitudes on the job, but also something about their families, and what they liked to do off duty. Most were single. More than half of the enlisted men in the DMC remained unmarried until they retired. Nearly a third of the officers in the Corps also remained single during their military service—or held off on marriage until they were nearer to leaving than to entering the Corps. There was no sense of urgency on Dirigent about starting a family. Excluding the chance of being killed in military service, the average lifespan was 120 years. "Old age" was not considered to truly begin until a person hit the centennial of his or her birth.

If any problems have come up with families, I'll find out tomorrow, Lon thought. It would take time for news of the company's return, and its quick turnaround, to spread to all of the families. Not all of the men had been in contact with relatives before starting to head for the gate for reunions— or to crowd in as much carousing as possible in sixty hours.

Precisely an hour had passed since Janno's departure from Lon's quarters when there was another knock on the door. Lon opened it. Janno was there in the corridor, but not alone. Dean Ericks and Phip Steesen were with him.

Lon looked at Belzer and grinned. "You figured you need more moral support than me?"

Janno looked sheepish. "Safety in numbers."

"He's buying the first round," Phip said. "And the last, if any of us are sober enough to remember. That's the price Dean and I set for going along on this contract."

"Do we head straight for the Dragon Lady or make a stop or two on the way to drink up a couple of quarts of courage before you face Mary?" Lon asked.

"I don't know about anybody else, but *I* sure don't want to face Mary sober, not to tell her that we're shipping out again in two days," Janno said. The others had a good laugh. Janno, Dean, and Phip were nearly inseparable. Before Lon won his commission, he had shared that close bond. Although all of them tried to hold on to the past, Lon's new status always put *some* restraints to it.

"Anyone think about eating first?" Lon asked.

Phip laughed. "Just takes longer to get proper drunk if you eat first. Besides, if we wait until after Janno breaks the news to Mary, we can eat while he's holding a raw steak to the black eye she's gonna give him." Dean and

Lon laughed with Phip at that. Janno's groan was impressive—as if there were actually a chance that he believed that Mary might hit him.

"You're not helping," Janno said. "I need moral support, I get jokes."

"We'll make sure you get to a trauma tube fast," Phip said.

"Hey, the longer you guys jaw here, the longer it is before we get any beer in our bellies," Dean said. That argument overrode the jokes. Drinking time was always precious.

Dirigent City and the main base of the DMC had grown together over the centuries. The world exported only soldiers and munitions. Everything revolved around the DMC. The linkage was so complete that the General and the Council of Regiments were also the leaders of the civilian government. Corps headquarters also served as Government House for Dirigent, or vice versa, and the affairs of the world were directed from within. Local government was democratic, but the overall affairs of the world were not entrusted to the whims of popular opinion.

The street that the main gate of the base opened onto was not crowded with taverns and the other haunts of soldiers, though. Instead, it boasted government and professional offices, and monumental facades to impress visiting dignitaries—especially those who might offer contracts to the Corps or the munitions industry. "Camo Town"—the area that existed to service the needs and desires of off-duty soldiers—was beyond that facade, close enough for all but the most desperate thirst.

Lon and his companions walked. It was three-quarters of a mile from their barracks to the main gate. There was no "public" transportation on base. Once they hit the street beyond the gate, there was a moment of discussion. There were buses and taxis available. They decided to keep walking.

"We hit the first bar," Janno said.

"That's MacGregor's, if we're taking the most direct

route to the Dragon Lady," Phip said instantly. "Mac-
Gregor's, then the Purple Harridan, then . . ."

"Enough!" Janno said. "I've got to be conscious when
I get to Mary."

MacGregor's, a simple pub that claimed to be a perfect
replica of an authentic early 21st-century Earth pub right
down to the recipes it used for its beers and ales, was little
more than two blocks from the main gate, stuck halfway
along an alley. It was out of sight from the boulevard that
connected the base with the city's spaceport, which was the
route that visiting diplomats and businessmen traveled.

Phip and Dean carried the conversation during the short
walk. Lon had always been the quiet one of the group, even
before winning his lieutenant's pips. Normally, Phip and
Janno were the talkers, the ones with a ready joke on any
subject, but Janno was quiet now, anxious about breaking
the news to his fiancée. He scarcely heard the gibes of his
friends. Responding was out of the question. Dean had to
fill the gap.

Lon listened to the chatter with amusement. Although he
was the youngest of the four, he had always felt a gener-
ation older. He walked a little apart from the others, an
unconscious token of the difference in rank between them—
maintained as much by his three friends as by him. Even
after a long evening of heavy drinking, there would be that
gap. There had always been a degree of reserve. When they
had first met, Lon was an officer-cadet, needing only the
baptism of a combat contract to earn his commission. The
others had known then that he would become an officer and
might well command them.

It was not yet three in the afternoon, which meant that
MacGregor's was not busy. Like almost all of the busi-
nesses in the district, MacGregor's depended almost exclusively on soldiers and ex-soldiers for trade. It would be six
or seven in the evening before Camo Town really came
alive.

When the four soldiers reached MacGregor's, Phip was
in the lead, pushing open the door with one hand and half
tugging Janno along with the other. "You're buying the

first round,'' Phip reminded his nervous friend. ''We can't have you getting lost just when we're here.''

They headed straight for the bar, where the bartender seemed relieved to see them. ''What'll ya have, lads?''

''Four pints of your best,'' Phip said, pulling Janno up to the bar. ''My friend with the long face here is buying.''

Lon turned and scanned the room while he waited for his ale. There were only two other customers—two men who looked as if they might have retired from the Corps decades earlier sat bent over a table along the side of the room playing draughts and nursing their pint mugs. MacGregor's did not waste money on extravagant lighting, music, or decoration—or on any of the other devices that many of the bars in Camo Town used as bait to attract and hold customers. The room was dim, lit only by two neon beer signs behind the bar, a small bulb over the till, and what little light came in through two windows covered with filmy sheer drapes. The lights would be turned up later, when there were enough customers to justify it—or when someone complained that he couldn't see the dartboard well enough to play.

''Here you are, gents,'' the bartender said as he slid the four mugs into place before them. ''Enjoy yerselves. There's plenty more where that came from,'' he added as Janno paid.

''Bottoms up!'' Phip said, doing his best to empty his mug in a single gulp. Then he wiped his mouth with the back of his hand. ''So much beer and so little time,'' he complained.

Lon took a first sip and forced himself not to grimace. He far preferred chilled lager to ale served at what was laughingly called room temperature—about fifty-eight degrees Fahrenheit. But Phip had done the ordering, and in MacGregor's he always ordered ale. He really seemed to see no difference in types or brands. Malt beverages were malt beverages to him, and the more potent they were, the better he liked them.

Janno's hand was shaking when he set his mug down after drinking a third of it. *He's really worried about what*

Mary's going to say, Lon thought sympathetically. He liked Mary Boles, had from the first time they met. Although she was quite capable of taking care of herself in a pinch, she was not a violent person. Lon had never seen a hint of bad temper in her.

Phip and Dean each ordered a second drink after the others declined. And those were done before Lon forced down the rest of his pint. Phip was anxious to move on. Janno did not seem particularly eager to move closer to the Dragon Lady . . . and his own personal dragon lady, as he now seemed to consider her.

Another hour passed before the men entered the Dragon Lady. Loud music greeted them. Strobing lights assaulted their eyes. The afternoon had progressed enough that there were some customers in the main bar room, and undoubtedly more in the other public—and private—rooms. One of the most profitable enterprises in Camo Town, the Dragon Lady tried to satisfy as many of the wants of its clients as possible—liquor, food, games, and women.

One of the waitresses spotted Janno and his companions. She waved and grinned, then made her way over to them. "Mary's working the dining room, Janno," she said.

"Thanks, Looza," Janno said. "I guess we'll go straight on up." Like the other waitresses at the Dragon Lady, Looza was dressed simply. Other than shoes, her only garment was an apron—more a belt with two pouches to hold an order pad and tips.

"Why don't we have a beer down here first?" Phip asked. "I'm thirsty."

"You're always thirsty," Dean said.

"There's beer upstairs," Lon said. "You won't die of thirst before you get there." Lon spoke lightly, needing to make certain that the others knew that it was a joke. He was sensitive about such things—more, perhaps, than they were.

"Yeah," Dean added. "Anyway, since when do you get so impatient when it's your turn to buy?"

"My turn? I bought the last one," Phip said.

"Just for yourself. You've been drinking two for our

one," Dean said. "You're on your way to a three-killjoy night and the sun isn't down yet."

Lon stopped the talk by pushing the two of them in the direction of the stairs. Janno moved with the group as if he were on a leash . . . and reluctant to continue the walk. Looza grinned and shook her head, then headed toward a pair of customers at one of the tables.

"Before we went to New Bali," Janno said while they climbed the stairs, "Mary said that all the girls here were planning to throw her a big bridal shower as soon as we got back."

"So now they'll just have longer to plan," Phip said. "And more time to talk themselves into more expensive gifts." Janno made a sound that was halfway between a growl and a groan.

When they reached the dining room—called that only because it was the public room nearest the kitchen; it also had a bar—Mary was transferring plates with sausages and hot chips from a tray to a table with four soldiers at it. Mary's back was to the doorway. She didn't see her fiancée. Janno seemed prepared to stand where he was until she noticed him, but Lon touched his sleeve, then pointed toward an empty table when Janno turned to see what he wanted. "We might as well sit," Lon said.

"I'll get the beers," Phip said.

"Lager for me," Lon said. "I've had enough ale."

Phip grinned. "Not a snifter of brandy?"

"No, no old grape juice," Lon replied. *If anyone's still conscious enough when we get back to the barracks, maybe this is the time to open that bottle of djorja,* he thought. *Or wait until tomorrow and start with that. No sense in letting it sit and age for however long we're gone on this next contract.* There was almost superstition behind that, though Lon would not admit it, even to himself—the thought that leaving something unfinished at home might lead to not returning from a contract.

Mary spotted them as they were moving toward the table, but needed a moment to finish her chore before she could head toward them. Although displays of affection were frowned on in the public rooms of the Dragon Lady—though not in the private rooms, where the waitresses served more than drinks and food—Mary threw her arms around Janno and gave him an almost suffocating kiss. He had to put his arms around her waist and hold on to keep from being carried to the floor by her ardor.

"I love you, Janno Belzer," she said when she finally pulled her mouth away from his.

"I love you too," he replied—nearly stammered.

"Should I give my notice tonight?" she asked.

"We're going back out in two days," Janno said, spitting out the bad news quickly. "Another contract."

Lon could see the way the news hit Mary—like a pail of ice water. She let go of Janno and took half a step back. "Tell me you're joking," she begged.

Janno shook his head, and did not even think of trying to disguise his own anguish. "We got the news almost before we got off the buses this morning. A big contract, the whole regiment."

Mary looked at Dean, and then at Lon, hoping that one of them would contradict Janno. "It's the truth, Mary," Lon said. "We're going right back out, and we don't know how long the contract will be."

"That's not fair!" Mary said.

"I won't argue that," Lon said. "But it's how things are." When they first met, Lon had been bothered by the fact that Janno's fiancée worked as both waitress and prostitute, but his attitudes came from Earth. On Dirigent, prostitution carried no stigma. *There's really not much difference between prostitution and what we do—we all sell our bodies,* Lon had been told. He had needed time to get past his prejudices, but he had come to like Mary, and he had enjoyed meeting several of her coworkers—both socially and professionally.

Mary abruptly turned back to Janno. "Two days?" she asked, and he nodded.

"We've got to be back in by three o'clock tomorrow night, Thursday morning."

"Then we can't waste any of that time with me working

and you drinking yourself silly," Mary said. "I'll go tell the boss I need the rest of the evening off. I was scheduled to have tomorrow off anyway."

By the time Phip returned from the bar with the drinks, Janno and Mary were gone. "Okay by me," Phip said when Dean told him what had happened. "That just means two beers for me this round." He took a long drink of the first of them before he added, "I guess she took it better than he expected."

Dean laughed. "At least in public. Hard telling what she'll do once she gets him alone somewhere."

"I know what she'll do," Phip said with a wink that was supposed to be lascivious. If he had not already been well on his way to intoxication, it might have worked.

"How about some food before we get too far gone?" Lon suggested. "We left before supper."

"Hell, we didn't even bother with lunch," Phip said, setting down an empty beer glass and reaching for the second. "Why put food into space that could hold more of this?"

"Because you'll stay conscious long enough to drink more if you eat," Dean said.

Phip hesitated, then nodded. "I buy that," he said. "But who's buying the food?"

"Everybody buys their own food," Dean said. "That's the way we always do it."

"It was worth a try," Phip said with a shrug.

4

It was 0745 hours the next morning when Lon's complink buzzed to alert him to an incoming call. He was sitting on his bunk buffing the shine on his dress shoes. He got up, crossed to the entertainment unit, and touched the "Accept" button. "Lieutenant Nolan," he said.

"Sir, this is Corporal Vajerian at battalion headquarters. Captain Orlis asked me to call to make sure you remembered the officers' call at oh-nine-hundred."

To make sure I was awake and sober, fit for duty, Lon thought. "I remember, Corporal. Thank you for calling."

There was no excuse for being drunk or hung over on duty. Killjoy-patches could get the alcohol out of the system, and an analgesic could get rid of any headache. Lon had no idea how many patches he had used the night before, but he had wakened at the first call from his alarm, in plenty of time to shower and make himself presentable. He had, however, elected to skip breakfast despite grumblings from his stomach. *I'll get a snack out of one of the machines before we go to the briefing,* he had promised himself. He was to meet Captain Orlis and Lieutenant Hoper in the orderly room, the company office, thirty minutes before the briefing.

There was no one up and about in the hallway when Lon left his room. He did not bother to look into any of the squad rooms. The men were off duty. They did not need, or deserve, to have him popping in to disturb their rest. In any case, he doubted if half of the men would even be around, and most of those would be sleeping off the night's celebrations . . . and resting up for one more round.

He stopped in the dayroom to get coffee and doughnuts from the food service machines. He ate one doughnut and sipped enough coffee to make transporting it simpler, then took the stairs down to the orderly room. It was empty. There was not even a CQ—Charge of Quarters—on duty. The company's communications links were remoted to battalion headquarters. Lon sat at one of the two desks in the outer office to finish his makeshift breakfast while he waited for the other men. Captain Orlis arrived just seconds before the scheduled rendezvous time, and Lieutenant Hoper was actually almost a minute late.

"Sorry, Captain," Carl Hoper said as he entered the orderly room and saw the others. "I stopped to get coffee." He gestured with the cup.

"Close enough," Matt Orlis said in a tired voice. "I almost didn't make it on time myself." Orlis was married and lived in the officers' housing district on base, about twenty minutes by floater—ground-effect vehicle—from the barracks. "We've got plenty of time before the briefing."

"I've been thinking," Hoper said. "From the little that Colonel Flowers told us, this could be one hairy contract."

"Wouldn't surprise me," Orlis said with an economical nod. "In the middle of a war between neighboring worlds. That means at least one is space-capable on its own. The soldiers are likely to be at least arguably professional as well."

"A *real* war?" Lon asked.

Orlis grunted. "They're all real," he said—mildly, without reproof, "but this one could be worse than most of the contracts we see. It depends on just what resources Calypso and Belletiene have available."

"We should have some idea before long," Hoper said, glancing at the clock.

"Before I forget," the captain said. "I'm going to want both of you here and passably fit when oh-three-hundred rolls around in the morning. We may have to chase down anyone who's late getting in. I don't want to take the slightest chance of having anyone miss transport tomorrow.''

Hoper and Nolan both nodded. Discipline was not a serious problem in the Dirigent Mercenary Corps, but things could happen, and missing transport heading out on contract was a certain route to dismissal from the Corps.

''I'll be here myself, along with Sergeant Ziegler.'' Jim Ziegler was the company lead sergeant. ''If you happen to see your platoon sergeants anytime today, let them know.'' Orlis shrugged. ''You've both got good platoon sergeants. They're probably ahead of all of us on this.''

''Aren't they always?'' Carl Hoper asked.

The commanders of the other companies in 2nd Battalion had already been through a regimental mission briefing, along with the battalion commanders and staff officers. That had been held before Alpha Company returned from New Bali. But the company commanders were all present, along with their junior officers, for the battalion briefing. By five minutes before nine o'clock, all of the officers from the battalion's four line companies were seated in the briefing room. There were complink monitors in front of each of them, and a large monitor at the head of the room, on the wall behind where Lieutenant Colonel Flowers would stand to deliver the briefing. Flowers and his executive officer, Major Hiram Black, came in precisely at 0900 hours, followed by Battalion Lead Sergeant Zal Osier, who would operate the controls of the complink during the briefing. Osier was the only enlisted man in the room.

''Good morning, gentlemen,'' Flowers said, glancing around the room. There were no military formalities about a contract briefing. This was business. ''Let's get straight to work.''

The complink monitors came to life with a three-dimensional chart of a solar system. ''We'll get the geography out of the way first,'' Flowers said. ''We have an unusual physical setup here, one of the rare instances of two inhabited worlds in the same system. Both are well within the parameters for colonization. Calypso is closer to their sun. Each world has a population of more than three million, with Belletiene slightly more populous.

"Our client is the government of Calypso. They have reason to fear that Belletiene is on the verge of invading. There have been ultimatums and propaganda claims and charges. Relationships between the worlds have been difficult for more than a century, and the tension has increased markedly in the last decade.

"It is only within those ten years that Calypso has started to build an army, something more than the usual colonial militia. Six years ago, a detachment from our 3rd Regiment spent half a year training that army, and setting up a local training protocol for the Calypsans. They have also purchased much of their military stores from Dirigent. That means that we will be working with troops who know how we operate, who have had training designed by us, and who use weapons that come from here.

"That's the good news. The bad news is, first, that the Calypsans have no space defenses worth mentioning, nothing more than a few interceptor rockets of questionable design, vintage, and manufacture. Their atmospheric defenses are almost as primitive—one squadron of fighter aircraft that were obsolete when they were designed two hundred years ago. Second, Belletiene is capable of transporting its soldiery to Calypso, and has a fleet large enough to put the equivalent of two of our regiments on the ground at once, with the naval power to protect their transports and fighter craft that can operate from orbiting carriers to cover the landings and attack targets on the ground. Their capacity in that regard is not large, but apparently sufficient for their purposes. It's been a long time since we faced an enemy with the potential of Belletiene, but we are not going in unprepared. Besides Seventh Regiment, the General is dispatching a four-ship task force to provide cover for us and the Calypsans—three cruisers and a fighter platform."

Colonel Flowers took a long pause, looking around the room. "As I said, the Calypsan government has reason to believe that invasion is imminent. Since Belletiene does not have to make any Q-space transits to reach Calypso, it is possible that the invasion will have taken place before we get there. If that is the case, we will dispatch a message rocket back here and a second regiment, or more if that seems necessary, will be dispatched to reinforce us. But, if at all possible, we will go in immediately." He paused again. "If that is the case, we will face at least thirty days of combat before our reinforcements can arrive, with only such resources as we bring with us, and what survives of the Calypsan military."

The briefing continued for another two hours. Colonel Flowers, spelled occasionally by Major Black, gave information about the number of troops that Calypso had, the geographical situation and conditions on the world, likely centers of conflict, economic details, and so forth.

"We will start moving the regiment up to the transports at noon tomorrow," Flowers said eventually. "That should be completed by twenty hundred hours, and the fleet will start moving out-system shortly after that. Questions?"

There were none at the moment. Everything that the colonel had said, and much more information, would be available to the officers through their complinks. And there would be plenty of time in the next two weeks—during the voyage to Calypso—for questions and discussions. The officers were dismissed.

"Captain," Lon said after they were outside the building, "I've got an untouched bottle of green djorja from New Bali back in my room. The stronger variety. I think now would be a fine time to open it." He nodded toward Carl Hoper. "I think all three of us could use a quick belt."

Orlis grinned. "I don't usually drink during the day, but this does seem like the time for an exception. We are off duty."

"I know *I* could use a bracer," Hoper said. "*Green* djorja? How many colors do they make it in?"

"Just the two, I think," Lon said.

"We'll have to hold it to one drink," Orlis said. "That stuff needs food to make it safe."

• • •

No one from Lon's platoons missed the deadline for returning to barracks. Janno Belzer was the last man to check in, and even he made it with a half hour to spare.

Lon had returned several hours earlier, sober enough to work. He had sat in his office and gone through the entire data file for the Calypso contract—all the information that the DMC had, both from the client and from its own databases. The latter was unusually extensive because of the prior contract. Since the government of Calypso had seen Belletiene as its primary—or only—potential enemy then, the Corps had gathered additional information about that world. The file on Calypso included video and hundreds of still photographs, two- and three-dimensional, showing the areas of the world that the mercenaries had visited while there to train the colony's new army.

We're not flying blind this time, Lon thought. *We know we have a lot of reliable information.* That was not always the case. Often, the Corps had little more than what the client was willing to provide, and some clients concealed pertinent, even vital, information from the mercenaries they were hiring. The consequences could be disastrous.

"Another tropical paradise," Lon said softly, shaking his head. Beaches and ocean, people running around in minimal clothing. Bright sunlight in cloudless skies. He keyed a query to find climatological information. It was somewhat reassuring. Calypso should not be as uncomfortable as New Bali. The primary centers of population were more subtropical than tropical, and edged into the world's southern temperate zone. The world's capital and largest cities were on the seacoast, and there were—according to the data gathered by the first Dirigenters to spend time on the world—prevailing breezes off the ocean that kept those cities relatively cool even during the hottest months of the year. The highest temperature they had recorded during the training contract was twenty degrees below the average highs that Lon's company had endured on New Bali.

Livable, Lon thought. *Maybe not as bad as Dirigent City during August.* Except for the chance of getting killed in combat. Lon logged out of the database and keyed the complink to standby mode.

5

Lon Nolan was no longer a rookie. The shuttle trip up to the battalion's transport, *Long Snake*, was just another ride, no more interesting than the bus from base to the spaceport on the other side of Dirigent City. Besides, Lon had responsibilities now, two platoons of soldiers. For seventeen of those, mostly in fourth platoon, Calypso would be their first time in combat; New Bali did not count—not as *combat*—though it had given Lon a chance to observe the new men in something more than a training exercise. Even this early in the mission, Lon had to reassure a few of them, and he had questions to answer.

Moving the entire regiment up to the ships took time. Buses and trucks had to make several round trips between base and spaceport. The port could only handle so many shuttles at once. And flight control preferred not to get the route between Dirigent City and the parking orbits of the fleet *too* crowded. There had been a lot of *hurry up and wait*. The waiting did not end once the shuttle docked with *Long Snake* and the men were marched to their quarters. The fleet would leave Dirigent together, in loose formation, and the last men would not board their vessels until two hours after Lon and his men arrived.

Long Snake carried the entire 2nd Battalion of 7th Regiment, along with supplies, baggage, and enough assault and transport shuttles to get them all to the ground at once—*and* its own crew and everything they needed. The ship was four miles long, but even so the troop compartments were cramped. A platoon was crowded into one bay, except for its platoon sergeant. Two sergeants shared a

47

cabin, and each officer had his own stateroom. Lon's was eight feet by five. It contained a berth, a fold-down desk with built-in complink, and two storage drawers under the bunk. The bathroom that went with it was scarcely large enough for a person to turn around in it.

Lon's duffel bag had already been delivered to his cabin when he arrived. It was lying on the bunk. Before he could sleep, he would have to stow his things in the drawers. *Later,* he decided. *After I eat.* Supper would be served in just a few minutes. One company would fit into the mess hall at a time. Alpha was first on the schedule for this meal. Tomorrow it would be last. The companies rotated in strict order.

"The contract is basically open-ended," Lon told third platoon the next morning. "The initial term is for six months, but with provisions to extend it as needed. Calypso apparently has plenty of money in its coffers. They've found so much gold and platinum that they make New Bali look poor." Those precious metals were always in demand, and only minimally for jewelry. With perhaps half a trillion humans on several hundred worlds, electronics alone required huge quantities of gold and platinum. Spaceships were also major users. A single Nilssen generator—the device that allowed a ship to jump through Q-space and provided the artificial gravity that made transportation comfortable—required eighty ounces of gold and seventeen of platinum. And a ship like *Long Snake* had three Nilssens, and more electronics that also required the metals.

"They also have a growing tourist business," Lon said, pausing then for comment.

"Tourists?" Phip asked. "*Tourists from other worlds*? Who's got that kind of money?"

"Enough people that Calypso gets between six and eight thousand of them a year, for stays that average six weeks."

"As long as there's a few lovely young heiresses," Phip said, earning his round of laughter from the platoon.

"Don't get too hopeful," Lon said. "The female population of the world is only forty-seven percent of the total."

He paused before adding, "Calypso would like to increase
its tourist business. To do that, they need some certainty of
peace. Another reason for our little junket. To get back to
what I was saying before, the contract is open-ended, but
if it goes longer than six months, we're to be relieved by
another regiment. Give someone else a turn at contract pay
and bonus money." He looked at Janno Belzer. The news
that his absence from Dirigent would be no more than
seven months—six months on Calypso and a month for
travel time—did not seem to cheer him up.

"Any chance it'll be less than six months, Lieutenant?"
Dean Ericks asked after also glancing at Janno.

"Always a chance," Lon said. "If peace breaks out and
Calypso no longer feels threatened, there is provision for
early termination of the contract. However, since this is
scheduled to be a long contract, provision will be made for
you to send message chips to family and friends on Dirigent. They'll go with the regular MRs that the colonel sends
with his progress reports. And you'll receive mail from Dirigent the same way, with the routine official stuff they send
us."

"How often will there be MRs going?" Corporal Heyes
Wurd of first squad asked.

Lon shrugged. "I doubt that the routine stuff will be
more often than fortnightly," he said, "and it may only be
once a month. MRs are a trifle more expensive than kites.
Okay, I know. It's not much. But it is something."

There was no plan of attack to brief the men on. If fighting had not started on Calypso when the Dirigenters arrived, the regiment would land at the capital's spaceport,
or at other locations. They would have time to move into
defensive positions and make preparations to meet a Belletiener attack. If enemy troops were already on the ground
on Calypso, then plans would have to be made once the
fleet emerged from its third and final Q-space transit of the
voyage within the star system that contained the two
worlds.

Lon spent an hour with third platoon, giving them the
information he had on Calypso and answering questions.

Then he repeated the process with fourth platoon. The men would all have a lot of time on their hands through the fifteen days of the trip. Apart from the need to keep their areas tidy, the only duty for the men was an hour of physical training each day. The rest of the time was their own. Eating and sleeping could not use up all the hours.

Lieutenant Colonel Flowers had entered the DMC on his eighteenth birthday, almost thirty years ago. The colonel had not bothered to prevent or correct the graying of his red hair, which he wore short. He was six and a half feet tall and weighed 220 pounds—solid and muscular. There was nothing soft about his appearance except for his green eyes.

"To success, gentlemen," Flowers said, standing at the head table in the officers' mess. He raised his glass of wine, then waited for the rest of the battalion's officers to stand and raise their glasses for the ceremonial toast.

"To success," came the chorus of echoes. Everyone drank deeply. *Long Snake* and the rest of the armada were four days out from Dirigent. In another eighteen hours the ships would be making their first Q-space transit of the voyage. The toast was ritual, in 7th Regiment, during the last supper before the first jump on the way out to a combat contract.

Colonel Flowers sat, followed by the rest of the officers. The meal was over, but—this time—no one would leave before the colonel. He leaned back and pulled a cigar from his shirt pocket. Despite the almost universal use of molecular health implants that prevented illness, physical debilitation, or addiction, smokers were a small minority in the DMC.

"Indulge yourselves, gentlemen, if you care to," Flowers said, gesturing vaguely. There were several boxes of cigars open in the room, on various tables. Flowers peeled the wrapper from his cigar and used his steak knife to nip the end from it.

Lon looked around, more than a little nervous, concerned whether he should take one of the cigars. Captain Orlis did.

So did Carl Hoper and maybe a third of the others.

"Never smoked, Nolan?" Matt Orlis asked softly.

Lon shook his head minimally. "They grow tobacco back where I was raised," he said. "Not much, of course, but there's apparently still a market for what they call the 'real stuff' instead of what's produced by a machine. I've seen it growing in the fields, seen people who smoke, and even chew the stuff, but I don't think I was ever really tempted to try it myself, even when some of the kids I hung around with did."

"I don't myself, as a rule," Orlis said. "Once in a great while, like now. It won't kill you."

"Though you might think differently when you get your first lungful of smoke," Carl Hoper said with a short laugh.

Lon shifted his glance from the nearby box of cigars to the others around him. Then he shrugged and took one for himself. He watched Carl prepare and light his, then copied him.

Lon coughed, and felt his face getting red. Orlis and Hoper both laughed, but not loudly. "I warned you," Carl said. "It takes getting used to."

"Why?" Lon asked when he felt he could dare to speak without going into more coughing.

"Beats me," Matt Orlis said. "People who do it regularly seem to get some sort of pleasure from it."

"All the rage in some circles," Carl said. "Why, I know some people who'd rather have a good smoke than a good beer."

Lon took a second, far more cautious, draw on his cigar, holding the smoke in his mouth rather than allowing it to travel any deeper. This time he noticed the taste, the mild tang and almost a sweetness, before he expelled the smoke.

"I feel a little dizzy," he said.

"Just because you're not used to it," Carl said.

"You do this often?" Lon asked.

Hoper shrugged. "I go through phases."

"Gentlemen!"

Colonel Flowers rapped on the side of his glass with a fork and spoke loudly enough to make certain that he got everyone's attention. The private conversations in the room ceased.

"There's no way to know what we'll face on Calypso," Flowers said, waving smoke away from in front of him, then leaning forward. "We may have to fight our way in, or we might land and spend six months waiting for something to happen. If you've spent any time at all looking through the database we have on Calypso, you will have noted that it offers a lot of . . . temptations. We're going to have to be careful about discipline, if we do have time on our hands and find ourselves stationed in or very close to one of the major population centers." He paused long enough to drag on his cigar.

"I know that the Corps rarely has problems with discipline. A large part of that is the spirit that we instill in all of our men, the knowledge of what the Corps stands for, and the certainty that breaches are treated most severely. But the rest of that success comes from having officers and noncoms who will do whatever is necessary and possible to prevent having anything happen that would require disciplinary action." He cleared his throat and scanned the room. "Something to think about," he said. When the colonel leaned back and turned toward Major Black, his executive officer, the other conversations resumed.

"More routine?" Lon asked.

Captain Orlis shrugged. "Not especially. But he's right. If the men have time on their hands and temptation wiggling in front of their eyes, there could be trouble."

"Just let your sergeants know that the colonel is concerned about discipline," Carl suggested in a whisper. "They'll know if there's any cause for alarm before you will anyway."

Lon nodded. *Sometimes I wonder why they need us at all.* He stared at his cigar and wondering about that as well. *Dendrow's been in the Corps since I was eight years old, and Jorgen has been in even longer. I need them a lot more than they need me. Lieutenants are like these cigars, a questionable habit.*

•   •   •

Lon found himself thinking about home that evening—his *real* home, Earth, not Dirigent. His parents were still there, and most of his childhood friends—those who had survived to adulthood. It had been several months, before the New Bali contract, since he had last received a message chip from his parents, with news of home and friends and relatives. Sending message chips by interstellar transport was expensive. Each one had to be used entirely, which meant several months worth of occasional notes sent together. Lon had known when he left Earth that there was little chance he would ever return. But there had been an element of desperation to the decision. His choices were to leave and take a chance of getting the military career he wanted on Dirigent, or staying home to be drafted into the federal police force of the North American Union when his class at the military academy graduated.

The only thing Lon had ever wanted to be was a soldier.

It was unusual for Lon to have trouble getting to sleep, except during a contract when sleep might allow danger to overtake him, but this night, he did. He lay awake for more than an hour, restless, unable to shut out memories of home. When he closed his eyes he could almost see his mother, hear her talking to him—way back when he was seven or eight years old—and almost smell a special Sunday dinner cooking. On Sundays, they had always splurged and had natural food, meat and vegetables from nature instead of from the food replicator. On Dirigent, natural food was commonplace, as common as the more modern substitute. But Lon had never escaped his earlier . . . respect for grown food. His mouth started watering. There was a hunger that no available meal could possibly satisfy. When he finally did fall asleep, he dreamed of pot roast with potatoes and carrots, brown gravy, coleslaw. . . .

He was never aware of the few tears that wet his pillow in the night. They had dried before he woke the next morning.

6

The gymnasium, the only training facility available to Alpha Company on *Long Snake*, was small, cramped, and minimally equipped. Each company had a similar room. There was only space for one platoon at a time. Lead Sergeant Jim Ziegler posted the schedule the first evening the battalion was aboard.

Lon alternated his own schedule, taking his exercise with each squad in his platoons in rotation. Some days, he went through two sets in the gym, not so much for fitness as to keep himself occupied. On *Long Snake*'s eighth day out, he was in the gym with Tebba Girana's squad. He paid little attention to the men around him. Lon was too focused on his own exercises, pushing himself, using exercise to keep his mind somewhere near where it needed to be— instead of drifting back to Earth and the family he could not reasonably expect to see again.

It can't be homesickness after all this time, he told himself. *It's not the way it was during the trip from Earth to Dirigent, or my first weeks in the Corps. This is different.* He could not explain it any other way. It was nothing as simple as a retreat from fear. He did not know what was coming on Calypso, and even if he had been certain of the most desperate combat, that was something he could accept. That was his profession. Until an answer surfaced in his mind, he compensated by pushing his exercises almost to the point of abusing his body. Subconsciously, there was the faintly ridiculous thought that self-torture might force his mind to produce the answer, or set aside the weakness that had come.

"Lieutenant?" It took a few seconds for the word to penetrate Lon's concentration. Lon blinked. He had not noticed Sergeant Dendrow standing five feet in front of him.

"What is it?" Lon asked, almost gasped.

"The platoon has finished, sir," Dendrow said, moving a pace closer once Nolan halted his almost frantic workout. "And the bridge made the thirty-minute warning for our next Q-space transit."

Lon looked around. Tebba's squad had left the gym. He and Dendrow were alone. Lon shook his head. "I guess I got a little carried away, Ivar. I was so focused that I didn't even notice."

"Yes, sir. I got that impression." If there was an undertone of concern in the platoon sergeant's voice, it was too subtle for Lon to notice. But Dendrow *was* concerned. Any real or suspected aberration in a commander was cause for concern.

"How long ago was the warning for Q-space?" Lon asked.

"Been eight or nine minutes now, Lieutenant."

"We'd best be getting back then, hadn't we?" Lon said. The full power of all three Nilssen generators would be required for the transit. *Long Snake*'s occupants would be deprived of artificial gravity until the ship returned to normal space. The hiatus was rarely more than six to eight minutes, during which the ship's position might alter by scores of light-years.

"Yes, sir." Dendrow paused. "Are you all right, sir?" he asked then, hesitantly.

Lon did not answer immediately. He turned the question over in his own mind a couple of times first. "I'm fine, Ivar. This is going to sound a bit ridiculous, but I've just been feeling a little homesick the past few days."

"Not Dirigent, I gather?"

Lon shook his head. "No, Earth—the one planet in this galaxy I know I'll probably never get to again."

For the duration of the Q-space transit, *Long Snake* was effectively in a universe of its own. The Nilssens generated a bubble of Q-space—quantum space—around the ship. The ovate bubble's long diameter was barely greater than the ship's length. Looking out from *Long Snake*, all that anyone could have seen was a featureless dark gray, lit only by the few exterior lights on the ship. Theoretically, the bubble of Q-space was contiguous with every point in the universe of "normal" space. By stressing the Q-space envelope around it at the proper point for the proper length of time, *Long Snake* could—in theory—reemerge in normal space at any desired point. But the stresses did require calculation. In practice, that was why ships normally made three separate Q-space transits during each voyage—one from the point of origin out to a customary "shipping lane," one along that well-documented route, and a final jump from it to the point of termination. The days spent in normal space before and after each jump were meant to reduce the chance of variable fluctuations that could affect the accuracy of the calculations. There was no measurable distinction between one Q-space bubble and any other. It was merely an inescapable part of interstellar travel, no more remarkable for the traveler than transferring from one bus to another in a large city.

During the three days between the second and third jumps, the approach of the end of the voyage, with its uncertainties and possible danger, gradually took Lon Nolan's mind from Earth and the melancholy memories.

Long Snake emerged from its third transit of Q-space in Calypso and Belletiene's star system, eighty hours out from Calypso. The first order of business was to reestablish contact with the other ships of the armada, all of which emerged in normal space within the space of less than a minute. The fleet was, of necessity, well dispersed by this point. DMC policy was to require considerable separation between ships when they entered and exited Q-space, to minimize turbulence.

The second order of business was to learn the latest news from Calypso. Less than two hours after the end of the final

Q-space transit, Colonel Flowers called his officers together.

"Belletiene's invasion of Calypso began five days ago,"
Flowers said as soon as everyone was assembled. "I don't
have many details yet. Regiment and fleet CIC"—combat
information center—"are still trying to determine what the
situation is. What we do know is that fighting continues.
We can expect to either make a combat assault landing or
to enter combat shortly after arrival. As soon as I know
anything more definite, I'll pass the news along to you."

Rumors had a short lifespan in the transports of 7th Regiment. Colonel Arnold Gaffney, the regimental commander,
and CIC aboard his ship, *Star Dragon*, processed information from Calypso as quickly as it could be obtained. At
times there were as many as four separate communications
links open between the ship and Calypso. Colonel Gaffney
shared what he was learning with his battalion commanders
and their staffs, who passed each bit of solid news along
to their subordinate officers. Facts killed rumors, but—
phoenixlike—gave birth to new rumors.

The history of the fighting was compiled and distributed—troop movements, battles, and various intelligence
estimates of the relative abilities and equipment of the two
sides. There was even video of the Belletiener landings and
many of the firefights that had taken place. In the Calypsan
army, only officers and sergeants had video cameras in their
battle helmets, but those were of Dirigentan manufacture,
so the quality was as good as video from the helmets that
the DMC used. The video of the enemy landings came pri-
marily from other sources, including the cameras of tourists
and the civilian complink nets.

"Don't wait for someone to tell you what you should or
shouldn't bother with," Lon told third platoon during one
of his briefings. "There are plenty of complinks available.
Use them. The more you know about what's going on down
there now, the better equipped you'll be when we hit the
ground."

"Lieutenant?" Corporal Wurd of first squad raised a hand.

"What is it, Heyes?" Lon asked.

"Any idea yet when that'll be? When we go in, that is."

Lon shook his head. "Not when or where. Regiment hasn't firmed up a plan of attack yet. We're still forty hours out from attack orbit, so it's going to be at least that long before we go in. My best guess is that we won't wait too long after that. Our employers might not take kindly to the paid professionals sitting safely in orbit and watching while they take all the heat. We'll reach our orbit about sunset in Oceanview, the capital. Figure that a landing is most likely that night, or dawn the next morning. But that's just my guess, worth what you paid for it." During the trip, the diurnal cycle had been gradually adjusted so that time aboard the ships would coincide with time in Calypso's capital.

"Night won't give us an advantage here," Corporal Girana of second squad said; it was definitely not a question.

"Expect the Belletieners to be equipped as well as we are," Lon said. "That means weapons as well as electronics and full night-vision capability. They've spent liberally over the past twenty years to build and maintain a modern army, shopping anywhere they could find good gear."

"We gonna be facing anything made on Dirigent?" Heyes Wurd asked. "Damn near all my relatives work in military industries." That garnered nervous laughter from about half of the platoon.

"Dirigent hasn't sold anything to them directly, I do know that," Lon said with an appreciative grin. "And it's unlikely that anyone has transshipped anything in the sort of quantities they've been buying."

Lon conducted at least two sessions a day with each of his platoons, answering questions and sharing information—doing what he could to keep his men loose, ready for action. That had started during the interstellar part of the voyage, and the sessions got longer once the fleet was in-system.

At least for the length of time that the sessions lasted,

Lon was able to set aside his own concerns about the contract. The closer to Calypso that the fleet got without a definitive battle plan from regiment, the more nervous he got. Lon was not the only one. Matt Orlis and Carl Hoper both admitted to nerves as well. "I don't know what the colonel's problem is," Matt said when the three officers gathered in the captain's stateroom after supper, one day out from Calypso.

"Yeah, you'd think he would have approved at least a preliminary plan by now," Hoper said. "Something to let us start preparing the men for. No matter how fluid conditions are on the ground, CIC should be able to come up with *something* reasonable."

"With all the policy about being open, you don't suppose they're holding something back from us, do you?" Lon asked.

Orlis shook his head quickly. "Not Gaffney. I've served under him too long to think that's even conceivable. And he's got twenty years more in the Corps than I do. The only explanation I can come up with is that there must be some sort of argument going on, that the Calypsans want us to do something that the colonel doesn't want to do. *That* I could understand. The locals probably want us to drop right on top of the largest enemy concentration, and the colonel would resist that."

"Too costly," Hoper interjected.

"Colonel Gaffney won't spend men thoughtlessly," Orlis said, nodding. "And, with him, I'm sure it's more than just because it's bad for business." Mercenaries looked at the idea of last stands or suicide charges with total horror. Casualties, deaths, were part of the business, but a mercenary needed to *know* that he had a reasonable chance of surviving any contract.

"If it's something like that, wouldn't he just pass the word?" Lon asked. "That way we'd know what's going on and wouldn't be worrying over it the way we are—and the way the men must be too."

Matt Orlis looked at the floor between his feet for a moment. "If we haven't heard anything by morning, I'll ask

Colonel Flowers, and ask him to ask Gaffney if he doesn't know.''

Medwin Flowers anticipated the questions at breakfast the next morning. ''You're all wondering why we haven't been given at least a preliminary plan of attack.'' He paused. ''Perhaps I've been remiss. I should have anticipated your concern sooner.''

Lon and Carl Hoper exchanged glances, but no one spoke. Colonel Flowers had obviously not finished.

''I know you've been studying the action reports we've been getting,'' the colonel said. ''There are two zones of fighting, one near the capital and the seacoast, the other in the area of the most productive gold mines. Those are the obvious primary targets for the invader. The Calypsan army is, for the time being, holding its own. The situation is fluid, changing dramatically, almost hour by hour. Our CIC has come up with three equally feasible scenarios for us. Calypso's Defense Command Center has one other—and is pushing hard for it.

''Colonel Gaffney decided that it would be counterproductive to issue preliminary assault plans based on several possible, and contradictory, scenarios. He intends to wait as long as possible before making a final choice, depending on the latest information. He plans to put us down where we can be most effective, *at that moment*.'' Flowers paused to make certain that everyone caught his emphasis. ''I talked to Colonel Gaffney just before coming here. He assured me that he will try to give us a minimum of an hour before we head for the shuttles to study the plan he chooses.

''We should be going in tonight, sometime. You all know the routine for today. No exercise periods. Give the men all the time possible to eat and sleep. Do what you can to reassure them. It's certainly not *bad* news that's holding up a final plan.'' He almost allowed a smile to sneak across his face. ''Besides, you all know that even the best battle plan tends to get buried within minutes after we ground.''

• • •

After breakfast, Lon passed the news to the men in his platoons; then—after the usual question-and-answer session—he went to his cabin and settled in for a morning's work. He pulled down the folding desk and logged onto the complink net. *What would I do if the choice were mine?* Lon asked himself as he called up the files on Calypso. It was an intellectual exercise, a holdover from his days as a student officer, first at the North American Military Academy on Earth, and then as a cadet-officer on Dirigent. It was also a practical exercise, one more way to help fix details of the situation on the ground in his mind, and prepare for action.

The bulk of Calypso's population was concentrated in a thin strip along the east coast of the one continent that was heavily settled. It was in the southern hemisphere, so there was no danger from hurricanes. The capital, Oceanview, was relatively small, an enclave devoted to governmental business a couple of miles from the largest city on the world. A secondary concentration of people was located in the principal mining region, in the mountains two hundred miles west of the coast. There were no large towns or cities, but several dozen small villages, some little more than mining camps. Most of the mining activity was between two ranges, in the valleys and along the flanks of the mountains.

A spine for the continent, like the mountains in the Americas, from the Rockies to the Andes, Lon thought, as he added the topographical element to his map. Thinking of home was no distraction now—his mind was too focused. Everything going between the coast and the mountains went by air. There were no improved roads connecting the regions, no bridges or tunnels, and—so far as the available database knew—no one had ever attempted to make the journey on land. The area had been well charted, but only from space and from the air. *No telling what might be in there.* Lon grinned. No systematic survey of flora and fauna had been made, except in the areas where people lived—or thought they might want to live in the near future. Calypso could still hold plenty of surprises, even for its residents. In a rare moment of whimsy, Lon annotated his working overlay of the map with *"Here There Be Drag-ons!"* then leaned back and chuckled. It made him feel better, more relaxed.

CIC had put together an animated log of the fighting and troop movements with a voice-over commentary. A panel across the bottom provided numbers and links to supporting data. Belletiene had committed thirty-five hundred troops to the initial assault—slightly more men than were in a standard DMC regiment. The bulk of those troops had been targeted against the population centers on the coast. Only five hundred men had been sent west to threaten the mining region. The initial assault had been given limited air cover. According to the available information, Belletiene only had one fighter carrier, and its capacity was apparently twenty-four aerospace fighters. At least three of those fighters had been shot down by Calypsan air defense, and—if the government's claims were valid—possibly as many as seven.

Lon went through the entire animation once without pause, watching as the two armies maneuvered for position and fought. So far, the Calypsan army had done its job well, protecting the cities and avoiding a decisive battle that might go against them. In the west, where only one company of the Calypsan army was normally stationed, the slack had been picked up by local militia groups supplied by the mining contractors. Gold and platinum mines always faced the possibility that they might need protection. The contractors had been prepared. The largely untrained units they had assembled might not stand for long against professional soldiers, but there were enough of them to keep the invaders occupied. Just hours before the Dirigent fleet emerged in normal space coming in, the Belletiener commander had moved another 250 troops west as reinforcements.

"The bullion is the vital link," Lon muttered. "That's the whole point of the invasion. Belletiene wants the precious metals." He leaned back and shook his head. *Why didn't they put their whole army in there? They could have overpowered the local opposition and started hauling ore out, or the refined metals. Make Calypso come in after them. That would have given the Belletiener force the security of defending good ground.*

He thought it over. *Okay, I can see a couple of reasons for not doing it that way. Maybe they can't sustain a long campaign without a broader base. They might be forced to cut and run, or get pinned down and destroyed piecemeal. They're not in this just to raid what they can and run. They want the whole kit and caboodle, all of the gold and platinum, the refineries, and the industry that has grown up to exploit the deposits.*

The most radical alternate scenario was harder to deal with. *Then why not forget about the mining area altogether until the real work was done? Put all your resources to defeating the Calypsan army and taking the government and population centers.* The only answer Lon could see was that Belletiene wanted the threat in the mountains to distract the Calypsans.

Okay, that's the situation, he thought at last, *however they got to where they are. Now, how would I use the regiment to do the most good in the shortest time, at the lowest cost?* That was, after all, supposed to be the point of this exercise.

Lon started by noting objectives. The first was "Protect the government." The paymaster, the boss. The second, "Protect the main population centers," was a corollary of the first. The government of Calypso needed its base of support, and would have little power if its main cities were captured. "Force a quick, economical end to the fighting," was the third note Lon made.

There could be infinite ways that 7th Regiment *might* be used on Calypso. Lon had to start with broad strokes, making basic assumptions, to narrow down the possibilities. It did not take him long to get to the point of writing "Land along the coast, near the primary action, but not immediately *in* it. Put the main Belletiener force in pincers between us and the Calypsan army, pressure them toward ground favorable for us, then force them to surrender or face destruction." That meant ignoring the Belletiener soldiers in the mining region. Once the main force was neutralized, they would no longer be a serious threat.

"Now, how do I go about this?" Lon asked himself softly. He was feeling very pleased with his progress. In the long run, it would matter not at all that his deductions were entirely wrong.

7

"It doesn't make sense, Captain," Lon said with some heat. "It just doesn't make sense." He pointed at the complink monitor in Orlis's cabin. "Belletiene has pulled more men from the seacoast and sent them to the mining region. If the numbers we're getting are right, they've split their force almost right down the middle now."

Orlis shrugged. "Don't get so lathered up, Nolan. If they want to make things easier for us, let them. Don't ask me to make excuses for them."

"They *have* to know we're here," Lon said. The transports were less than thirty minutes from being in position to launch shuttles, nearly sunset in Oceanview. The cruisers were pushing in faster, heading for a confrontation with the Belletiener troopships, which were armed with rockets and both energy and projectile guns. There was no sign of the aerospacecraft carrier. The estimate was that it had gone home. Belletiene had no cruisers or anything else over Calypso, and there was no sign of traffic along the route between the two worlds, which were currently about 80 million miles apart. "You'd think they'd be massing to meet us."

Orlis sighed. There were things he would rather be doing, but educating junior officers was part of the job. "There are good reasons for dispersing troops when faced with attack from space. And it's almost always beneficial to do the unexpected. If Belletiene's moves confuse Colonel Gaffney and CIC the way they have you, that's justification enough, don't you think?"

"Maybe," Lon conceded reluctantly.

"According to the record of the campaign Belletiene has waged up to now, there's no reason to suspect that their commander on Calypso is incompetent," Orlis said. "They appear to have done a creditable job so far. And—assuming that they have decent intelligence about our fleet—it would make sense for the Belletiener commander to use his shuttles before we can interdict air travel for them, get all his people where he thinks they'll do the most good, or be in the least jeopardy."

"But . . ." Lon started, then stopped. He shook his head, a gesture aimed more at himself than at the captain.

"Don't worry about it," Orlis said. "You're just upset because this makes all your wargaming for the contract obsolete." That was a guess, but from the startled look that flashed onto Lon's face, the captain knew that he had struck the primer. He held up a hand to stop whatever Lon was about to say. "I know. We all do it. I just hope you got your share of sleep this afternoon. If we go in tonight, hard telling when you'll get a chance to get any real sleep next."

"I got what sleep I could," Lon said, his tone almost pouting. Altogether, Lon doubted that he had managed two hours of sleep during the past ten. But he was not tired, not sleepy. His mind was wired, thinking ahead to the landing and the combat that might come almost immediately after that.

"Too late to get any more," Orlis said, glancing at the clock. "We ought to be getting an assault plan from regiment any minute now."

"I hope so," Lon said, half under his breath.

"Look, I've seen contracts where we didn't get *any* plan until we were in the shuttles, and even then it was nearly obsolete before we landed. We had to start improvising within five minutes after grounding. You can't count on the enemy doing what you expect. If you do, you're in serious trouble."

"Yes, sir," Lon said. "It's just so frustrating."

"Goes with the territory, Nolan."

Lon left the captain's cabin and went back to his own. There was no room to pace in the tiny stateroom, which was what Lon felt like doing, but he did not want to start walking up and down one of the passageways where he might be seen by enlisted men. Officers were supposed to remain unflappable. Any sign of nervousness might infect the lower ranks. In the troop compartments, things would not be so tense. It seemed that every squad had at least one man who had some way to ground the static of worry among his mates. In Girana's squad, the lightning rod was usually Phip, with his unending wisecracks and sometimes sardonic observations, often aided and abetted by Janno and Dean. There were times when their antics could distract the entire platoon.

"Relax, dummy," Lon told himself. "Don't get so keyed up." *Don't use all of the adrenaline before you get down where you might need it.* He sat on the edge of his bunk, then lay down. He tried breathing exercises to relax. To some extent it did work, but not as much as it might have if he was not also trying to listen for the first note of a signal from the complink that an action plan had come through—or orders to muster the men and start moving to the shuttles.

After a few minutes Lon started working through the latest troop movements and dispositions on the surface—the last he had seen before his excursion to Captain Orlis's room. New positions, new possibilities. *Take out one or the other of the enemy concentrations,* he thought. *It's almost a toss-up which to attack first.* He needed only a few seconds to proceed from that to *On balance, I guess I'd concentrate on the enemy force threatening the capital and the cities on the coast. Once they're neutralized, there's plenty of time to see to the rest.*

He did not fall asleep. Most of the time his eyes remained open, though he was really not seeing the ceiling. He did lose awareness of passing time, as if his mind had created a Q-space bubble around him, making time almost irrelevant. He was thinking about the possibilities, where he might land the troops if he were in command, how they would put the enemy in an unfavorable position and then move in. Lon focused on that, and found nearly as much relaxation in his musings as he might have in sleep.

. . . Until his reverie was interrupted by a worried *What time is it?* He was so startled by the sudden realization that time had passed that he almost levitated from his bunk. He turned toward the complink monitor and the timeline across the top.

Twenty hundred hours.

Lon got to his feet, fighting back the thought *It can't be.* By twenty hundred, they should have had orders at least, if they were not already en route. Lon moved to the complink and keyed in the self-test programs—a useless gesture, because even if the set, or the entire net, had been out of order, he would have heard. Someone would have come to the door to fetch him, or to tell him that they had their action plan.

The complink ran its tests without complaint and announced that everything was functioning properly. Lon barely glanced at the screen. He started toward the door, ready—without thinking through the decision—to run down the passageway to Captain Orlis's room to ask what the problem was. He had his hand on the door handle before thought caught up with instinct. *You'll just look like a fool,* he told himself. *Again.*

Think, dummy. He took a deep breath, then released the door handle and returned to the complink. He keyed in a search for late additions to the files on the coming operation. New intelligence had been added about the latest movements on the ground, and a report that the Belletiener troopships were accelerating toward home, fleeing from the Dirigenter cruisers, but there was no new analysis from CIC—and no action plan.

I can't just sit here and twiddle my thumbs, Lon thought. *I could go to the mess hall and get a cup of coffee. Maybe check with Ivar and Weil to see how the men are bearing up.* It would use up some time. There was also a chance that he would run into Captain Orlis or one of the other officers. They could chat. *I'll just have to act calm,* Lon thought. *I can do that.*

• • •

Nearly half of the battalion's officers were in the officers' mess, drinking coffee, tea, or soft drinks and chatting. Some turned to look when Lon opened the door. There was a quick subsidence in the level of conversation as men waited to learn if he might be the messenger who would tell them that orders had finally come. When he headed directly for the drink caddy at the end of the serving line, the conversations resumed.

Carl Hoper was sitting alone at one of the tables. Lon joined him once he had his coffee. "I guess I'm not the only one getting a little antsy," Lon said sotto voce.

Carl grinned. "I don't know about the rest of these people, but I just got tired of being by myself."

Lon grinned back. "Yeah, me too. It was either come up here or go bother the men."

"Matt came but only stayed for about two minutes, long enough to drink half a cup of coffee. Said he was working the kinks out."

"You suppose someone forgot to wake Colonel Gaffney from his afternoon nap?" Lon asked, looking to see that no one was close enough to overhear. Gaffney was a popular commander.

"You're the third one to ask me that in half an hour," Carl replied. "It's the joke of the day."

"It's not just me, is it?" Lon asked. "I mean, this *is* unusual, this stooging around waiting for some sort of plan?"

"It's unusual," Carl agreed. "Not unheard of, but not something you expect to run into. And, no, I don't know why. Hell, maybe the Calypsans want to renegotiate the contract. Strange as it may seem, that has happened before, other places. They get to thinking that maybe they can dicker the price down a little once we're on the spot."

"You're kidding."

"Look up the Dinwaith contract when you get the time. Seven or eight years ago, I think it was. Our Fourth Battalion waited overhead for nine hours while the governor of Dinwaith tried to talk down the fee. That wasn't the first time. It's just the one that comes to mind." Carl got up to get another cup of coffee. Lon took a couple of long drinks of his, then went to the machine as well to refill it.

"I think I'll get a couple of doughnuts or something," Carl said. "Once we do get moving, hard telling how long it'll be before we get a shot at halfway decent chow again."

Lon was not especially hungry. He had eaten to capacity at supper, five hours earlier, and that was still sitting firmly in his stomach. But he took a doughnut for himself—something to nibble at to help fill the remaining waiting. Besides, Carl was right about one thing. Once they went into action, it might be a long time before they had anything but packaged battle rations to eat, and although those were nourishing, they were not noted for being tasty or filling.

It was past 2100 hours before the loudspeakers said, "All officers of Second Battalion will report to the officers' mess immediately." Several more officers had drifted into the mess before the announcement. Few had left.

Lon and Carl stared at each other.

"Now we find out," Carl said.

Lon nodded. "At last." He looked around, not actually counting noses, but checking. "Not too many people missing, other than the colonel and his staff."

"I think I'll get another cup of coffee before the briefing starts," Carl said. As he stood, he added, "Assuming that this is going to be a briefing and not just another 'Well, we still don't know what we're going to do, but soon now' sort of excuse, or—worse yet—news that the contract has been canceled and we're going home."

"It *can't* be that," Lon said.

"I hope not" was Carl's less than optimistic reply.

The remaining officers started arriving within seconds of the end of the announcement over the public address system. Inside four minutes, every officer in the battalion was present but its commander and the executive officer. Matt Orlis joined his lieutenants after getting coffee.

"I hope you two haven't had so much of that go-juice that you won't be able to sleep if the orders are that we don't go in until just before dawn," Orlis said as he sat.

"You think that's likely?" Hoper asked.

Orlis shrugged. "I don't know what to think. I don't suppose our mere presence overhead is going to be enough to make the Belletieners suddenly surrender, but . . ."

He did not finish the thought, because the door opened and Lieutenant Colonel Flowers strode into the room followed by Major Black and Battalion Lead Sergeant Zal Osier. They went straight to the head table. The two senior officers sat. Sergeant Osier remained standing behind them. The company commanders and platoon leaders—those who had been standing when the commander entered—hurried to find seats.

"Gentlemen," Flowers said in his usual soft voice, "we have our orders." He did not have to speak loudly. There was not another sound in the room.

"The rest of the regiment will be boarding their shuttles within the next thirty minutes."

Don't tell me we're going to be held in reserve! Lon thought during the brief pause the colonel left after that statement. There were a few sounds in the room in that gap, small noises—murmurs and involuntary movements, feet shuffling.

"Our turn will come soon enough," the colonel added, looking around. "Here are the basics. The other battalions will land close enough to engage the Belletiener forces in the mining region. CIC estimates that the enemy will attempt to shift more men to deal with that threat. If they attempt to use the shuttles they have on the ground to move those men, our Shrike fighters will have a crack at them— which could save us some work. In any case, the landing of our main force in the west should provide some stress for the enemy commanders, and maybe even a little confusion. Those landings will be accompanied by fighter cover, with our pilots striking at enemy positions. Then, at oh-three-hundred hours, we will board our shuttles to land near Oceanview just before first light there.

"This might be tricky. Just after sunset this evening, Belletiener soldiers reached the outskirts of the capital. Calypso is contesting their advance, holding them to a very slow pace, but how long they can continue that successful resistance is open to question. We will come down on the right flank of the Belletiener force—which will outnumber us about three to two.

"The immediate objective for Second Battalion is to get between the invaders and the government of Calypso. We will operate as a separate force, but we will be in close cooperation with the Calypsan army, coordinating our moves with the local commander. Remember, the Calypsans have shown their abilities. Many of them were trained by our people, and those who weren't were still trained by those who had. They are a serious military force, not haphazard militia.

"When you get back to your rooms, you will find more detailed briefing information on your complinks. Get with your noncoms. Give them the word and let them pass it on to the men. I won't pretend that the plan we have is comprehensive. Everything after the actual landings is up in the air, depending on the conditions that prevail then. CIC has scores of scenarios ready to act upon, depending on how Belletiene responds to our grounding and the outcome of the early fighting."

Flowers paused again, but only briefly. "I'm not going to ask for questions now. "We'll try to deal with any of those later, when we're ready to head for the boats—after you've all had time to read through what CIC has provided. By the time we get ready to leave, we should have some idea how the Belletieners are reacting to the rest of the regiment." He stood and the rest of the officers immediately followed suit.

"Once you've briefed your noncoms, try to get at least a couple of hours of sleep, and that goes for your men as well. Reveille will be at oh-one-forty-five hours, followed by a quick breakfast. For now, gentlemen, let me just add, good luck, and may God go with us all." Flowers, Black, and Osier left immediately. The rest of the officers were slower to depart, but there was still not much of a delay, just long enough for men to express their reactions to the news.

"This doesn't even come close to any of the possibilities I saw," Lon said. "And if I had thought of it, I probably would have dismissed it without a second thought."

Captain Orlis's short laugh was almost a bark. "Let's just hope that the enemy is as much in the dark as you were, Nolan. Now, let's tell the men what's up. And, you two, if you've got too much coffee in you to sleep naturally, use patches. I want you as fresh as possible when reveille comes."

8

The weight of full battle kit was more comfort than
burden for Lon. He scarcely noticed the load as he moved
to the shuttle bay with his platoons. That might change once
he had been on the ground carrying it for some time. Camouflage battledress, helmet, rifle and pistol, ammunition,
mapboard, canteens, and pack—it added up to sixty
pounds. He had managed nearly two hours of sleep, though
it had taken a patch on his neck to knock him out. There
was no drug "hangover" from the medical device, and the
sleep was as restful as any could be. He was alert now,
clear-headed, and only moderately tense.

There was no time to worry about himself. He had a
hundred men to take his attention. Lon watched and listened. He detected no unusual signs of strain among his
men. There was the usual joking and good-natured grous-
ing. They moved from the barracks compartment to the
armory to draw weapons, then went on to the hangar and
into the shuttle.

Lon was the last man to board. He stood at the entrance
to the shuttle and counted men as they boarded. The hangar
bay crew chief, a member of *Long Snake*'s crew, stood
opposite Lon and also counted. When the counts matched
and every man in third and fourth platoons was accounted
for, the crew chief—a petty officer—saluted. Lon returned
the salute, then boarded the shuttle and hit the button to
close the hatch. The crew chief checked the telltales, then
left the hangar. Once the shuttle pilot confirmed that his
lander was pressurized and on its own air supply, the hangar could be depressurized for launch.

Inside the shuttle, the men were already strapping themselves in. Most had lowered the tinted faceplates of their helmets. Privacy. Whether they wanted solitude for prayers or just to prepare themselves mentally for what was to come, it was something that most Dirigenters craved at a time like this. Lon remembered the almost-terror he had experienced when he was about to go into combat for the first time.

Lon stood near his place while squad leaders worried about the eleven men under their command. Platoon sergeants checked on squad leaders. And Lon checked his platoon sergeants before he strapped himself in. He waited until the shuttle pilot informed him that the hangar was being depressurized before he spoke to his men—by radio, over his all-hands channel.

"You all know the basic plan," Lon said. "We're going in hot, but with any luck we'll get down and out of the box before the enemy can react. Down and out, and set up a quick perimeter to let the shuttles get back off safely. After that, we'll pretty much be playing it by ear. Remember, we're going against trained soldiers, and they have *some* combat experience. They're not going to faint dead away just because they see our pretty uniforms." Lon was relieved to hear a few laughs. The last news from the surface was that, so far, Belletiene had not attempted to move any additional troops from the east coast to the mining region in response to the earlier landing by the rest of 7th Regiment. The invaders were continuing their assaults on Oceanview and the nearest of the larger cities, The Cliffs.

"Let's keep calm and do our jobs. Tonight is just the start. We might still be here for six months." Even though the fact that the Belletiene invasion had taken place was supposed to trigger the deployment of a second DMC regiment, there was no guarantee that 7th Regiment would be sent home early, even if the fighting ended quickly.

Lon felt, rather than heard, the massive outer hangar door open. The air had been evacuated from the hangar, so sound could not be transmitted. But vibrations did pass through metal.

"Lock and load," Lon said, an order that army officers had been giving for a thousand years. Men checked safeties, then slid magazines into rifles and ran the bolts to put a round in the chamber. Lon did the same with his rifle. He had loaded his pistol at the armory. After that, Lon remained silent. He continued to monitor his all-hands and noncoms channels, but he let the sergeants and corporals deal with the routine reminders for everyone to make certain that they were strapped in tight and that their weapons were secured before the shuttle left the hangar and lost *Long Snake*'s artificial gravity.

Don't let me fail my men, Lon thought—prayed. *Don't let me screw up and get men killed.* "Unnecessarily" was understood.

The shuttle was lifted out of the hangar and released by the grapple. The pilot used cold gas jets to maneuver away from the ship. All of the battalion's attack shuttles would rendezvous before any of them accelerated toward the ground, using their own power more than gravity to get them in as quickly as possible. Once the descent started, the passengers on the shuttles would be subjected to as much as four times standard gravity. But, for the present, they were virtually weightless.

Some people never got used to weightlessness. A few got sick nearly every time they experienced it; others did occasionally. It was one ailment that medical science had not eradicated. Those who were prone to it knew they were; nobody in this shuttle was on his first trip. Those who sat close to the likely victims were certain to insure that they had a bag handy to catch vomit. Lon listened for the sounds, but the minutes of microgravity passed without incident. The shuttles rendezvoused and started to accelerate toward the ground. As soon as there was some semblance of weight—a *proper* physiological notion of up and down—the greatest danger was past.

A hot descent could be a hell ride for passengers. It was a power dive starting from orbit, with the pilot accelerating toward the ground, then reversing thrust and pulling out of the dive at the last possible second, pushing the lander to the limit the troops could physically stand without protective gear to counter the push and pull. The rationale was to get the troops on the ground and out where they could fight as quickly as possible, to give any enemy as little time as possible to target the shuttles in flight. An error in judgment by the pilot could have troops graying out from the gee-forces, or plowing into the dirt. The boat itself could stand much more than its passengers.

Though they might complain about the procedure, few troops would have opted for a slower insertion into a combat zone. While they were aboard the shuttle and strapped into their seats, they were powerless to defend themselves.

Here we go, Lon thought as the acceleration became noticeable. There were video monitors spaced along the bulkheads so that everyone could see at least one. They now provided infrared views of what was in front of the shuttle. Once they got closer, it might be possible to get some hint of conditions around the landing zone.

If the Belletieners had not moved any troops in the last few minutes, the LZ would be two and a half miles from any known enemy positions. That *should* be sufficient to let the shuttles touch down, unload their troops and equipment, and get back into the sky burning for orbit before the enemy could get close enough to bring them under fire. *If the intelligence is right,* Lon thought, *and if luck hasn't taken time out and let the enemy move right into the LZ.* He took a deep breath and let it out slowly. *We'll know soon enough.* There was that about a hot landing: The trip was over in short order.

Oceanview was a planned city. In the earliest decades of the colony, the capital was the nearby city known as The Cliffs, from its site on bluffs overlooking the ocean. Prosperity and a longing for a more "proper" showplace led to the decision to create a special capital, a place for local governmental business and—more important—for nurturing interworld trade agreements. Oceanview was marked by broad avenues, extensive parks, and—unlike most colonial worlds, except for the oldest and most heavily populated—monumental buildings. There had been plenty of money for all of the efforts. The government reserved fifty percent of the proceeds from mining for "the benefit of all Calypsans"—that is, for itself.

Government House was the center of the city, and the largest structure in it. The building and its grounds covered ninety acres. The center portion of the building was in the shape of a five-story step-pyramid, with broad patios on each level—a design continued in the terraces that elevated the building above its surroundings. To either side were large square wings, with extensive courtyards in the center. One wing held parliament, the other the main courts of law. The designers of Government House had wanted plenty of air, and broad vistas. The edifice was built with future expansion of the bureaucracy in mind. After more than a century of use, there was still no crowding. Even rather minor officials could claim private offices.

In the area around Government House, a group of not-quite-so-imposing buildings housed ancillary agencies, trade organizations, and the headquarters of the world's major industrial companies. The next "ring" of the city was given over to professionals and to the essential service sector. Those rings extended only around two-thirds of the city, though. The side facing the ocean, with a flowing slope down to one of the best beaches along the coast, was left without buildings. The offices and official quarters of Calypso's elected governor had excellent views of the natural vista.

To the south and west, the city continued with residential neighborhoods and shopping districts. Everywhere there were extensive greenways and wide streets. And, again on every side but the east, the city was surrounded by a two-mile thick belt of native forest where no construction was permitted, a screen to insure that Oceanview would retain its sense of isolation.

It was in that strip of forest where the Calypsan army was attempting to stop the invaders. Against the standing law, trees had been felled. Defensive lines had been erected, and antipersonnel mines planted.

• • •

One thought came to torture Lon's mind in the last minutes of the descent. *If something hits us, will I have time to know what's happening before I die?* Trussed up inside a box with no way to defend themselves or affect the outcome, this was when soldiers felt most vulnerable. A missile could strike the shuttle and explode. Would there be an instant of realization before fire or shrapnel brought an end to everything? *I don't want to know,* Lon thought fervently. *I don't ever want to know.*

He always had to fight the urge to hold his breath through the last minute or two of one of these landings—even in practice runs on Dirigent when he knew that there would be no enemy firing live ammunition. The maneuver had its own dangers. A hot approach always seemed to be one step short of playing "chicken"—trying to see how close to utter disaster one could come without crossing the line. The slightest miscalculation by a pilot, or a malfunction in any of dozens of pieces of equipment, could leave a shuttle half buried, with everyone aboard dead.

The pilot gave Lon a warning when they were thirty seconds from landing. Lon passed that information to the men. That half minute seemed as long as the rest of the trip down from *Long Snake*. He tensed up, as if to protect himself against a crash landing—a useless gesture that he had not yet learned how to prevent. The gee-forces were extreme, reversed now, with everyone thrown forward against their restraining harnesses.

The shuttle touched down. There were no wheels. Nearly frictionless skids were part of the belly of the craft. Braking was accomplished solely with the engines reversing thrust. The noise level inside the lander was intense. The boat rocked. For an instant, Lon thought that it might be turning sideways, but either he was mistaken or the pilot corrected it quickly.

Then the lander was motionless.

There was no stopwatch on. Lon needed a few seconds, or perhaps it only seemed that long, to react to the cessation of forward motion. He hit the release on his safety harness while giving the order for the men to get up and out, into their initial perimeter. They drilled at this often enough to do it in their sleep—or when half crazed with fear. Each man knew exactly where to go and what to do. There were two exits from the troop compartment of the shuttle. Platoon sergeants and squad leaders were there to move their men along, to make certain that no mistakes were made, that assignments were not forgotten in the heat of the moment. The men had the safeties off on their weapons before they went out the door, jogging toward their positions.

Nine shuttles came down together, within the space of twenty seconds, in an area no more than a thousand yards in diameter. The pattern was routine, part of the drill, so that the troops would always have the same series of movements to perform to get into position. The Dirigent Mercenary Corps had been using this maneuver for generations. It was rare for any shuttle to be more than a few dozen yards out of its assigned position.

It was also part of the drill for the shuttles to take off again as quickly as possible. During the minute or so that they were on the ground, they were vulnerable, as they would be during the first stage of their subsequent ascent. DMC shuttles were not defenseless, though. They had rockets and multibarrel cannon, covering themselves and the troops until the defensive ring was established and the landers were free to leave.

Lon took a deep breath as he left the shuttle. It always seemed so much easier to draw in air after going through that hatch, as if the air in the shuttle had been oxygen-deficient. He started trotting toward his platoons' section of the perimeter, looking around to make certain that his men were moving in proper order, and searching for any threat that might materialize in these first seconds.

The landing zone was southwest of Oceanview, at the far edge of the insulating line of native forest. There had been no indication of enemy troops in this area at the time the shuttles left *Long Snake*. The nearest Belletiener force was north of 2nd Battalion, trying to force its way along a narrow stream toward the capital. The other major enemy force was fifteen miles to the south, entering The Cliffs.

Darkness was no barrier. His helmet's night-vision system was the best available, and he had plenty of experience interpreting what he saw through it—still able to monitor the head-up display that the visor also provided, and monitor and answer radio traffic, switching among the many communications channels with practiced ease.

It took no more than a minute for the battalion to establish its initial perimeter. Men were prone, weapons pointed out from the circle. The shuttles throttled up and made short takeoff runs, tilting back almost as soon as they were off the ground in a nearly vertical climb toward safer levels. With only surface-to-air missiles to worry about, shuttles were only vulnerable during the first two miles of their ascent. Once they reached ten thousand feet, they would be able to outrace anything launched from the ground.

After the deafening roar of nine shuttles at full throttle, ears needed time to readjust, to become aware of the lower levels of noise that might be found in the environment. Any wildlife in the area would certainly need even longer to recover from the sonic assault. In the first minutes, any sound beyond the perimeter would likely be hostile.

There was no nearby gunfire. More than a minute after the shuttles took off, Lon thought that he could finally hear the dull sound of more distant conflict, perhaps rifles and grenades. But he needed longer to be certain that he was actually hearing those sounds and not just imagining them.

By that time, CIC's updates to the helmets and mapboards of the battalion were current. Lon unfolded his mapboard and checked the overlay for enemy electronics. That was one of the hottest areas of military competition, the twin drives to shield one's own electronic emissions against detection and to improve your capacity to intercept enemy emissions. It was not—except under the rarest of circumstances—a matter of eavesdropping on enemy communications. Complex digital encryption schemes and patterns of switching a single transmission around through as many as a dozen different channels made that virtually impossible. But just knowing where the enemy was, and in what

numbers, could make an immense difference —often, literally, between life and death.

DMC electronics showed as green points on the mapboard; those of the Calypsan army were in yellow; and
enemy or unidentified emissions were in red. There were
no red blips within a mile of 2nd Battalion's perimeter. *If
they're closer than that,* Lon thought, *they're being careful
not to use active electronics.* Only transmissions—voice,
telemetry, and some rangefinding procedures—would be liable to interception, either by troops on the ground or by
scanning from orbit. Standard operating procedures were
different when you knew or suspected that your enemy had
modern electronics and the means to detect your transmissions. There would be no idle radio chatter between men
here. And command use of the radio channels would be
kept to a minimum. Where possible, hand signals would be
used to direct men, even though the fact that the enemy's
ships had been chased away meant that the Belletieners
would be limited to what their people on the ground could
pick up, and the intercept range for helmet-based sensors
was very limited.

"We move in two minutes. We've got the left flank."
Lon recognized Captain Orlis's voice. "Follow first platoon
out."

Lon made a clicking noise to acknowledge, then passed
along the orders in as terse a fashion to his platoon sergeants. Third platoon would go ahead. Fourth would be
rearguard for the flank.

There was nothing more on the radio until Orlis's one-
word command came through. "Go." Lon used hand signals to his platoon sergeants, who directed their men. In
near silence, the eight hundred-plus men of 2nd Battalion
got up and started moving north, into the native forest. Toward the enemy.

Alpha Company was on the left. Delta had the right
flank. The other two line companies and Colonel Flowers's
headquarters detachment were in the center. The columns
moved in parallel, eighty to one hundred yards separating
the columns. Within each column, the gap between men

averaged eight yards, greater on the flanks, less in the center, spreading the formation over a considerable distance. Scouts and rearguards, both sent out from the center column, extended it even more.

Lon positioned himself in fourth platoon's first squad, just behind Corporal Wil Nace, the squad leader. They did not speak, but acknowledged each other with a nod. They shared the close bond that only men who have survived combat together when many others did not ever really know—something more than mutual respect for each other's abilities.

The pace of the battalion was little more than a casual stroll—except that there was nothing casual about the attitude of these men. They moved with alert expectation, eyes and ears tuned to any hint of a threat. The enemy had to know that they were on the ground, and almost as certainly knew approximately where they had landed. One way or another, the Belletiene commander *had* to react to their presence.

A walk in the woods, Lon thought, scanning the trees and undergrowth ahead and to his left. He was most concerned with ground level. The majority of the trees he could see had high, straight trunks, unbroken by limbs or leaves below the thirty- or forty-foot level. That did not mean that snipers could not be in them, but this soon it was unlikely. There was far more cover for the enemy on the ground. This was no manicured park. There were bushes and thickets separating sometimes broad avenues under the forest canopy. People used this forest for picnics and other outings.

Colonel Flowers stopped the advance with the point a half mile from the nearest known enemy positions. Flowers took less than a minute to confer with his company commanders and give new orders. Captain Orlis gestured for his two platoon leaders to come to him and relayed their orders face to face.

"We attack," Orlis started. "Alpha and Bravo will advance until we engage the enemy. I want three platoons up front; fourth in reserve until we see where they can best be used. Carl, your platoons on the left. Charlie Company will drop back and move around to the left to cover our flank and—if the opportunity presents itself—move to cut off any retreat to the west by the enemy. Delta will use one platoon to physically link us with the Calypsan army. The rest of Delta will be held as battalion reserve. We move in three minutes. Get back to your platoons and get ready.''

Lon jogged toward his platoons, gesturing for the platoon sergeants to join him. As quickly as he could relay the necessary information, it was time to get the men moving. The skirmish lines had scarcely had time to settle into position before the order came for the advance.

The DMC front spread across a quarter of a mile. The pace slowed almost to a hesitation step. Squad leaders watched to keep the advance even. Everyone knew that contact with the enemy was close, and that the first warning might be the sound of gunshots—or the tear of bullet through flesh.

Lon was between third platoon's first two squads. Ivar Dendrow was between the other two squads. Both men were a step behind the skirmish line, along with one fire team each from first and third squads.

Lon's breathing became shallow and slow, suppressed in his desire to hear the enemy as soon as possible. His palms were sweating. Almost unconsciously, he wiped them, one at a time, on his trousers. Fear was there, but mostly as an extra rush of adrenaline, making his observations perhaps a little more acute than they would have been without. Time seemed to slow. Each step forward seemed to occupy a unique place in time, with measurable gaps on either side.

Like the men in front of him, Lon moved in a crouch, shoulders hunched forward, arms tight to his sides, presenting a minimal target to any waiting enemy. The tautness in his muscles would become uncomfortable after a time, but while it lasted, it would give him an extra edge if he had to propel himself to the ground, or to one side or the other. It was something he did not notice at all now.

In ten minutes the advance covered 150 yards. Lon noticed the time and distance only because that was when he heard the first gunfire directed at the battalion—well off to the right, facing Bravo Company. Momentarily, the advance stopped and men went to the ground, in firing position, until it was determined that Bravo had only run into a Belletiener patrol, a single squad. That squad retreated quickly after several quick bursts of rifle fire, and the advance resumed . . . slower than before.

The pause was just long enough for Lon to become aware of sweat trickling down his neck, but there was nothing to be done about that. He had his men to watch over, and a section of forest to search for other enemy patrols— or a force that might outnumber the entire battalion.

Three minutes after the advance resumed, Lon thought that they might have finally run into that force.

9

Automatic rifle fire came first. There were no tracers, no glowing arcs to follow back to their source, but muzzle flashes could be seen blinking rapidly 150 to 200 yards away. A scattering of rocket-propelled grenades followed. Before they arrived, all of the Dirigenters were flat on the ground, behind the best available cover, even if that was no more than a high clump of grass.

No order had to be given to return fire. Some of Lon's men were shooting as they dove for cover—more than a simple reflex, if less than carefully aimed. Lon found himself rolling into thick brush at the base of a tree. He needed a few seconds to realize that he was caught in the tangle of a vine hanging from the tree. He freed an arm from one loop of the vine and slid forward on his stomach until he could see ahead.

There was no need to observe radio silence during a firefight. It was obvious that the enemy knew where they were. Squad leaders conferred on what they were seeing, or gave orders. Lon heard two separate calls for medical orderlies.

"Ivar?" Lon asked on the channel connecting him to the third platoon sergeant.

"We're okay, so far, Lieutenant," Dendrow said. "I think we've hit a wall, though. This isn't just a patrol."

"We were supposed to go forward until we found the enemy," Lon said.

"You think we should let them know we're there?"

Lon smiled. "Let's get the men moved somewhere they can fix themselves a little cover first." Now that the fighting had started, Lon felt less tense. He was not going to freeze with fear. *"The second time can be worse than the first,"* an instructor had once told him. *"The second time you know what to expect. Forget that 'fear of the unknown' crap. A man's more likely to freeze when he knows exactly how much danger he's in."*

"Have your men dig in as best they can," Captain Orlis said over the radio. "We're to hold where we are for now. The Calypsans are going to put pressure on from their side."

"Already working on it," Lon replied. "Should I bring fourth platoon forward or leave them back?"

Orlis scarcely hesitated for two seconds before he said, "Leave them be for now. Have them dig in too."

Lon passed the orders along, then got his entrenching tool off his pack and started scraping at the hard ground next to the tree and piling the dirt in front of him. Not everyone could start digging at once, but the work would get done. The men in each squad would take turns, one digging while two others continued to return fire.

This was one maneuver that they had never drilled at—digging a slit trench—a shallow hole just large enough for a man to lie in, with the dirt piled up around it to give him a little extra protection while lying prone, under fire. It was hard, cramping work. Some of the gunfire was uncomfortably close. Lon paused several times, long enough to fire a short burst or two with his rifle. The head-up display on his visor allowed him to safely fire past his own men—their positions were clearly shown on the faceplate.

We can't just lie here and exchange fire forever, Lon thought after six or seven minutes of scraping at the dirt. He had a depression two inches deep, slightly wider and longer than his body, with most of the dirt piled up in a shallow arc in front of him, giving him another few inches of protection. With a tree at one side, and the tangle of vines above, he felt *almost* secure. Even with good night-vision gear, there was a tendency for rifle fire to be high in the dark, even when shooters tried to compensate for that well-known tendency.

Lon clicked over to the radio channel that connected him with all of his noncoms. "Remind the men not to get too loose with ammunition," he said. "We've only got what we're carrying until we get a supply shuttle in."

Only gradually did Lon become aware of an increase in the volume of gunfire off to his right. *That must be the Calypsans,* he thought. *Ought to be about time for us to start putting more pressure on the enemy too. Maybe send Charlie Company around in back to make them worry about getting encircled.* That was a possibility that had to make any commander nervous. Trying to second guess what his own commanders—as well as the enemy—would do next was second nature for Lon, and for most junior officers. It was another five minutes before Lon learned that, this time, he had been right.

"If you hear noise off to the left, don't sweat it," Captain Orlis told him over the radio. "Charlie's on the way around. Colonel doesn't want us to get old where we are."

"Any idea how many of the enemy we've got in front of us?"

"At least nine hundred," Orlis said. "Maybe eleven or twelve. Or more. We don't have any definite intelligence on where they've got everyone."

So what else is new? Lon thought. Even with the best sensing gear in the galaxy, battlefield intelligence was often woefully inadequate. The ships overhead would be scanning for electronic and infrared emissions. In theory, the equipment was sensitive enough to give a fairly accurate count of warm bodies, but thermal shielding in battledress and cover overhead could diminish that accuracy—sometimes to the point of making the estimates worse than useless. Misleading

"Move your fourth platoon up, spread them across the entire company front to add to the firepower," Orlis said then. "The idea is to put as much pressure on as possible, end this stalemate as quickly as we can."

Lon passed the orders along to fourth platoon's sergeant and squad leaders. "Keep your heads down," he added. "We still can't replace those."

Then he switched over to talk to the rest of the noncoms, to pass along the "request" to increase pressure on the enemy. "That's become more urgent than conserving ammo," he said. "Maybe a few more grenades in as well."

Lon checked his mapboard to see what progress Charlie Company was making. It had to circle behind the rest of the battalion, then move west and north to turn the flank of the Belletieners. At a minimum, it looked as if they would need another ten minutes before they could make their presence felt. But the pocket the enemy was in was already shrinking. The Calypsan army appeared to be tightening in on the north, threatening that flank of the enemy.

Belletiene has to withdraw, Lon thought after staring at his display for twenty seconds. *They have to pull back before the circle closes.* He folded the mapboard up. *Or they have to hit us from behind, somewhere, try to break up our attack.*

"Captain?" Lon said, after switching to his link to Orlis. "Did we leave any eyes behind us? Might not take many of the enemy hitting us from where we don't expect it to make a difference."

"Delta has men out, and they've planted snoops," Orlis replied. "I'm glad I'm not the only one who got that itch."

Lon hardly noticed the implied compliment. "The enemy commander must have something up his sleeve, or they'd be pulling back by now."

"Maybe not. They don't have any eyes overhead doing surveillance. They might not know about Charlie yet, or just how much of the ring we've managed to close around them."

Maybe, Lon thought. He switched channels to talk to Sergeant Jorgen. "Weil, pull two men out. Have them drop back to where the platoon was before. I want them watching behind us, the whole circuit, just in case the enemy tries to sneak in between Delta and us." There was not, Lon thought, any need for him to clear that decision with Captain Orlis. Lon was responsible for the safety of his own platoons. The captain had enough to worry about without a minor detail like this.

''Right, sir. I'll send Nace and Headly. They're the best I've got at that sort of thing.''

Lon nodded to himself. ''Fine. Get them moving. They see or hear anything that doesn't belong, have them call me directly. Other than that, I want them on passive electronics only, nothing that will let the enemy know they've moved, and I don't want either man firing a weapon unless it's absolutely necessary.''

Jorgen clicked an acknowledgment, and Lon returned to scanning the terrain. For a moment he switched his faceplate to full magnification, but that did not show anything major.

This would be a good time for a couple of fighters to make a pass over the enemy, Lon thought, *in from the east so the enemy will have the sun in their eyes as the Shrikes come over the horizon.* But it was unlikely, unless the battalion got itself in real trouble. Most of the Shrike fighters had been used in connection with the landings in the west, in the mining region, and pilots could not operate forever without rest.

It was difficult for Lon to tell that dawn had actually arrived. Besides the general cover of the forest, he was under his thick tangle of vines and leaves, leaving him in almost night-dark shadow.

If we're going to be here much longer, the men need to dig in better, Lon thought, but that was not something that called for immediate action on his part. The men would improve their positions little by little, as they got the chance, without any encouragement beyond the bullets coming their way. Another glance at his mapboard showed Lon that Charlie Company was making progress. They had gone farther west than he had expected before making the turn north.

They should be getting into the fray any minute now, Lon thought. Once the Belletiene commander became aware of Charlie, *something* should happen, fairly quickly. Almost two-thirds of a circle would have closed around the Belletieners then.

''Fairly quickly'' was a good estimate. The action picked

up less than a minute later. There was considerable gunfire and the explosions of a dozen or more grenades, all close together, well off to Lon's left. Almost simultaneously there was a marked decrease in the fighting in front of Alpha and Bravo Companies, and over toward the Calypsan army.

"We're pushing forward in two minutes," Orlis said a couple of minutes later. "I want two skirmish lines forty yards apart. We'll take as much as Belletiene lets us like that, switch to fire and maneuver if they try to make a stand. Nolan, pull your fourth platoon back as company reserve again, fifty yards behind the second skirmish line. You stay with them. If I have to send them in anywhere, I'll want you to lead them."

Two minutes was not a lot of time. The two men sent back from fourth platoon had to be recalled. Orders had to be passed to the rest. Fourth platoon would stay in place as the skirmish lines started forward, then consolidate behind them. Little more than the length of a soccer field separated Alpha Company from the enemy. How great that distance would feel to the men when they moved forward would depend on how vigorous the opposition was.

The first skirmish line got up and started moving slowly, six to eight yards between men. They fired as they advanced, and the second line of men provided covering fire from their positions—carefully, to avoid inflicting friendly casualties.

The Belletieners responded. There were casualties in the first DMC line. The men switched to standard fire and maneuver tactics, half a squad moving forward to the next cover while the rest covered them, then switching jobs. That had to slow the advance, but it was safer.

Lon moved to where fourth platoon had assembled—the men down on the ground, not exposing themselves uselessly. "Wouldn't it be better to get all of us in this now?" Wil Nace asked Lon when the lieutenant settled to the ground next to him.

"Not my decision, Wil," Lon said. "Captain thinks this is better, just in case the enemy has any surprises for us.

They've got people we haven't accounted for, some-where.''

The second skirmish line started forward, holding their pace down to that of the line in front of them, using fire and maneuver tactics as well, even though they were draw-ing less fire than the first line.

Then, suddenly, the incoming fire stopped almost com-pletely. The two skirmish lines continued on as they had been for another thirty seconds. Only when it became ap-parent that the enemy had given up this fight did they start moving forward without the interruptions of men leapfrog-ging each other. There were no more than a dozen Belle-tiener soldiers still firing toward the two advancing companies of 2nd Battalion—covering the withdrawal of the rest of their force from the pocket.

''Captain?'' Lon spoke only the one word.

''Hang tight,'' Orlis replied. ''Steady advance. Remind your men to be on the outlook for booby traps and land mines. Belletiene has had time to cook up a lot of nasty surprises for us. And have your people watch for Delta on the right. They're between you and the Calypsan army.''

''Right. Should I move my fourth platoon in?''

Orlis hesitated before he replied. ''Yes, but not too close. I want that platoon back from the positions that Belletiene vacated, just in case we have to move you in a hurry. This isn't over yet, not by a long shot.''

10

There was, finally, time for a few minutes rest for Alpha Company. Charlie Company was following the withdrawing Belletiener force, harassing them, not giving them an opportunity to stop and regroup. Bravo and Delta were on the perimeter. There was a certain amount of confusion as the Dirigenters and the Calypsan army met for the first time. Colonel Flowers had been in radio contact with the commander of the Calypsan force defending Oceanview, and Delta's commanding officer and one of his platoons had been in more direct contact with the nearest elements of the local defenders. But coordinating actions brought complications. The respite after dawn provided time for the commanders to sort things out.

Four men in Lon's platoons had been wounded. Lon took a few minutes to talk with them. None of the injuries was serious enough to require time in a trauma tube. Injection of molecule-sized medical repair units to boost the victims' basic medical maintenance systems sufficed. No bullets had to be removed; that would have required a trauma tube.

"Check on remaining ammo," Lon told the platoon sergeants. "The captain is trying to find out when we can expect a supply drop, or if we can get anything from the Calypsans. They use the same rifles we do, so the cartridges should be interchangeable."

Ivar Dendrow laughed softly at the note of skepticism in Lon's voice. "If the rounds work in their rifles, they'll work in ours, Lieutenant. They just might not work the same way, if they've messed with the specs too much. You know, weight of the slug, weight and type of propellant."

"If they've got ammo to spare, we'll be glad to have it, even if we can't put three shots in a ten-inch cluster with it," Weil Jorgen said. "They should have plenty. The way I understand it, Calypso's been gearing up for this for years."

"That's what they tell me," Lon said. "Just find out what we've got ourselves. If the colonel or Captain Orlis comes up with a job for us, I want to be able to tell whether or not we've got the munitions to do it." Both sergeants acknowledged the order. "Tell the men to grab a bite to eat while they can," Lon added. "I don't think we're going to get time for sleep, but food should help."

Lon moved a few yards from where fourth platoon was resting. He sat with his back to a tree, leaned his head against it, and closed his eyes. There was always a reaction after the flood of epinephrine, after tension and danger. As soon as there was relative calm, the body tried to purge itself of excessive levels of the hormone. The body's medical maintenance system worked to mediate the flow and ebb to avoid dangerous extremes.

I should eat now, while I've got a minute free, Lon thought. *Nobody's going to come along and order me to eat.* When he first joined the company as a cadet, that had happened with annoying frequency. He had been unable to fathom why everyone seemed so preoccupied with getting him fed regularly.

Sleep would be better . . . But sleep would have to wait. Lon forced his eyes open. Eating would help him stay alert for a few minutes—for the duration of the meal, at least. He slid out of his pack's straps and opened it to pull out the first battle ration packet he put his hand on. He ate slowly, methodically, paying little attention to what he was doing. Five minutes after he finished, he could not have said what he had eaten.

There were interruptions. He received the reports on ammunition from his sergeants. Third platoon was shorter than fourth—they had seen more action. When Captain Orlis called to ask about ammunition, Lon had the information ready. It was worth a thin smile. *Anticipated that one*, Lon thought.

He leaned back again. He could afford to close his eyes for a few minutes and rest—doze, if not actually sleep. It was something most veterans learned, to take even a few minutes whenever they could. Save energy, do what little he could to replenish it. Lon quickly started to nod off. His head would slide toward one side or the other and he would start, then drift back to the same state . . . until the next time. *If I could just sleep for ten minutes,* he thought during one interval of near alertness. *Be good for another twelve hours then.*

It did not matter that he had not been awake for all that many hours, or that he had slept as much as he could during the voyage from Dirigent. His body and mind wanted sleep *now*. After several failures, Lon got himself in a position where his head was supported better. Then he almost did manage something approaching sleep, except for a fitfulness that came from knowing that he might be called upon to react alertly any second.

"Nolan." At first, Lon thought he was dreaming. It was not until Captain Orlis called a second time that Lon jerked awake.

"Yes, sir?" He scarcely paused before he added, "I guess I nodded off for a minute."

"God, I wish I could," Orlis said. "And I wish I could let you and your men rest longer, but it's time to get back to work."

"Yes, sir."

"There'll be a local floater here with ammunition —rifle magazines and grenade clips—shortly. Get fourth platoon resupplied as fast as you can and have them ready to move out. You'll lead. Let Dendrow know that he'll be in charge of third. Anything comes up while you're gone, he should call me directly."

"Yes, sir," Lon said when Orlis paused.

"Belletiene has stolen a march on us," the captain continued. "While we were concentrating on the force in front of us, they moved a larger force around behind us on the east, up from The Cliffs. Calypso doesn't have enough men in position to stop them. You're to take fourth platoon and delay them as long as you can, give the rest of us time to get into the city.''

"Yes, sir. Just how large a force do we need to delay?"

"A thousand, maybe eleven hundred," Orlis said. "You're going to have to buy us at least a half hour. Split the platoon in two. You know the drill. Give the Belletieners enough to think about that they've got to slow down."

Lon nodded. He did not ask for detailed instructions, or voice misgivings over the odds. For this type of assignment, step-by-step orders would be impossible. *See what you can do when you get there.* A judgment call. And using a small force to harass and delay a larger enemy was . . . not unheard of.

"You will have a little help," Orlis said. "Colonel Gaffney is releasing two fighters to make a pass over the enemy, to try to tie them up long enough for you to get into position."

Lon nodded. "That should help."

"Here comes that supply truck now." The captain pointed. Lon glanced that way. "Get busy. I want you moving as fast as possible, before the Belletieners get too far into Oceanview."

"Yes, sir." Lon started toward the truck, ready to call Sergeant Jorgen to get the platoon there to meet him, when Captain Orlis stopped him briefly.

"Good hunting, Nolan," the captain said. "And good luck."

Lon gave Jorgen the news piecemeal, first just telling him to get the platoon up and moving toward the truck. Only after the men were on the way did Lon give him the rest of the news, in capsule form. Details—as far as Lon knew them—could wait until they had stocked up on ammunition and started moving toward the enemy.

A quick survey of his mapboard gave Lon a good idea where he would have to take his platoon to get in front of the enemy. The Belletieners were already entering the residential district at the southern edge of Oceanview. Some of the civilians in their path had fled northward. Others were apparently holed up in their houses, hoping that trouble would pass them by. The invaders were apparently not conducting house-to-house searches. They seemed intent on moving through to the government district as rapidly as they could.

"We'll have to hit them here, Weil," Lon said, pointing out the location he had decided on. He had adjusted the scale on his mapboard to show a fairly detailed view of the edge of the commercial and professional district just south of the governmental core of Oceanview.

Jorgen nodded. "We'll have to move smartly to get there ahead of them. The locals have any mines or booby traps planted between here and there, anything we're going to have to watch for along the way?"

"Not that they've told us about," Lon said.

"We're ready to go," Jorgen said.

The platoon moved out at a brisk march, in two columns, with intervals more those of a hike than an advance toward the enemy. Once clear of the other Dirigenters, Lon alternated the pace between march-step and double time. They had to move north, through the woods, for a half mile before turning east, into the early-morning sun.

Twice they passed companies of Calypsan soldiers who were trying to regroup and replenish their own ammunition. They also passed a field hospital, where local soldiers were being treated. *They got hit hard,* Lon thought, looking as he moved past the open-sided tent. There were a dozen trauma tubes under the canopy, and several dozen wounded soldiers waiting their turns.

Finally the platoon turned east, through the outskirts of Oceanview. The streets were almost deserted. Only an occasional police or military vehicle was moving. Civilians were staying indoors, or had moved to safer ground ahead of the fighting the night before. The army had sentries posted, and a couple of shorthanded squads out as scouts.

Lon heard the sounds of explosions to the south, and the

rapid fire of the multibarrel guns that the DMC's Shrike fighter aircraft carried. He looked in that direction, but saw nothing. The fighters were either risking everything to get very low or—more likely, he thought—staying high enough to give them a good chance to evade any surface-to-air missiles the Belletieners might launch. The fighters would not be around for long. If they had come in with full loads of munitions, they might make three passes over the enemy—rockets and gunfire. Then it would be time to burn for orbit, to return to their ship.

"Give them hell," Lon whispered.

Two minutes later, just after the last rocket explosions to the south, it was time for Lon to split the platoon. He kept first and second squad and started south again. Platoon Sergeant Jorgen took the other squads and continued east. They would go another quarter mile before turning south to intercept the invaders. There was no double-timing now. Lon did not want his men to be winded when they encountered the enemy. After the two sections had separated, Lon gave his two squads a minute to rest.

"It's going to be hit-and-run and watch your asses," Lon told Wil Nace and Ash Bocker, the corporals who led the two squads. "That means use the men with beamers as long-range snipers when possible." Each squad had one man with an energy weapon. "Grenades at maximum range, from cover. Duck into buildings to take a few potshots, then get out before the enemy can respond. Our job is to slow the enemy down, give the rest of the battalion and the locals time to put a more credible force between government center and the invaders."

Nace nodded. "We know the drill, Lieutenant."

"You'll operate separately," Lon continued. "If necessary, break your squads into fire teams. Wil, I'll stay with you, but it's your show, tactically. I've got the entire platoon to manage. If I get any ideas, you'll hear them, but don't wait for me to say what to do from minute to minute. Now, let's move."

• • •

The broad avenue made Lon nervous. He and his men were too visible. They stayed close to the buildings, near cover, but that was only a partial solution. They were heading toward the enemy, and one Belletiene column was advancing along the same avenue—just the other side of a park, no more than seven hundred yards to the south. As soon as possible, the two squads moved to either side, heading for alleys and the spaces between buildings, to areas where there was some cover.

Wil Nace halted his squad and sent Loe Gavish, his beamer, and another man to the top of a building to try for a shot at the enemy. Then Nace deployed the rest of the squad, talking to two or three men at a time, telling them where to go, what to do.

"We'll operate in relays," Nace told Lon. "Leapfrog each other. If the enemy goes after the first men who hit them, they can beat it, and we'll let the enemy run into the next ambush."

Lon nodded. "Do what you think best, Wil. You've had more experience at this than I have." Lon had no qualms about admitting that. He trusted the veterans under his command, and he was always willing to learn from them. The Corps operated that way, generally. Young officers were not given the opportunity to nurture delusions that the red and gold pips they wore were worth more than years of experience. "I'll stick with you. Maybe I'll even get a shot or two at them myself."

"I got no problems with that," Nace said. "Just remember, this kind of operation can get dirty in a hurry."

Lon glanced around. He had already noted how clean, how *new*, everything about Oceanview looked. It was almost as if the city had just been built and no one had moved in yet. But the city was not new, simply well maintained, even in the face of an enemy invasion. *Not even Dirigent City is kept up like this,* Lon thought, and he had been impressed with how clean the capital of the mercenary world was. It had been so distinct a contrast with the cities he had seen on Earth.

"Whenever you're ready, Wil," Lon said.

Nace nodded. "I'm just waiting for Gavish to report that he's ready. With a little luck, he might get off two or three shots with the beamer before the enemy knows that anything's happening."

Loe Gavish reported that he was in position and had the enemy in sight. Nace gave him the go-ahead, then alerted the rest of the squad. "Well, Lieutenant," he said then, "I guess it's time for us to get out of the street before we get arrested for vagrancy." The others had already disappeared from sight, into buildings and between them, moving into position.

Lon gestured toward the door nearest them. They were standing by the rear entrance to a three-story office building. There was no glass in the door. "After you, Wil."

"Right, Lieutenant. Just for the sake of an old corporal's nerves, let's treat this as if there might be a squad of hostiles on the other side."

Lon nodded, and brought up his rifle and checked to make certain that the safety was off. Nace did the same with his weapon. The two men looked at each other and lowered the faceplates on their helmets.

Will he just kick it open or try the latch first to see whether or not it's locked? Lon wondered as Nace moved toward the door. The corporal moved to the hinge side of the door, then glanced at his lieutenant. Lon nodded and moved to the other side of the door.

"You want to try the knob?" Wil asked.

Lon reached for the knob as Wil brought his rifle up. The knob turned freely. "Ready?" he asked, holding the knob. "Ready," Wil replied, and Lon pushed the door in.

Nace did not wait. As soon as he saw the door start to open, he pushed forward, accelerating quickly, throwing his shoulder against the door and diving for the floor inside. Lon crossed behind him, his rifle searching for any hint of a target. Lon did not do a rolling dive. The fraction of a second between Wil's entrance and his own had not brought any gunfire.

They were in a corridor that ran the length of the building. To the left were stairs and lift tubes. At the right were three doors. The first appeared to lead into a service closet. It was locked. The rooms behind the other two doors both housed lawyers, judging from the signs on them. At the far end of the corridor, glass double doors looked out on the street.

Wil Nace got to his feet. "I'll check the front door to make sure it's not locked. We might be glad of a choice of exits. Then we'll go upstairs and see what we can find."

They did not take anything for granted, looking into each office suite they passed, ready for ambush . . . or any other surprises. The office doors were locked, but there were glass panels in each. The building's front doors were unlocked. Then the two men took the stairs up—one at a time, with Wil going to the next landing before Lon left his post at the bottom. On the second floor, they took a few seconds to glance into each of the three office suites there—testing doors and looking. These doors were also locked. Only a pair of restrooms, at the back of the hall, were open. And empty.

It was while they were checking the restrooms that Loe Gavish reported in. "I'm sure I got two of them, Corp," he told Nace. "Maybe a third. A few of the enemy got off shots, but they didn't know where to aim. We're beating it out of here now, before the rest get up and start looking for us."

"Loe said that there was gunfire," Nace told Nolan. "I didn't hear anything, so the sound insulation in this building is pretty damn good."

On the third floor, they found no easy access to the roof. There were no stairs, only a metal access panel in the ceiling. "Nothing we can do about that," Lon said. "We'll have to make do with the windows on this level."

"We'll have to break into all of the offices," Wil said. "I hope they've got working windows. The ones out here in the corridor don't open. And we probably can't break them, not easily anyway."

Lon nodded. Window "glass" was rarely real glass on any urbanized world. There were far superior substitutes, nearly as secure as plate steel. It might be easier to knock the windows out of their frames than to break the panes. "We don't have much time. The Belletieners will be in range soon."

"I just hope the locals haven't gotten too cute with these doors," Wil said. If the tenants, or their landlord, were overly conscious about keeping the premises secure, the door might be impossible to get through without the key or explosives. Wil moved to the first locked door and turned to give it a powerful side kick, next to the lock. Years of marching, hiking, and practicing unarmed combat had given him extremely muscular legs, and he knew how to place the kick for maximum power. They heard something crack, and the door was loose—but not yet free. Nace turned around and delivered a second kick, with the other foot, to the same spot, and the door flew open.

"I hope you can handle the next one, Lieutenant," Wil said. "That smarts."

Lon went along the corridor to the next door. He tried the knob, just to make certain that it was locked, then backed up. He had never attempted to kick open a door before. He took a deep breath, then made his first kick. The shock of impact ran all the way up his leg to the hip, but he felt only the slightest give to the door. A second kick put a little play in it, but he needed a third to finally break the jamb.

For the third office door, they took turns. Nace hit it first, and Lon finished the job with his kick. Then the two men split up to check the windows inside the three suites.

Lon had the suite at the front of the building. The interior doors were not locked. The windows were hinged at the top and opened outward, but only eight inches. Lon tried to force the first window farther, but could not.

He had been monitoring the talk in the two squads, not at all confused by the jumble of voices. He could identify each of his men, even from a couple of words. Sorting out the conversations was little more difficult.

The ambushes and withdrawals had been in progress for ten minutes, and the tactic *was* having some effect on the advance of the Belletiene army. Instead of parading along the avenues, they had been forced to stop and maneuver more carefully. Each time a few of Lon's men hit, the enemy commander had to make certain that it was only harassing fire—and not a gambit to draw all of his force into a killing zone. Loe Gavish was working around to the side of the enemy column, looking for a place to hit them from behind with his beamer—to further confuse the issue.

They'll be in view before long, Lon thought as he made the circuit of the suite, opening all the windows. Then he went back out to the corridor. Nace was already going into the third suite, at the back of the hall, to get those windows.

"We'd better just hit them on the street side, Wil," Lon said. "Keep their attention there while we scoot out the back."

"You want the honors, Lieutenant?" Wil asked. "I can keep watch out the back way, make sure they don't show up out there before we're ready to vacate the premises."

"Might as well, since I'm already up here," Lon said, moving to the window that had the best view along the avenue.

"Give me a shout before you shoot, Lieutenant."

"Right. One quick burst, then we're out of here," Lon replied. He got down on one knee, his right side against the wall, adjusting himself to the best position he could find. The barrel of his rifle was just above the windowsill, where it would not be visible to anyone on the ground, even two blocks away. "It shouldn't be long now," he added.

He turned down the volume on his earphones, to help him concentrate. The radio chatter was still audible, but softer than before. Seconds dragged as he worked to make his breathing regular and shallow, and stared down the street for the first view of the approaching enemy.

One quick burst at the point man, he reminded himself. That was all there would be time for. Anything longer, and the enemy might respond before he and Nace could make good their escape from this building.

"In sight, Wil. Anything out back?" Lon asked when he saw the first enemy uniform. The man was moving slowly, half in a crouch, along the far side of the street, down at the limit of Lon's possible zone of fire.

"We're clear," Nace said.

"Here goes." Lon had started tracking his target as soon as he came into sight. The barrel of his rifle rested on the windowsill. His finger constricted on the trigger, firing a three-shot burst. Lon was already moving back from the window before he was aware that the man had been hit. The accuracy of his shooting was almost irrelevant.

Nace was waiting at the top of the stairs when Lon came out of the front suite. They ran down the stairs almost at full bore, three or four steps at a time, grabbing the newel posts to check their momentum and turn them at the bottom of each flight. Lon felt a rush of exhilaration such as he had not known since he was a child running from some prank in the Asheville circus neighborhood back on Earth. The two men paused only briefly when they reached the rear exit. Wil went out first and ran across the alley, looking to make certain that they were alone. Then the two men turned left and ran, anxious to put distance between themselves and the scene of the ambush.

11

As he could, Lon provided a narrative of what he was doing, and why. Anything he said inside his helmet would be recorded. He could, if he chose, shut off the recorder, but he generally left it on. Later, assuming there *was* a later for him, he would have the opportunity to edit his annotations and conversations and provide a gloss before they became part of the permanent archives of the Dirigent Mercenary Corps.

Keeping track of his men, with all four squads broken down into smaller units and moving independently, kept Lon too busy to have time for anything other than the essentials—since he was moving and fighting at the same time. From the time he had taken his first shot at the enemy until the cat-and-mouse game ended for his fourth platoon, only fifty minutes passed. When he had a few minutes to rest afterward and thought back over all that he and Wil Nace had done, Lon was amazed to discover that it had not actually been two or three hours.

The rest of 2nd Battalion, and nearly three battalions of the Calypsan army, moved into the city and worked hard to block the invaders. Lon's platoon withdrew through the newly formed defensive line.

"I lost two men, Captain," Lon told Orlis when he reported in. "Just at the end." He had to concentrate to keep his voice matter-of-fact, free of the emotion he felt. "Valentin and Roschev from third squad. No one saw what happened, but we lost their vitals just as Nace and I were coming through the lines. My guess is that they were both taken out by the same grenade. I'd like your permission to take a squad back out to look for them.''

There was a pause before the captain replied. ''No, we can't, not now. If they were wounded and needed help, that would be different. I know you don't like the idea, but that's the way it has to be. It could have been worse, Nolan. I know it's rough, but you and your men did a damn good job. You gave us the time we needed. Colonel Flowers said to pass along his 'well done.' ''

My ass, Lon thought. It was not quite bitterness he felt. He had been in combat before, seen comrades die. But this was the first time that men under his command had been killed. *Under his command*—his responsibility. All the leadership training he had received could not take the pain out of that.

''Any of your men require medical attention?'' Orlis asked.

''No, sir,'' Lon said. ''We could use a few minutes to catch our breath, but we're ready for whatever.'' The sounds of fighting were audible, and not extremely distant. It was not just scattered actions involving a few men. A couple of times already, Lon had heard what sounded like company-sized actions.

''Take ten minutes, then move back to rejoin us. I can't give you more than that.''

We'll manage, Lon thought as he switched channels to pass the news to his platoon sergeants and squad leaders.

Lon knew that he needed rest too, even if only ten minutes, but there were other demands on his time. He moved among the squads of fourth platoon, talking face to face to as many men as he could, passing along the news, both good and bad. ''The colonel says you did good work. We're going back to the rest of the company. I don't know what comes next, but it's not time to kick off our boots and sleep yet.'' He added personal words to some of the men, appreciation, encouragement, condolences. He tried to defuse the gripes that many had about not being given more than ten minutes. A few men had their rifles fieldstripped, in the process of cleaning them, when they got the news about the "rest" and the subsequent move.

"Hey, if you wanted easy," he told part of first squad, "you should have studied for a chauffeur's license and gotten a job driving a cab. Sit on your butt all day and breathe climate-controlled air, ferry people back and forth around Dirigent City." By the time he had made the rounds, the ten minutes were gone. Lon allowed himself a silent sigh. *Maybe next time,* he thought after giving Weil Jorgen the order to get the men formed up for the move.

The platoon marched in two columns, one at either side of the street, close to the buildings. The men carried their rifles at port arms, ready for action. It was clear that they were moving toward the sounds of gunfire. Even though they were supposedly behind the lines, away from any enemy, no one took that for granted. They had not been in action long enough for exhaustion to nullify caution.

Captain Orlis came on the radio to talk with Lon again. "We've had word that the rest of the regiment is handling the Belletieners in the mining region easily enough," he said.

"With the manpower advantage the colonel has, it *should* be easy," Lon said. "They going to send more men to help us?"

"Not before tonight, at the earliest," Orlis said, ignoring the almost petulant tone in Lon's voice. "Maybe not then if the Belletieners are still putting up any resistance there."

"Even one more battalion would be a big help here."

"I know, Nolan, but we'll make do for as long as we have to." There seemed to be a trace of annoyance in the captain's voice, so Lon did not press it.

The battle lines in the southern district of Oceanview were not as fixed or regular as Lon had imagined or hoped. Neither side had settled into a static defense posture. Both commanders were attempting to maneuver. The only place where lines of soldiers actually faced one another from fixed positions was in one of the greenbelt parks that separated the residential neighborhoods from the commercial and professional strip. That stretch—less than a quarter mile wide—was a pivot point. On either side there was movement, and urban fighting of the most dangerous kind, building to building. To the right, the DMC was moving south, into blocks that Belletiene had already come into. On the left, the Calypsans were struggling to keep Belletiene out of the office blocks. The situation there was, according to the reports that filtered through to Lon, "extremely fluid."

"Back home, that'd mean our people are up the creek," Ivar Dendrow commented when Lon gave him the report.

"Where I come from too," Lon replied. "That means we're liable to get jerked over there to hold the line."

"Whatever," Dendrow said. "It all pays the same."

Pay doesn't mean a thing unless you're alive to spend it, Lon thought. "We'll take it one step at a time, Ivar. That's all we can do."

Captain Orlis had held third platoon back, using its squads to investigate buildings that had—supposedly—already been cleared of any enemy troops, and to watch that the enemy did not outflank the rest of the battalion on the west. Once third and fourth platoons were reunited, that changed. Slaving Lon's mapboard to his own, Orlis told Lon exactly where he wanted him to take his platoons.

"We've got to put pressure on the enemy's left flank, and try to start closing a circle around them, make them break off the attack on their right."

"Take the pressure off of the Calypsans?" Lon suggested.

"Give them more time to regroup," Orlis said. "They've been in this constantly for a week now. They've lost a lot of men, and there haven't been all that many chances for them to sleep. You know what it's like."

Lon nodded to himself. He was two blocks away from the captain, so Orlis could not see the gesture. "I know," Lon said. *The way we're liable to be in a few more days if we can't end this in a hurry.*

"Get the enemy's attention. Get in his face. Start something. Then we move more men in to exploit the situation."

"Yes, sir."

"They're not paying enough attention to their rear and flanks. Their orders must be to take Government House no matter what. That gives us a little leverage. Use it, but don't take foolish chances. Remember, our resources are limited."

Lon's platoons moved west before they turned south again. The Belletiener advance was narrow, a spear-thrust toward the center of Oceanview. Apparently, only widely spaced sentries and a few roaming patrols of no more than squad strength were all that covered the flanks and rear of that advance. The invasion force was not large enough to stake out large tracts of ground and hold it while they expanded the territory they controlled.

"We'll start by taking out any sentries and patrols," Lon told his platoon sergeants. "We'll move a few blocks east then, as if we're heading toward the solid line in that park from behind. I don't know how far we'll get, but that should certainly get their attention."

"I'd just as soon they took notice of us sooner rather than later," Sergeant Jorgen said. "Before we get too far from help. I don't mind a little action, but I'd hate to get in a position where it might take too long for our reinforcements to arrive, if you know what I mean."

I know what you mean, Lon thought. "The captain didn't say anything about racing," he said. "We'll do as much as we can."

There was little need for Lon to worry over the mechanics of getting his men to their jumping-off spot. The men moved in two columns, as close to cover as they could, taking care at intersections, and whenever they might come under observation . . . or enemy fire. Lon sent one squad ahead to clear the way and move toward the first enemy sentry whose location was known from his helmet electronics. So far, the Belletieners in Oceanview had shown no inclination to shut down their systems to avoid detection, though the force to the south, in The Cliffs, had apparently started to shut down unnecessary emissions.

"We got the sentry," Corporal Frehr reported, on a link

that connected him both to the platoon sergeant and to Lon. "He never had a chance to take a shot."

"Good work, Ben," Lon said. "You see anything I need to know about?"

"I'm not certain, Lieutenant. Maguire thought he maybe saw movement a block over, but he wasn't certain, and there were no electronics registering from that direction. I didn't see anything."

"Maybe a stray dog or something like that?" Lon asked.

"I don't know, Lieutenant. Maguire said he thought he saw a battle helmet with a different camouflage pattern, but like I said, no electronics."

That doesn't prove anything, Lon thought. "Keep your eyes open. Maguire's not one to see things that aren't there."

Less than a minute later, Lon had a call from Captain Orlis. "Something more for you to watch for. The Calypsans just passed along a message they got from a civilian in The Cliffs. Belletiene has started moving troops our way, breaking off from what little resistance the Calypsan army had been able to put in front of them there."

"Any idea how many, or how soon they might get here?"

"No, and I'm not certain how long ago the message was sent. The colonel is trying to find out more, but it's iffy. They may be moving without electronics, which cuts down on the chances of the fleet spotting them from above. Calypso has scouts out, and people working their complink nets, but we don't have any confirmation yet. Just be careful."

"Any change to our orders?"

"Not for now. But if you run into these new troops, give me a holler at once."

You can bet on it, Lon thought. He passed the news to his noncoms. "We do everything we can to keep from being surprised," Lon told them. "If we run into any enemy concentrations, I want to know about them before they know about us. We move as if we were trying to infiltrate a known enemy position. Move one squad from each platoon at a time, use the rest to provide cover. The enemy might be observing electronic silence, so don't count on seeing blips on your faceplates." He felt self-conscious reminding longtime veterans of such basics, but did not let that stop him. Nor did any of the noncoms object to his lecture.

There were the little things, habits. For Lon, that always included checking the safety on his rifle. It was off, as he wanted it. He glanced at the timeline on his head-up display. He surveyed the overlay that showed him the positions of his men, even though he could see all but one squad from where he was.

Lon was with third platoon. It was not simply a matter of dividing his time between the platoons in the most equitable fashion, moving with third now because he had been with fourth before. It was also a matter of comfort. He was more at ease with third platoon. That was where he had served as an officer-cadet. He knew the men of that platoon, especially its second squad, better than he knew any of the others. For the same reasons, he attached himself to the platoon's second squad, taking his position just behind Tebba Girana.

"You think this is going to get hairy, Lieutenant?" Girana asked over a private link.

"Why do you ask?" Lon replied.

"That's when you're most certain to show up here," Girana said with a soft chuckle. *Like running home to Mommy,* he thought but would never say—to anyone. He had too much respect and affection for his lieutenant to cause him any embarrassment.

"Could be, Tebba. At least with the bunch of you, I've got a damn good idea which way everyone will jump if something *does* happen. You'd better be careful, though, doing all that thinking. Someone's apt to notice and transfer you to Corps Intelligence."

"Bite your tongue, Lieutenant," Girana said with horror that was not completely feigned. "I'm no egghead, no more'n I gotta be to stay alive."

The conversation was slow, interrupted often, resumed

when possible. Neither man let the talk interfere with watching over the men, and watching for trouble. Lon also had to switch channels to talk with the sergeants and the other squad leaders now and then. The two platoons reached the spot where the enemy sentry had been killed, and turned east. Ben Frehr's squad had gone on. It was several blocks away now, stalking another of the isolated Belletiener sentries.

"Weil, put one of your squads out on the right," Lon told Sergeant Jorgen. "If there are enemy troops coming up from The Cliffs, I want to know as early as possible."

"Right, sir," Jorgen replied. "I was gonna suggest that."

Lon looked up at the sky. Midday. The sun was bright in an almost cloudless sky. Day or night made little difference against an enemy who also had night-vision equipment, but like most soldiers, Lon felt safer operating in the dark. It gave an illusion of security, like a child pulling a blanket over his head to hide from "night monsters," but it was also something more. The night-vision systems in most battle helmets (not only those of the DMC) provided minimal resolution at a distance. The range of danger was lessened somewhat.

One squad from fourth platoon split off and moved in a different direction.

I hope I'm not forgetting anything important, Lon worried. That was something he worried about often, the nagging fear that somehow he would fail because he was not good enough. He occasionally had nightmares that men died under his command because he had screwed up, made some inexcusable mistake, or overlooked something basic. He feared that more than he feared the possibility of his own death. The most extreme version of the nightmare had him as the only survivor of his platoons.

"Weil, I want your platoon farther to the right," Lon instructed after both platoons crossed one of the broad avenues. "The next street or alley. Give us a little more room."

Jorgen acknowledged the order and redirected his men.

Lon turned his attention to the area directly in front of third platoon. Two blocks over was another of the many green preserves of Oceanview. "If Belletiene hasn't claimed it first, that would make a comfortable spot for us to waylay them," Lon said when he pointed the park out to Tebba. "If that was what we were out here for."

"It'll get us out of the open for a few minutes, anyway," Girana replied. "We can go in and pick where we want to come out. That park manicured or wild?"

"Somewhere in between, I think. Most of them at least have paths and clearings so the locals can enjoy them." Lon got out his mapboard, unfolded it, and adjusted the view. "It almost connects with the city boundary strip," he said after scanning the image at the best magnification the mapboard could provide. "A permanent structure right in the middle, octagonal, about a thirty-foot diameter. Maybe a band shell or something like that. So the rest of the park is probably 'improved' as well."

"Might not be much cover at ground level then, past those bushes we can see right at the edge," Tebba said. "Less chance of running into an ambush if the enemy has got there first."

"If there's an ambush, it will likely catch us trying to get into the park," Lon said. "Men at windows in buildings surrounding the park, just waiting for targets to show up. But they shouldn't be waiting for us, not yet. It's too soon, even if they noticed right when they lost that sentry."

Lon was wrong. Gunfire came from behind, from the west. The start of the attack was coordinated, more than a dozen rifles opening fire simultaneously. The Dirigenters dropped to the ground quickly. The reaction was instinctive, drilled into them in training and honed through each combat contract. *Get down, then worry about where the gunfire is coming from and how you're going to respond.* Despite quick reactions, there were casualties. Four men were wounded and two men were dead.

"Get the men around the corner, out of the line of fire," Lon ordered. "Keep down, but move." He had the platoon sergeants arrange for covering fire. The troops nearest the enemy would respond while the rest moved. Then they would pull back once the rest of the men in the two platoons were in new positions and could work to suppress enemy fire.

At first, Lon stayed back, turned toward the enemy. He was an expert with both rifle and pistol, and this was rifle work. He could not be certain how many Belletieners were present. They had obviously had time to prepare their surprise. In addition to men on the ground and sheltered by the corners of buildings, they had men in windows and doorways in the next block. He reported on the backdoor ambush to Captain Orlis as he started firing short bursts toward the most exposed targets.

"I've got men down, dead and wounded, but—for the moment, at least—we're coping. Must be at least a platoon, more likely two platoons or more. If they've got other troops moving around to intercept us, I can't tell yet."

"The colonel doesn't want to put more men in until we're certain that we've got something major going, Nolan," Orlis replied. "Find out as quickly as you can."

"I've got squads out looking. Neither has reported coming across any of the enemy yet." Lon emptied the magazine in his rifle and replaced it. A few seconds later, Ivar Dendrow called.

"We're set up back here, Lieutenant. You and the others should start pulling back now."

Crawling backward, and continuing to spray short bursts of rifle fire while he did, took concentration. And time. The movement was awkward. But finally, Lon found himself at the end of the building, close to the covering fire of rifles and grenade launchers. He ducked around the corner and sat with his back against the wall, taking a few seconds to catch his breath—and to let his mind catch up with the rest of him.

Then it was time to get on the radio, to talk to the leaders of the squads that had been moved away before the attack. Fourth platoon's scouts had already started moving around to try to assist. They were almost in position south of the

Belleticners. Third platoon's scouts had been farther off.

"Find out how many got in behind us," Lon told both squad leaders. "If you can do it without letting them see you, so much the better. We're okay now. We got everyone back." *Everyone who was still alive.* The wounded were receiving first aid. Two men were hurt badly enough that they would need time in a trauma tube—soon—to survive.

Lon called Captain Orlis to tell him that. "If someone can't get to us, I'm going to have to turn loose a squad to take them to the medics," he said. "So far it looks as if we haven't hit a really large enemy force. My scouts are moving in on both sides, and neither of them has seen anyone. But I've got two men who have to have medical help without delay."

"Have a squad bring them in," Orlis said. "I'll have medics meet them." He gave Lon map coordinates, and then the street names of an intersection. "How long will your men need?"

"They can be there in ten minutes if they don't run into more trouble along the way," Lon replied.

"Your orders are to continue your mission," Orlis said after a pause during which he dispatched the men to meet Lon's wounded. "Get free of this ambush if you can, or stay there and fight it out if you see a chance to inflict damage at minimal cost to your own men. We still want to draw out more of the enemy."

"We obviously aren't going to give them much of a surprise, Captain," Lon said. "They've got to be expecting a counterattack, and that might be when we find they've got more people than we expect." He did not pause long enough for the captain to say anything. "I reckon that would give the colonel what he wants. We'll give it a try."

12

Lon sent all of the wounded toward the rendezvous, not just the two men who needed more attention than they could get where they were. With one squad to escort the wounded, and two others already separated from the platoons, both working their way around toward the flanks of the Belletiene ambush, Lon only had five squads left to deploy, with two of those shorthanded.

"I'll keep one squad from each platoon," he told the platoon sergeants. "We'll work our way through the buildings between us and the enemy. I want the other squads to circle around, join up with the men already out there, to hit them from both sides. You two will have your own men there. If all we're up against is a couple of platoons, they might retreat rather than risk having the horns close around them." He paused. "If there are more Belletieners waiting, we should find out soon enough."

"We going to all hit at once?" Weil asked from his position behind the building across the street from Lon and Ivar.

"The squads I keep will try to keep them occupied until the rest of you get into position," Lon said. "Once you're hitting them from both sides—and yes, I want that coordinated if possible—we'll start working in from this side. If the enemy takes you under fire first, respond, but if we have a choice, I want both horns to open up together. Check on the squads you've already got out. Link with them if you can. Now, get started."

Lon kept Tebba Girana's squad from third platoon and Wil Nace's from fourth. While the others pulled back and started their encircling maneuver, Lon briefed the two squad leaders on what they were going to do. "We don't know if we're going to run into fifty of the enemy or five hundred. Or more. Be ready for anything. We may have to beat a hasty retreat if we bite off more than we can chew."

Two men on either side of the street were sent to break into the nearest buildings between them and the enemy, to make certain that the Belletieners did not use those covert routes. The rest of the men in the two squads faced the enemy directly, with rifles and rocket-propelled grenades. They did not try to overwhelm the enemy with volume of fire. This was not a time to be spendthrift with ammunition. All Lon wanted was to keep the enemy occupied.

It took ten minutes for his flankers to get into position. Neither Dendrow nor Jorgen reported any sign of additional enemy soldiers waiting to pounce. "That don't mean they're not there," Weil added, "but if they are, they're inside buildings and being damn cute about it."

"Wouldn't you be, in that situation?" Lon asked. He did not wait for a reply. "Assume that they know cute as well as you."

Both platoon sergeants were on the link. Lon said, "One minute from now, start hitting them. Then we start moving." As soon as the sergeants acknowledged the order, Lon told Nace and Girana to be ready as well. While he was doing that, Lon slipped a new magazine into his rifle.

For a change, the waiting went quickly. The added volume of gunfire was immediately audible. The noise level nearly doubled.

"Let's move!" Lon said—almost shouted—on the channel that linked him with Girana and Nace. "Inside and on."

Janno Belzer and Phip Steesen went through the door as if they expected the room beyond to be filled with enemy soldiers, even though Lance Corporal Dav Grott and Gen Radnor had already gone in to secure the building against that possibility. Girana was the next man through the door, and Lon followed him, with the rest of the squad close behind.

The building was a professional arcade. The center of

the building was a large atrium with a lightly tinted skylight that gave a soft pink touch to everything. Offices surrounded that on all three floors. On the ground floor, the center was arranged as an indoor garden with small trees and several beds of flowers around a fountain and reflecting pool.

Many of the interior doors had been broken open. Grott and Radnor had been busy. Girana had his men briefed. Grott was sent to the right, to keep watch on that side of the building. Radnor was sent to the far end, nearest the Belletieners. The rest of the squad moved into offices to find windows they could use as vantage spots to fire on the enemy—half on the ground floor and half on the levels above. Lon glanced upward, tempted to go to the third floor to see what was visible, but instead he moved through the center of the building, past the fountain, to the door at the far end where Radnor was posted.

"See anything?" Lon asked when he knelt on the other side of the doorway.

Radnor shook his head. "There's that next building in the way. I haven't seen anyone shooting from that, so maybe the enemy isn't in there."

A paved courtyard stood between the arcade and the next building. There were a half dozen plascrete tables with benches and large umbrellas over them in the courtyard. Several small pieces of sculpture lined the street side of it.

Lon nodded, then called Corporal Girana. "Tebba, when we move out, I want Ericks and Steesen upstairs providing cover until the rest of us get into the next building." For close work, those two were the best marksmen in the squad, and both would keep their heads no matter what they came up against.

"Yes, sir. When do we move?"

"Hang on a second while I check with Nace." Lon switched channels to see how the squad across the street was faring.

"We're ready to move whenever you give the word," Nace replied. "Not much here in the way of vantage. I've only got three men where they can bring the enemy under fire.''

"Okay, let's move." Lon gave Girana the same order.

The first few men through the doorway came under gunfire. A few Belletieners were located where they could cover that terrace. But the incoming fire stopped quickly, and none of Lon's men were hit. The plascrete tables and benches provided excellent cover. The door to the next building to the west resisted efforts to open it. Two men working together could not dislocate door from frame, and the lock resisted two attempts to shoot it open.

"That's gonna take a shaped charge, Lieutenant," Girana said. "And that's something we don't have."

Lon shrugged. "Maybe we don't need it," he said. Weil Jorgen was talking to him at the same time.

"They're pulling back, Lieutenant," Jorgen said. "No more than forty of them, looks like. Do we keep after them?"

Lon hesitated, almost ready to call Captain Orlis and pass the decision to him. Then he shook his head. *Original mission,* he thought. "No, Weil. Hang on while I bring Ivar into this." When he had both platoon sergeants on link, Lon said. "Keep them under fire as long as you've got targets but do not, repeat *not,* pursue. As soon as they're out of range, pull back and we'll go on with what we were doing before. That's still the assignment."

He waited for their acknowledgments before he asked, "Any additional casualties?"

"Not here," Ivar replied, "but the enemy lost a few men."

Weil had one more man wounded, but it was not serious, and he would be able to continue on with the rest of the platoon.

After a time, the senses of an infantryman in combat become almost feral, attuned to his environment with a fineness that cannot be duplicated except under circumstances that might prove lethal. He hears and sees, he *notices.* Even his sense of smell can become abnormally acute, filtering

out the smells of gunpowder and fear, and whatever may-
hem he may have been through, for any hint of new danger.
He can move with exaggerated caution, patiently stalking
the enemy, or onto ground that might be under observation,
but the surge of adrenaline that will propel him to whatever
new physical exertions are required is never more than a
heartbeat away.

The men under Lon's command moved with the preci-
sion of men on a drill field, accomplished veterans. Routine
maneuvers could be done without conscious thought, leaving the mind free to concentrate on greater need. That was
one purpose of all of the drilling and field exercises. Remove, as far as possible, the need for the individual soldier
to think when he was in danger. Drum all of the predictable
moves into him so thoroughly that they will be done automatically—at need . . . or on order.

Lon moved with Girana's squad, to the left of the re-
formed advance. Once more, a single squad had been sent
out on each side, as scouts and flankers. The objective was
still the park where the center of the Belletiene line was
holding strong—unless they were intercepted first. Twice
they encountered three-man enemy patrols. The first group
managed to escape. The second was pinned down. Two of
those men were killed, the third wounded. The wounded
man was given first aid, then stripped of weapons and helmet, and bound. Lon had no men to spare for guarding a
prisoner.

The two skirmishes were the only obstacles they encountered until the park was in sight one park of so many
in the city. Lon never questioned that it was the right one.
Even without the sound of battle in front of him, he had
the enemy positions on his mapboard and, once he was
close enough, on the head-up display of his helmet's faceplate.

"Get the men into cover," Lon told his platoon sergeants
when the point men were within a block and a half of the
park. "Into the buildings. Something isn't right here. Give
me time to check with the captain."

Orlis listened patiently. "Not a bit of reaction, Captain,"

Lon said. "We're almost close enough to spit on them, and it's as if we were completely invisible. They're in there, in the park, but they're taking absolutely no notice of us."

"I thought sure that you'd draw them in before this, Nolan. You've got your men under cover?" When Lon replied in the affirmative, Orlis said, "Stay put. I've got to buck this one up the line, see what we do next."

It took fifteen minutes before the captain called back. "It looks as if things might get hotter for you, soon. As near as we can tell, Belletiene has moved virtually all of their men north out of The Cliffs. We've only managed a few isolated intercepts of electronics, but the main enemy force can't be more than six-tenths of a mile south of you, and they might be a lot closer. To your west, things have settled down a little, but with Belletiene in control of the area near you, you're going to have to head east. That's the only possibly safe route. Belletiene's troops have advanced farther our way on that side, so there shouldn't be much more in your way than sentries and scouts, what you've been dealing with."

"Yes, sir, take the men east. Any idea how far we'll have to go before we can circle around to rejoin you?" *There's an ocean not too far away,* Lon thought.

"I'm not sure yet that you'll be able to circle around. The fighting extends almost all of the way to the beach. I'll pass along any intelligence I get, but if anything unexpected happens, be ready to use your own judgment. You'll likely have a better idea what's possible than I will. Understand?"

"Yes, sir. Use my own judgment." *Take the responsibility . . . and the consequences,* Lon thought. It was as close to independent action as any junior officer in the Dirigent Mercenary Corps was likely to come. "I think we'll have to start by moving a little south before we turn east, Captain. We're too close to the Belletiene lines here."

"I'll do what I can to keep track of you, and pass the information along to CIC. If they spot anything pertinent, they'll be able to notify you directly if there isn't time to go through me or through battalion."

More fingers to point, Lon thought as he acknowledged the captain's information.

After he signed off, Lon took a moment to collect his thoughts. *You don't* know *that this is going to be trouble. It might be a walk in the park.* He grimaced at the unintentional pun. *Don't panic. Keep your head. Do everything by the book. As long as we don't get boxed in by a far superior force, we can come through this,* he told himself— almost with confidence. He took a couple of slow, deep breaths and let them out, then called his platoon sergeants to let them know what the situation was. Dendrow grunted at the news. Jorgen gave no reaction at all that Lon could hear.

"What's our status on ammo?" Lon asked.

"Never enough," Jorgen said, "but we're not in desperate straits. We watch what we're doing and don't get bogged down in a major firefight, we should be okay for several hours. If this lark goes on much past sunset, then we might have to worry."

"Depends what we come up against," Dendrow said. "I've got a couple men down to half a standard load, but I've already had words with them. The rest of the men are in pretty good shape."

"No one with physical problems that could slow us down?" Lon asked next, and both sergeants replied in the negative.

"We're going to electronic silence, as far as possible," Lon said next. "Once this conference finishes and you've had time to brief your men, I want passive scans only, no radio transmissions unless it's vital. Hand signs and face-to-face when possible." He did not need to define "vital." The platoon sergeants, squad leaders, and most of the men could make that distinction reliably. If anything, they would generally err on the conservative side.

The two platoons moved south, staying inside buildings as much as they could, and using them as a screen between themselves and the enemy in the park when they had to move outdoors. Lon kept his men as dispersed as he dared, with one squad tailing well behind the rest as rearguard, another out in front, and a third on their right flank. For the moment, he did not put a squad out on the left, the side nearest the known positions of the enemy. The Belletiener lines were simply too close to take that risk.

Their progress was slow, cautious. Lon hoped to rely on stealth more than speed to see them safely across to the sea, or as close to it as they had to go before they could turn north. *We get to the far edge of the fighting, there might be a way for us to sneak through the lines,* he decided, though that might mean waiting for dark. In the dark, observing total electronic silence, Dirigenters could penetrate all but the most closely guarded lines without detection. Lon had seen it. He knew what he and his men were capable of.

One Belletiener patrol held up their movement for ten minutes. Lon moved two squads around so their beamers would have clear targets and others would be close enough to move in to finish the job as quietly as possible if any of the enemy survived the silent assault of energy weapons. There were a few gunshots in the fight. *Maybe not enough to draw anyone's attention,* Lon told himself, but as soon as the nearest squad reported that all of the soldiers in the enemy patrol had been "accounted for," Lon hurried his men on. They moved the next quarter mile as quickly as they could. Only when they reached the next park did Lon give his men a few minutes to rest.

The trees and flowers that Lon saw in this park—about five acres in extent—all appeared to be terran species, an arboretum to remind the Calypsans of the homeworld from which their ancestors had come. Lon was not familiar with all of the varieties, but there were nameplates identifying each. Many were tropical. But he saw magnolias and dogwoods, both of which he had seen in abundance in the southeastern portion of what had once been the United States, now one of the three major divisions of the North American Union, where he had grown up.

In the arboretum, Lon called his platoon sergeants together, using hand signals. With their visors raised, Lon said, "So far, so good. There's an even chance that we'll be able to get through this next stretch without difficulty. The fighting on this side is all farther north." He paused. "At least it was the last word I had." Observing electronic silence meant not using his mapboard to look for enemy positions.

"It's what, a mile and a half to the coast?" Jorgen asked.

Lon nodded. "About that. I hope we don't have to go that far. There won't be any cover at all close to the ocean. A wide beach, long, gentle slope. Remember, this city was designed so that the government big shots would have a clear view of the sea from their offices."

"From a mile or more away," Ivar Dendrow commented. "Even at night it would be hard to cross that beach without being seen, if there's anyone looking."

"We know anything about what it's like in the water?" Jorgen asked. "Currents, tides, predators, all that stuff?"

"People swim in it. That's all I know," Lon admitted. "Not something that was covered in the briefing. I don't know if we could wade out and head north without abandoning most of our gear. Let's hope it doesn't come to that."

"I've got a suggestion," Dendrow said, and he waited for the lieutenant to nod before he continued. "Since we probably won't be able to go through the enemy lines until after dark—wherever we do it—this seems to be as good a spot to wait as any we're likely to find. We can make ourselves safer in this tree museum than in a building that the enemy could drop on us with a couple of RPGs, and we've got good fire zones and lines of visibility."

"Well, what do you think?" Lon asked.

"It makes sense, if we can risk being this far from the water for another six or seven hours. This city is full of parks. Chances are we'll come across another one between here and there. But either way would work, I think."

"The only argument against I can think of is that patrol we took out," Ivar said. "If someone comes looking, we're still not all that far away."

Lon nodded slowly. "Or maybe they wouldn't think of

looking so close," he said. "Let me think on this. We'll take thirty minutes anyway, as long as things stay quiet. I'll let you know then whether we're going to stay or move on." He shrugged. "Thirty minutes, everything might change anyway."

The three men separated. Dendrow and Jorgen passed the word to their squad leaders that they would—probably—be staying put for at least thirty minutes. Lon took five of those minutes to make a quick tour of the impromptu perimeter his platoons had established. *If we stay here, we'll have to plant snoops out where they'll give us some warning,* he thought. The electronic bugs would catch any sound around them, and miniature cameras would switch on to relay what they saw. *Too bad we don't have any mines to plant.* They had not carried any coming in, and had not been offered any from the Calypsan munitions.

Before he completed his tour, Lon had decided that Dendrow was probably correct that they were unlikely to find anyplace better to wait. But he did not rush his decision. He got off his feet, sitting with his back against a tree trunk, determined to get at least a few minutes rest before he committed himself.

I'm too tired to make any decision quickly I don't have to. The longer I can mull it over, the better. He yawned. He did not *quite* doze off. His mind would not let go completely of his responsibilities, and the many questions that forced themselves on his attention. *This is a crazy kind of fight,* he thought. *Nothing makes much sense. Everything's all mixed up, here and there.* It was nothing at all like the "clean" battle plans they had studied at the North American Military Academy, the fights they had looked at through the sieve of history, parsing decisions and performance, weapons and tactics—all to find the "inescapable" conclusion of why the winner had won and the loser had lost. *A man could make sense of those. Not like this. The Belletieners have to know that we're back here, doing whatever we please, but they're ignoring us. Colonel Gaffney sends most of the regiment off into the mountains when the important action is here, and most of the enemy.*

Lon's sigh was almost inaudible, even to him. *Maybe when we get home, Gaffney will explain why he made the decisions he did,* Lon thought. *Make it simple enough so that I can understand.*

Slowly, his mind got back to the immediate choice, to move on or stay put past the half hour he had promised. *There's got to be a better way than flipping a coin.* If he could just think through the situation with absolute clarity, he might find the one bit of data that would make the choice seem obvious. His eyes drifted closed a number of times. Once he realized that it was happening, he would open them quickly, as if afraid that someone might notice that he had almost fallen asleep. Each time, he tried to concentrate, but focus was hard to achieve.

I guess we can stay put a while longer, he decided after nearly all of the half hour had passed, but he realized that his decision was based more on inertia than anything else. Even then, he needed a couple of minutes longer before he started to move. He got to his feet slowly, as if he were infirm, and moved toward the center of the circle his men were in. As he moved, he gestured for the platoon sergeants to join him.

"Anyone seen anything?" he asked when they were face to face, squatting near the exact center of the two platoons.

"Nothing moving," Dendrow said. Jorgen just shook his head.

"I've had no word from the captain or from CIC," Lon said. "Maybe I'm too tired to think straight, but I can't see any reason not to stay where we are a little longer. If I'm beat, the men must be too. Keep them on half-and-half watches. With a little luck, maybe we can all manage an hour or so to nap."

He waited for the sergeants to nod. "Two hours will take us to about four o'clock, local time," Lon said. "If nothing pops before then, we'll start moving again, at least until we find the next good place to settle down." Neither Jorgen nor Dendrow offered objections, or advice.

13

Once Lon saw the men return from planting snoops beyond the perimeter, he made himself as comfortable as the location and his gear permitted. He knew that he had to get at least a few minutes of undisturbed sleep—if possible. One of the platoon sergeants would always be awake. There would always be someone in command and, theoretically, alert.

Relaxing his body was no problem. Clearing his mind was more difficult. It was some minutes before he started to drift off, more before his mind finally let go. . . .

"Nolan! Don't answer. Just listen." Lon came awake instantly at the sound of his name over the radio, though he needed a few seconds to realize that it was Captain Orlis on the link. "Colonel Gaffney has finished with the Belletieners in the mining region. The rest of the regiment will be coming to Oceanview and The Cliffs tonight, leaving their present locations shortly after sunset there. About twenty-two thirty or twenty-three hundred hours here. Arrival about twenty-five minutes after they leave their present location. If you can find a good spot, dig in and wait. Try to avoid detection. Belletiene is still moving troops north from The Cliffs." There was a short pause before Orlis said, "Click twice if you've heard this." Lon clicked his transmitter twice.

"If I can, I'll give you updates at five minutes past the even hours, more often if necessary. Off."

Lon got up and went to pass the news to his platoon sergeants. "Have the men dig in. We're going to be here for a while, so let's make it homey. Then make sure everyone eats. After that, we'll go back to half-and-half watches—if the enemy leaves us alone.''

It did not take long for the news to spread. Lon went back to his position and started excavating his own slit trench. He dug as close to the tree he had been sitting against before as possible. The ground was easy to work, mostly sand and humus. He needed less than half an hour to get down eight inches, working steadily, sweating freely from his labor.

He took his own advice and ate a full meal pack then, sitting in his new excavation, looking around at as much of his command as he could see. The new gashes in the terrain might seem obvious to anyone who happened to look, but they would not have to count on the trenches for long.

If trouble comes, they'll do a lot more good, he assured himself, *no matter how obvious they are.* Even a few inches of protection could make the difference in a firefight.

Lon had just finished eating when his platoon sergeants came toward him. ''Everyone's set, Lieutenant,'' Dendrow said when he slid to the ground at one side of Lon and lifted his faceplate. Jorgen took up a similar position on the other side and nodded his confirmation of what Dendrow had said.

''You two set things up so that one of you is always up,'' Lon said. ''I'm going to try to get a little rest, but I've got to be awake to get the updates from Captain Orlis. Make sure I am, on the even hours. Give me a few minutes to shake the cobwebs out.''

''We'll see to it, Lieutenant,'' Jorgen said.

''I hope they leave us alone, at least until dark,'' Lon said. ''Give us a chance to get back in touch with the rest of our people first. That would be even better.''

''When the rest of the regiment gets here, we should be able to finish this off in fair order,'' Dendrow said. ''Between us and the locals, we'll have Belletiene outnumbered and up against it.''

''Better them than us,'' Jorgen contributed.

"Just remember, that won't mean that we head straight for home," Lon said. "This contract could still last the full six months for us. The men start trying to talk themselves into thinking we've just got to beat this batch and collect our bonuses, stop them quick. Don't let them build up false hopes. They could crash all too quickly. Even after we quash this invasion force, there's nothing says that Belletiene can't send more men in tomorrow or the next day. They don't have to take two weeks to get here through Q-space."

Just make like we're not here, Lon thought after the sergeants had gone back to their positions, projecting his wishes as if the Belletieners might actually be influenced by them. *Forget all about us until the rest of the regiment gets here and keeps you too busy to remember.* It had not been necessary for Lon to reinforce the order for electronic silence, or to say anything about avoiding unnecessary movement. The sergeants and squad leaders would handle those details, should there be any need. But everyone seemed content to lie in their trenches and take their turns at watching and sleeping—or trying to sleep.

Now that he had time for it, Lon found that he was no longer as sleepy as he had been when it had looked as if he would have only a few minutes to nap. He was still tired, but his mind was working again. He listened, both for any hint of the enemy and for any unnecessary sounds from his own men. He thought back over what Captain Orlis had said, and kept looking at the time, to see how far away the next update was. Time crawled.

At 1605 hours, Captain Orlis had nothing new to say, and said just that. Two hours later, he said that everything remained on schedule, even though more of Belletiene's troops had joined the fighting on the southwest side of Oceanview.

After that, Lon did manage to doze. The several hours that had passed without any sign of enemy activity around the park had eased his tension a little. *Maybe we'll get away with it,* he told himself.

He was definitely asleep when Phip Steesen shook his shoulder and said, "Lieutenant!" in a sharp whisper.

"What is it?" Lon asked, blinking furiously.

"Enemy soldiers moving, west to east, north of us," Phip said. He was prone next to Lon's trench, keeping his head down. "At least a full company. The rest of the men are being wakened," he added.

Lon rolled over. He had been sleeping on his back. He lifted his head to look over the raised border to his trench. Almost unconsciously, he noticed that it was 1915 hours. The shadows were getting more acute, longer.

"I see them," he whispered, and Phip started crawling back to his own trench, snaking slowly across the ground.

The Belletieners were moving along the avenue next to the park. The point squad was just disappearing from sight to the east. The main body was coming along behind, moving along either side of the avenue, cautiously—as if concerned about the possibility of encountering hostile forces—but showing no hint that they knew that Dirigenters were so close.

Sitting ducks, Lon thought. His two platoons would be able to take out more than half of the enemy company before the Belletieners could react. The nearer line of the enemy was no more than eighty yards away. He watched, knowing that he would not give the order to fire unless the enemy did something threatening. There was no question of giving away the fact that they were present, even before he reminded himself that there might be more enemy soldiers close than those he could see. *Maybe the equivalent of a full battalion,* he thought. There were that many, and more, of the enemy who had not been accounted for, the last he had heard.

The invaders moved with proper discipline, alert. *They don't look as if they think they're whipped. They're not running scared. They're still ready for a fight.* It was something to think about. Lon considered breaking electronic silence to pass that news on to Captain Orlis—after these Belletieners were well away—but decided against it. *Not worth the risk. I'll get a chance soon enough, when it's safer.*

It was a few seconds later when he wondered where the enemy's flankers were. A company should have a squad out on either side, covering them. *On this side they should be moving right through this park or on the next street south,* he thought. He twisted around on his side so that he could look across to the far side of his platoons' perimeter. He could see nothing there, and none of his men was trying to get his attention to relay a message that he was seeing anything on that side. Then he looked west. There was no sign of trouble there either.

Unless there are other units moving east, Lon thought. *Close enough that they don't feel any need for flankers in the middle.* That made him more nervous. He could see one company—or maybe a little more—of Belletieners. If other companies were moving east in parallel, he might find himself in the middle of a royal mess. *If they see us.*

Once the main body of the enemy company moved out of sight to the west, Lon allowed himself a slightly deeper breath than he had been taking since Phip had wakened him. He did not move, though, waiting for the enemy's rearguard to move past.

But it was not a squad or even a platoon that trailed after the others, but another full company. *How many more?* Lon wondered. The more of the enemy who paraded by, the greater the chance that someone would notice something in the park, like freshly dug trenches or the low mounds of soil packed up in front of them. Lon started to think about the possibility of withdrawing, but knew that it would be impossible to move out of the park without being seen. Movement would give them away surer than anything.

Lon did almost jump when he heard a squawk over his earphones. He needed a second to identify the warning chirp from one of the snoops that his men had planted. He clicked a switch to accept the video and audio from the bug. Reception was passive, and the signal from the snoop would be too faint to be picked up at any distance.

He saw more Belletiener soldiers. This was not the view

north of the park, but south of it. *More of them,* he thought. *Are all of those missing soldiers going to troop past us?*

Having the enemy on two sides did squelch any further thought of withdrawing. There was no place left for Lon to take his men—no direction that would be *away* from the enemy. After dark they could take the chance, if necessary, but darkness was two hours away. Lon started sweating more heavily than he had while he was digging his trench, a different kind of perspiration. This was fear, a knot in his gut, an itch on the nape of his neck, a drum pounding in his head.

He took in a long, slow breath and held it for nearly a minute. Fear was no stranger. It was simply another weapon to use. He would not let it control his actions. It would not paralyze him. As long as none of his men did anything foolish, there was still a chance that they could avoid detection. *They've missed us so far,* Lon thought. *No reason to think some tail-end-Charlie is going to see us.*

On the north, the second company was past. On the south, that force—apparently company-strength also—kept moving east. On neither side was there any indication that the Dirigenters had been noticed. *Unless they're a lot smarter than they have any right to be,* Lon decided. *Smart enough not to show any reaction at all and to keep moving until they're out from under our sights before they turn on us.*

When a single squad showed on the north, trailing the two companies that had passed on that side, Lon felt a little less threatened. The rearguard. And only the single company—with one squad back as a rearguard—passed on the south. *Ten minutes,* Lon told himself, glancing at the timeline on his helmet visor to make certain of the time. *If nothing happens in the next ten minutes, we got away with it.*

Those minutes passed with excruciating slowness. Lon remained tense, to the point that he feared that his arms and legs might cramp. He had to consciously force himself to loosen his grip on his rifle, to make small movements with his arms and legs to keep them loose. He continued to think around the advisability of notifying Captain Orlis, or Colonel Flowers, about the enemy movement, but could not think of any way to do it without jeopardizing his command. *Don't break electronic silence. Don't give our position away.* Calling the captain would violate his orders. *If it was* our *people in immediate danger . . .* Lon thought. That would override his orders—make them obsolete. They would only be in that degree of danger if the enemy knew where they were. *Wait, just wait.*

As carefully as he could, Lon turned his head to look at the nearest men on either side of him. They might have been statues made from the same mold. His men were doing what they should, watching for the enemy, hands on weapons, ready, but not making a movement or sound. Lon returned to watching the street, waiting for any sign that the Belletieners were moving back toward them.

Maybe we should move as soon as they've had time to get well away from us, Lon thought. *In case they spotted us and passed the word on to their commander. We might be compromised here.*

Moving because of a possible threat to his command would fall within his scope of competence—and responsibility. He took a deep breath as the ten minutes he had allowed as the time of greatest danger passed without incident.

Not yet, he decided. They might move into trouble rather than away from it. He waited two more minutes before he crawled out of his slit trench, then got up and jogged to where Sergeant Jorgen was.

"I want you to send out two men, separately, to make sure those troops kept on moving," Lon told Jorgen. "They're to stay out of sight of the enemy, if possible, and they're only to break electronic silence if they come under attack. When they get back, have them report directly to me."

As soon as Jorgen nodded, Lon headed toward Ivar Dendrow, to tell him what he was doing.

• • •

"They kept going," Tarn Headly said when he returned from his reconnaissance. "Owl and I went three blocks over past the end of this park, a block apart, and the Belletieners just kept going, then finally turned north."

A few minutes later, Owl Whitley returned and made the same report. "They didn't hardly even look back," he added, "like they didn't have no reason to worry about what was behind 'em."

Lon had nodded and sent each man back to his squad. He had debated whether to send scouts out in other directions and had decided against it. The risks outweighed the possible benefits. *As long as we're safe, let it lie,* he told himself. *Don't do the enemy any favors by giving them extra chances at spotting us.* Once the sun set, he and his men would have an even better chance of remaining undetected long enough for Colonel Gaffney and the rest of the regiment to arrive. After that it would not, Lon thought—hoped—make any difference. Belletiene's soldiers should be too busy to worry about them.

The next update from Captain Orlis mentioned heavier fighting north and east of Lon and his men. That came as no surprise to Lon after seeing the enemy troops moving in that direction. For a few seconds, Lon again toyed with the idea of breaking electronic silence to tell the captain about those troops, before deciding against it yet again. There was no longer any urgency. Those soldiers had apparently already been committed to the fight.

Sunset came, and dusk. The waiting continued. Lon lifted his faceplate and looked around. Without the night-vision system of his helmet, it was already difficult to discern the positions of the men at the far side of the perimeter. As long as they remained motionless, they would be nearly invisible to any approaching enemy. The Dirigenters' battledress included enough thermal shielding to minimize their visibility even in infrared.

Lon had earlier put the men back on half-and-half watches, once the enemy troops had been tracked far enough so that he did not have to worry about them immediately. But he had been unable to get any additional rest himself. The danger of the passing enemy had driven the exhaustion away more surely than a full night of sleep would have. He was alert, edgy, and had difficulty even relaxing.

It was still two hours short of when Lon expected the rest of the regiment to leave the mining region when another of the snoops gave an alert, and the silent waiting ended for the two platoons.

14

The alarm came from the south. Lon pulled down his faceplate, accepted the feed from the electronic bug, and watched on his head-up display as enemy soldiers moved toward the park. He could not tell how many there were, just two columns of men moving straight toward his platoons.

Electronic silence had to be broken. Lon clicked to his all-hands channel to issue the warning. "Enemy soldiers moving toward us from the south. Don't move. Wait for my command before doing anything."

He turned around in his slit trench, facing the threat. He felt for the safety switch next to the trigger and firing mechanism on the receiver of his rifle to make certain that it was off. *Turn!* he thought, trying to will the enemy soldiers away. If they turned either east or west, his men might remain undetected, but if they kept coming, into the park, then they would move straight into Lon's platoons. Lon could not let the enemy get that close.

"Weil, you're closest," Lon said, switching to a channel that connected him with both platoon sergeants and all of the squad leaders. "They get within sixty yards of the perimeter, tell me. That's when we'll open fire." *If we have to.*

Jorgen clicked his transmitter in acknowledgment.

"If they do keep coming, I only want the men on that side of the perimeter firing at first, but I want a lot of volume, rifles and grenades. Do them fast, before they get organized."

Lon was already trying to plan for the next step, but that

would depend, in large part, on what the Belletieners did when—if—a firefight started, and how many he was facing. *If we can bounce them hard, then get away clean, that's the ticket,* he thought, trying to ignore the nagging worry that they might be attacking too large a force. *Move and take our chances until the rest of our people get here.*

There was one positive note. If a firefight started, he could call Captain Orlis and let him know what was going on.

"Sixty yards, Lieutenant," Jorgen said.

Lon did not hesitate. "Open fire."

Only two squads were given the order. The grenadiers were first, launching rocket-propelled grenades. Then the rifles joined in, as the first grenades exploded in and around the Belletieners. For a few seconds, Lon's men had the action all to themselves. Then the return fire started—sporadic and ineffective at first, then increasing in volume and accuracy.

"At least a full company out there, Lieutenant," Jorgen reported. "No way to tell if there's more coming up."

"They haven't started trying to flank us yet," Dendrow said on the same channel. "You want we should put out a squad on either side, Lieutenant?"

"Yes, out and around. Let them get in a few licks while they're at it. But I want everyone ready to move in a hurry. We get a chance, we're going to withdraw." He hesitated. "Unless Captain Orlis has other ideas. I'm going to call him now."

Lon changed channels. When Orlis answered, Lon gave him a quick summary of the situation.

"Try to determine how many you're up against first," Orlis said. "If the numbers are manageable, remain engaged. But if you are up against a company or more, get your men out if you can before they move in reinforcements."

"Yes, sir. The rest of the show still on schedule?"

"I haven't been told of any changes. The shuttles are on the way in to pick the others up. Anything you need right now?"

"Nothing that can't wait," Lon said, guessing that the captain was busy—most likely in his own combat situation.

Lon was prone in his trench. The enemy rifle fire was not all that far overhead. Several bullets hit the tree nearest Lon. He could see occasional muzzle blasts, bright flashes that could not be completely suppressed. The smell of smoke and powder was slow to reach him. What little breeze there was seemed to be coming from the west.

Two grenades exploded almost in the center of the area that Lon's platoons were defending—far enough from the perimeter that they were unlikely to kill or injure anyone flat in a slit trench. He had seen men move away from the perimeter on either side, but they had been going out.

"Lieutenant, we've got at least two companies out here, and they're starting to move around, farther out than we are," Corporal Girana reported. "We've hit them and moved. It slowed them down, for a minute or two anyway."

"Move back here, Tebba," Lon said. "Back and past. We're pulling out." Lon switched channels to tell all of his noncoms that, and to detail how he wanted to handle the withdrawal.

There was no time for intensive planning. Lon made his decisions and issued the orders quickly. The men on the north side of the perimeter, farthest from the enemy, were turned to face south. While the two patrols that had been sent out on the flanks withdrew, so did the men on the south side of the circular perimeter, pulling back through the northern half of the defensive position. That was slow. The men crawled the entire distance, below the fire of both the enemy and their comrades.

Lon finally had a chance to get his own shooting in. His concern was more with making certain that none of his own people were hit by friendly fire. That meant that his fire, and that of his men, was mostly too high to do much serious damage to the enemy. But if the volume helped keep the Belletieners in place, it served its purpose.

Then, after the first men passed through the northern half of the perimeter that was being abandoned, Lon and three squads were suddenly the front line, nearest the enemy, while the rest of his men took up new defensive positions across the street that flanked the park on the north—breaking into buildings and opening windows.

"We're set here," Weil Jorgen reported, ten minutes after he had passed Lon's position. "I've got men high enough to give you effective cover once you get out of the park."

"As soon as we can move," Lon said. "The enemy is coming toward us." Almost smothering the last words, a grenade exploded no more than twenty yards in front of Lon. He felt the concussion as he ducked his head and pulled in his arms—like a turtle trying to withdraw into his shell. The blast wave felt like a sledgehammer blow against his helmet, rocking Lon, stunning him. He was scarcely aware of the shrapnel and debris that showered him. He was completely unaware of the minor damage his hands and forearms suffered.

Lon was not badly wounded, but the concussion did leave him dazed for a protracted moment. Until the ringing in his ears muted, he could not hear anyone talking. Nor was he aware of several other grenades exploding close, if not quite as close as the first. It was instinct—honed by training and repetitious drills—that made him continue to withdraw from the edge of his slit trench, seeking sanctuary.

He was only marginally aware when someone dropped into the trench next to him, crowding him up against one side of the hole.

"Lieutenant?" Ivar Dendrow shouted, close to Lon's ear. He could tell that Lon was alive. He could read his vitals on his own head-up display. The platoon sergeant looked for injuries, a slow process since he had to stay low.

Lon groaned, a low sound that Dendrow did not hear. Lon only slowly became aware that there was anyone with him. "I'm okay," he muttered, before he was certain that was the truth.

"A lot of small cuts on your hands and arms, sir," Dendrow said, over his radio link.

That registered. Lon made fists, then relaxed the hands. They worked. "I'll be okay, Ivar. Just had my bell rung." He paused, then added, "It's still ringing. How are we doing?"

"Just you, me, and one squad left to move, sir, and I'd suggest we move now. The enemy is getting close."

"Casualties?" Lon asked as he reached for his rifle.

"The wounded have been moved," Dendrow said. "Three men dead. Grau and Davis from my first squad. Bocker from Weil's second."

While he talked, Dendrow nearly manhandled the lieutenant, getting him turned and moving. Lon was groggy, and his body appeared to be debating whether or not to cooperate. The last squad of men in the park provided covering fire while Dendrow and Nolan moved north. The platoon sergeant kept an arm around his lieutenant, and they staggered together. Lon had only minimal command over his body. Once they were out in the open, on the grassy verge before the street, Dendrow tightened his grip and hurried Lon on, supporting more than half of the lieutenant's weight as they moved toward the rest of the platoons.

They were halfway across the avenue before Lon started to feel as if he could take care of himself. He shook loose Dendrow's grip, stumbled, then caught his balance. "Let's get moving." Lon glanced over his shoulder. "Get that last squad moving too, while they still can."

He let Dendrow give the orders. Lon was still trying to clear his head. Awareness was a gradual thing, building slowly. He was not truly feeling his physical injuries, just the remnants of disorientation. And he was fighting that, working toward survival—for himself and his men. Everything else could wait until he could concentrate more effectively.

Lon tripped over the curbing on the north side of the street and nearly fell before he caught himself. The jarring misstep seemed to help clear his head. He paused and looked south, to where the men of the last squad were finally appearing at the edge of the park, moving slowly, ducking from tree to tree, still firing toward the pursuing enemy.

"We'd better get inside, Lieutenant," Dendrow said, hovering close. "Give the men a clear shot without worrying about us."

Lon nodded, almost absently, and started moving again, slowly, his attention divided. Dendrow guided him toward a doorway in the nearest building. Lon was only vaguely aware of the man with a rifle standing at the side of the door.

Inside, Dendrow guided him to the side, to cover, and almost forced him to sit against the wall. "Give me a better chance to look at those cuts," he said.

Lon set his rifle at his side, then pulled up the sleeves of his tunic. The backs of his hands and forearms showed more than a dozen tiny cuts, but the bleeding had stopped from most of them. Only now did they start to hurt.

"I'll be okay," Lon said, pulling his arms back when Dendrow made a move to take one arm to examine the cuts more closely.

"There might be bits of metal in some of them, Lieutenant," Dendrow said. "That can cause trouble later."

"Nothing we can do about it now, Ivar," Lon said. "If they're close to the surface, they'll work out on their own. And even if they're deeper, we don't have a surgeon or trauma tube here."

"I can get one of the medics to probe them," Dendrow said. "A little local anesthetic and you won't even feel it."

"Aren't the medics busy enough?" Lon asked softly. He had the faceplate of his helmet up, as did Dendrow.

Dendrow hesitated before he nodded. "They're busy."

"All I've got is a few scratches. If my body's health maintenance bugs can't handle them, I'll make a warranty claim when we get home. Make sure that last squad gets across safely. Then I'll want you and Weil to help me figure out what we're going to do next."

Dendrow moved toward the doorway, looking after his platoon, talking to all of his squad leaders. Lon gently rubbed the palm of each hand over the back of the other hand and forearm, feeling for any metal that might be lodged in the cuts. The probing was moderately painful. When he did come upon a piece of buried shrapnel, even a gentle touch hurt. Then he flexed his hands and arms several times. *I can still function,* he decided. That was reassuring, since there was no viable alternative. He still had tinnitus, but that had faded to a dull background buzz. He could hear several conversations over the radio, and he was able to focus on them.

He gave himself a minute to rest before he started to get to his feet, using his rifle as a prop to help him up. He leaned against the wall, bracing himself against a slight dizziness that came with motion. *Probably a touch of concussion,* he thought. That was no surprise. That grenade blast had been far too close for comfort. *Maybe I'm lucky my head is still on my shoulders.*

He took a deep breath. It was time he put his mind back to the problem of keeping his men alive and out of enemy hands. *The cat knows the mice are here now,* he thought. Even if they escaped this batch of the enemy, there would likely be other Belletiener units looking for them. And it would still be two hours or more before Colonel Gaffney and the rest of the regiment would arrive in Oceanview to give the invaders something more pressing to worry about.

Sergeant Dendrow saw that Lon was up and came back to him, lifting his visor so that they could talk without their radios.

"You think they had a chance to get a good estimate of our numbers?" Lon asked.

Dendrow shook his head slowly. "Hard to tell. They've got to know we're more than just a few scouts. They have to figure at least one platoon, and—the way these things go—they're as likely to guess they came up against a full company. That's how it works in a fight. If you can't get an accurate count, your estimate is apt to be way heavy."

"Which means they might turn a lot more soldiers toward looking for us than they'd need to put us down," Lon said. "We're going to have to move and keep moving, as long as we can. Try to stay two steps ahead of them."

The sergeant nodded. That was what he had planned on recommending, if Lon had asked . . . or suggested staying put. "Be a nasty game of hide and seek if it has to go on too long," he said. "But I can't see any better way, 'less they can free up a few fighters to give us one hell of a lot of close cover. And even that would be . . . uncomfortable."

Lon smiled. "It would," he agreed. "Hang on. Let's get Weil in on this." He pulled down his faceplate, and the conversation moved to the radio, on the channel that the three of them shared. Lon told Jorgen what he and Dendrow had been talking about, and the other platoon sergeant quickly agreed that it was the best they could do.

"We'd best be moving soon, Lieutenant," he added. "The enemy looks to have taken over some of our holes over in the park, and they've got to be moving more men around."

"Let's get going," Lon said. "One platoon leapfrogging the other. It may be out of the frying pan and into the fire, since we're going straight north, toward the rest of the fighting."

The plan was rough, but easily put into motion. Lon and his platoon sergeants continued to discuss it after the move started. They would stay, as much as possible, indoors, using each building in turn as a momentary refuge. A few men—less than a full squad—would cover each flank. Once they put a little more distance between them and the Belletiener unit they had been fighting, they could look at alternatives.

"How far you reckon we are from the main lines?" Jorgen asked.

"Not far enough," Lon replied. "Maybe less than three quarters of a mile. It could be just about anywhere now, though. I don't know how that fighting has progressed since we've been down here."

Third platoon was the last to move, keeping the enemy engaged while fourth moved north, through an alley into the next series of buildings. Once fourth was in position, third platoon could move past and find positions to cover the next stage.

"Too bad we don't have any mines or booby traps to leave behind," Dendrow said while third platoon was moving, pulling back through the building they were in to exits on the north side of it. "Something to slow the enemy down a little more."

"Put it on your list for Santa Claus," Lon suggested. "And tell the men to be careful of their ammo. We're going to be getting damn short if this goes on much longer." *Is it always going to be like this, worrying about running out of ammunition?* Lon wondered. He did not question the "standard load" that Corps operating procedures mandated. There was only so much weight that a soldier could carry and still be able to function. But the resupply problem could be acute, as it was now. There was simply no chance of getting a supply drop for two platoons behind enemy lines—not with that enemy too close to allow a shuttle a reasonable chance of getting in and out safely.

"I've been at the men from the start," Dendrow said. "And I'll keep at them," he added before Lon could suggest the same course. "I don't want to get to the point where all we've got is our bayonets. I'm too old for that sort of row."

Lon just grunted. Age had not diminished Ivar Dendrow's abilities to the point where it was noticeable. He was as good as most of his men in every variety of close-in fighting.

It was not until the second time that third platoon moved past fourth that the Belleticness behind them completely stopped firing. That was, technically, disengagement. They were out of direct contact with the enemy. But Lon did not consider halting the rapid pace of withdrawal. *We'll flip-flop twice more,* he decided, *then stop for a few seconds to figure out which way we're going next.*

He did not consider the movement a retreat. They were not blindly running from danger, but making a tactical move that would preserve the unit to fight when conditions were more favorable—in a few hours when the Dirigenters and the Calypsans they were supporting would have all of their forces in position.

"We're going to have to stop and fight sometime," he muttered under his breath, while he and third platoon were waiting for fourth to move past them. "All we're doing is trying to pick the time and place."

"You say something, Lieutenant?" Dendrow asked.

"Just talking to myself," Lon said. "I forgot I had an open line." *That was careless,* he chided himself. "I'm going to check my mapboard, get an update on known enemy positions. Those who are using electronics openly. It's time to start worrying what we're moving toward, not just what we're moving from."

The two men were forty feet apart. Their conversation had been over the radio. It would not do to have both of them wiped out by a single grenade or the same burst of gunfire. It was almost time to resume electronic silence, but Lon thought that he could risk a few minutes more. The enemy would have trouble figuring out where they were this soon.

Lon pulled the mapboard from the pocket designed for it on the right leg of his trousers and unfolded the instrument. He entered his password and keyed the "Update" button, then started narrowing the focus on the display screen until he was at maximum resolution—looking at an area that was five hundred yards in diameter, centered on his own location.

There were far more red blips, indicating enemy troops, than there had been the last time he had checked the display. Obviously, many of the Belletieners who had been keeping electronic silence before were no longer bothering. And it was not just enemy troops who were in contact with the Calypsan and Dirigenter defenders of Oceanview.

"Ivar. Weil. It looks as if our best bet is to head east. We'll be able to move faster staying out in the streets, at least for a while. If we have to, we can deke south again, go silent and try to throw any pursuit off the scent. But I hope we can avoid that, maybe find a place to lie doggo instead. I want to keep close enough to get into the main event when it starts.''

"Fine by me, Lieutenant," Weil said. "I'd rather sit than walk any day."

"Is there any place that looks good for that?" Ivar asked.

"I guess we'll know when we see it, Ivar," Lon said. "We're going to be getting close to the beach before long. There are fewer buildings this side of the city, and fewer trees."

"Be nice to find a place where we can see the enemy coming a long way off," Dendrow suggested.

"As long as they can't see us just as far off," Lon said. "That's getting too far afield. When we make the turn, I want to leave one squad behind for a few minutes to spring a surprise on the Belletieners, if they're still following. They might expect us to dig in and make another stand, so any opposition ought to make them stop and scratch their heads for a minute or two, give us that much more time to get clear and disappear."

"You got a particular squad in mind?" Dendrow got the question out before Jorgen could.

"Wil Nace's," Lon said. "I know that's the kind of thing he's good at."

"Right," Jorgen said. "Any specific instructions? Like, how long they should wait and what they're to do after they get the attention of the enemy?"

"Let's get Wil in on this and we'll work it out together," Lon said.

15

Three grenades burst almost simultaneously in the street. Lon's two platoons, minus the one squad that had not returned from its job of slowing down the pursuing Belletiener soldiers, had only a second to dive for cover when they heard the rocket-propelled explosive coming. The Dirigenters had been hiking along both sides of the avenue, close to the buildings as usual.

Lon had no time to ask questions even after the explosions, because rifle fire started immediately. There was no need for the "Where did those come from?" that had been ready to come out of his mouth.

"We need better cover," he told his platoon sergeants as soon as he could spare a few seconds. "Get out of the street. Fire and maneuver."

The platoons were already returning the enemy's fire, without great volume, but with some effectiveness. No one panicked. It was in moments such as this that training and experience were most valuable. On each side of the street, the squads worked together, one at a time moving out of the line of enemy fire, crawling to alleys or entranceways, taking wounded men with them. Lon was heartened to see that there were no dead.

"I don't think there are too many of them, Lieutenant," Ivar Dendrow said after half of the Dirigenters had escaped the most vulnerable areas. "Maybe no more than we've got."

"That's my take, too," Lon replied. It was dark enough for muzzle flashes to be easily visible. "All in one place, up in that next block. But we can't let them tie us down

155

long enough for them to get reinforcements. As soon as we get everyone out of this shooting gallery, we move around on both sides, force them out.'' *Or drop them where they are,* he thought. He switched channels on his radio. ''Weil, contact Nace and tell him what's going on, and that he's still got to slow that other batch down.''

''Yes, sir,'' Jorgen replied. ''I heard from him just before this ruckus started. He said they were about to tangle with the birds who were behind us.''

''Too much noise here to hear that,'' Lon said, more to himself than the platoon sergeant. Jorgen chuckled. There was no need to reply.

Lon and the squad nearest him—third platoon's second squad—were the last to pull out of the danger zone on the south side of the avenue. They had plenty of covering fire when their turn came. The platoon sergeants had done an effective job of deploying the rest of their men.

''Any serious casualties?'' Lon asked his sergeants once everyone was out of the street.

''No one who can't keep up and pitch in,'' Dendrow said. ''Not in third platoon, at least.''

''We're fine, too,'' Jorgen said. ''I've got three men with metal in them, but nothing that can't wait for a bit.''

''Keep track of them,'' Lon said. ''Now, let's get busy and return the favor to those men up there.'' *Those men*— the enemy.

''I've got two squads in position,'' Jorgen said. He was on the other side of the street. ''It looks like the Belletieners are getting ready to pull out. You want we should change their minds?''

''Drop a few grenades in if you can, Weil. Make sure they know what it feels like.''

''I've got one squad up there too, Lieutenant,'' Dendrow said. ''Let them join in?''

''Yes.'' Lon was already on the move with the rest of third platoon. He had Weil leave one squad where it was, in case the enemy tried to move west while the Dirigenters were moving east around them. He heard grenades exploding, and knew that—this time—his men were on the giving end. On the run, Lon called Captain Orlis, to let him know what was happening.

Orlis didn't give him time to say much, though. "Later," the captain said, very curtly, before he cut the connection.

I wonder what they're up against? Lon wondered. There was no time to ponder the question, though.

As they worked their way into position, the rest of his squads joined the fray. The Belletieners appeared to all be inside two buildings, one on either side of the avenue where they had staged their ambush. The first of Lon's squads had moved into position before the enemy could escape. They were trapped, unable to come out without facing Dirigenter gunfire.

"They can't do much damage now, Lieutenant," Weil Jorgen said. "But we can't just sit here and keep the cork in the bottle, and going in after them would be a bitch."

Lon hesitated. Going in to clear the two buildings of enemy soldiers might be costly, in men. But leaving them behind might be just as costly in the long run. Before he could come to a decision, there was a call from Wil Nace.

"Lieutenant, we're gonna be comin' up on you fast," Nace said. "Those bastards didn't take kindly to our ambush, and they didn't waste much time. We've got a company or more coming after us, and not much chance now to slow them up any more." Nace sounded completely out of breath. Lon guessed that he was talking while he ran.

"Can you flush them by moving to one side or the other?" Lon asked. There was a noticeable pause before Nace replied.

"I don't think so. They've got people out on both sides, almost got the horns around us."

"Okay, Wil. Keep coming the way you are. I've got you on my mapboard." He had taken that out and opened it up during Nace's report. "We'll hit them while they're chasing you. Come on through like you know there's no help for a mile. Got that?"

"Yes, sir."

"It might not work. If they're in contact with the batch we're involved with, it could all backfire, but I think it's worth a try. They might even figure to bag all of us at once.''

''It's better than anything I can think of.''

Lon had to work quickly, and get his men moving at once. He left two squads to try to contain the enemy soldiers in the two buildings, then took the rest back to set up an ambush for the Belletieners chasing Nace's squad. That required separating third and fourth platoons again, those squads that were left, to get in front of both of the Belletiener ''horns'' that were attempting to encircle Nace's squad.

I may be splitting my command into too many pieces, Lon thought. But he did not consider reversing his decisions. He shook his head, minimally, an unconscious gesture. *I'll just have to deal with whatever comes up. One way or another.*

There was no time for anything fancy. Lon stayed with the three squads of third platoon, moving to the right. Jorgen only had two squads of fourth platoon with him, but they would set up on the left. All anyone could do was get into the best position available in a hurry, and try to stay out of sight until the enemy was close enough to get hurt.

Lon settled into a good firing position. Unless the Belletieners changed course, they would come into view eighty yards from where most of third platoon was waiting. Soon. Nace and his squad went across the intersection a block over from where third platoon was set up to cover, and kept going as they had been instructed.

''Keep going, Wil,'' Lon said on a channel that connected him just with Nace. ''You're past our positions.'' Then he switched channels to talk to all of the squad leaders at once. ''Get ready. They'll be here any second. I want to let them get all the way out in the open before we start shooting.''

Make every bullet count, he thought, once more conscious of how short some of his men were on ammunition.

The Belletiener force came into view—a ten-man skirmish line in front, followed by two columns, one on either side of the street. They were moving almost at a jog, caught up in the pursuit—*too* caught up. Lon did not see any of them look to either side for possible trouble. By the time the skirmish line got within fifteen yards of the far side of the intersection, there were sixty men visible, with no sign that the end of the unit was near. But Lon did not want to give the vanguard a chance to make it to safety.

"Open fire," he ordered on a channel that connected him to the three squads of third platoon.

Lon had been tracking the near side of the enemy skirmish line. The order to fire was no more than out of his mouth before he squeezed the trigger of his rifle, moving it along the line of Belletiener troops, following them to the ground as they dove for cover. Lon was intentionally less frugal with his ammunition than he expected his men to be. He was far from being short. And the more of the enemy he could bring down personally, the less ammunition his men would need to use.

Grenades went off over to the right, down the street that the enemy had come along.

"Not too many more back that way, Lieutenant," Sergeant Dendrow reported. "We had nearly all of them out in the open before we showed our hand." That was extremely good news.

"It's not all of them, though, Ivar, remember that," Lon said while he ejected the empty magazine from his rifle and inserted a full replacement. "There's the batch Weil is hitting on the far side and however many there are behind Nace in the middle."

Jorgen's men had started shooting within seconds after third platoon started the firefight. He had reported that there were only sixty of the enemy facing them—slightly more than twice the number of men he had with him.

Lon switched channels to talk to Nace. "Cut right and go over a block. Get back and help the rest of fourth platoon." That would make the odds there slightly more equitable. Nace acknowledged the order with a single, almost breathless, word.

Closer in, the enemy was able to mount only sporadic return fire. This ambush had been, Lon told himself, almost spectacularly successful. "Ivar, let's move in closer to finish this batch off before we have to worry about the ones in the middle coming over to interfere." One squad moved while the other two provided covering fire. Lon gave the order to fix bayonets, in case the fighting came to that.

It did not. One by one, the surviving Belletiener soldiers in the intersection started to lay down their rifles and raise their arms in surrender. A couple called out for mercy, for an end to the fighting. *My God,* Lon thought, suddenly dismayed. *What the hell are we going to do with prisoners?*

He got to his feet and moved forward with Tebba Girana's squad. After transferring his rifle to his left hand, Lon pulled his pistol from its holster and held that pointed in the general direction of the surrendering enemy soldiers.

"Ivar, we'll collect their rifles and any ammunition they've got," Lon said. "That will give us some fallback if we run out of ammo for our own weapons. And disable their electronics."

"Right, Lieutenant," Dendrow said with what might have been relief at the fact that Lon had thought of that. "What are we going to do with our, ah, prisoners?"

We can't just shoot them, Lon thought, not quite with regret. It would have been the quickest, most expedient, solution, but it would have been an unacceptable precedent to set. Dirigenters did not fight that way, ever.

"Think we can scare up enough sleep-patches to put them out of business for a few hours?" Lon asked.

Ivar could not stop the one quick bark of laughter that welled up in him. "I imagine we can, Lieutenant," he said. "Always a few of 'em around."

"Give the wounded first aid, if we can without exposing ourselves too badly," Lon added. "But we've got more of the enemy to worry about in the next few minutes."

"I'll leave two men with medical kits once we know the rest of these are no threat. That'll free up the rest of us."

"Let's get busy. Weil could use some help, and there's still the third batch of them, the ones who were right behind Nace until this started."

"Probably only a couple of squads there, sir," Dendrow said. "Just enough to keep our boys from stopping in the middle. By now, they've probably gone over to join the fight with fourth platoon. Or turned tail, since they haven't shown up here yet."

"We still need to watch out for them until we know."

"Yes, sir." Dendrow's tone said, *I don't need to be told that.*

Making sure of the men who had been caught by third platoon's ambush took only another three minutes. Weapons and ammunition were gathered up and distributed among the Dirigenters. The Belletieners' helmets were taken from them and the electronics disabled so that they could not call for help or give any information on Lon and his men. The most badly wounded of the enemy were given quick first aid, enough to make certain that they would not bleed to death . . . as long as help got to them within a reasonable time. The enemy soldiers who had surrendered and were still capable of being an active threat were immobilized with sleep-patches. Those worked almost instantly, and once the men were asleep, it would be safe to leave them and not have to worry about them rejoining the fight.

Lon sent Dendrow and two squads to help fourth platoon finish up their firefight. He kept Girana's squad with him for a couple of minutes longer, to make certain of the enemy left from this fight.

"Okay, Tebba. Time for us to move," Lon said, turning to survey the area. He was taking a big risk, standing up in the middle of the intersection, but did not think about that. Any enemy would be unlikely to fire into the middle of this group right now, with some of their own as likely to be hit.

Third platoon had suffered no casualties in this firefight, not so much as a scratch. Lon offered a silent thanks for that, although he had never been particularly religious.

He glanced at the timeline on his visor display then. Unless something had gone wrong, the bulk of the regiment should be en route to Oceanview from the mining district, perhaps within ten or fifteen minutes of landing.

It can't possibly be soon enough, he thought as he started jogging along with Tebba and the rest of the squad. *Let's get this fight finished as soon as possible.*

16

The other fight ended as Lon arrived on the scene. The last half dozen Belletieners facing fourth platoon surrendered. Lon gave the same orders as before—take their weapons and ammunition, destroy their electronics, treat the wounded, and stick sleep-patches on the necks of the healthy.

"They have any last-minute help show up?" Lon asked Weil Jorgen. "We're trying to account for the troops who were in the middle, chasing Nace's squad."

"I can't say for sure, Lieutenant," Jorgen said. "We were too busy. I didn't *notice* anyone joining in, but that don't mean much, not under the circumstances."

Lon took a deep breath and let it out, scanning. This time he was not in the middle of an intersection, but near a corner, with a solid wall behind him. "We've got to get back to where we were," he said then, talking to both platoon sergeants. "See if we can finish off the men in those two buildings before more of the enemy shows up."

"Leastwise, we got a bit more ammo now," Jorgen said. Some of Lon's men were now carrying two captured weapons in addition to their own, so that the men who had been left to keep the Belletieners in those buildings penned up would have replacements, and they were toting all of the ammunition they had found. No one was complaining about the load.

Lon nodded, even though Jorgen was not close enough to notice. "There weren't many RPGs, though, were there?" he asked.

"We got three launchers, but only four grenades here,"

Jorgen said. "I don't know what the other platoon found."

"Not even that much, Weil. They had plenty of ammo for their rifles, more than we did, but we took one launcher and two grenades for it."

"Since we showed up, they haven't had any resupply from space," Jorgen commented. "I figured there wasn't much point in keeping more than one of the launchers."

"The rifles we're not taking with us, let's make sure the enemy can't use them again." *I wish I had thought of that before we left the other rifles,* Lon thought, shaking his head.

Jorgen chuckled. "We're already seeing to that, Lieutenant. They'll need to bring in spare parts before they can put them back together."

"Good. Let's get moving." Lon switched channels to include Dendrow in the conversation. "I want scouts out on all sides to give us warning of trouble," Lon told them. "Let's hurry it up. We've got to get back to the other squads."

It took a while for Lon to realize the change that had come over him. It had started sometime earlier. He was not certain when; it might have been when he and his men had opened fire on the Belletieners who had been chasing Nace's squad. Lon felt himself caught up in what was happening, almost exhilarated—both by the combat and by running toward the remaining firefight, the one that had been put on hold earlier. There was no room in him for fear now, and the concerns of command seemed less burdensome. He did not worry over every possibility, but gave the orders, made the decisions.

Maybe I'm fey, he thought, and a stark grin forced its way onto his face. As a child on Earth, he had read Norse sagas about warriors who experienced such unnatural buoyancy going into what—as often as not—would be their final battle. They were heroes cutting wide swaths through their enemies, demonstrating superhuman strength and endurance, caring nothing for their own safety. It had been a powerful image for an immature mind.

No, I'm not fey, Lon decided, exhaling softly. *I'm still in command of my mind, my actions. I haven't lost control.* That was important. He could not, would not, fail his men. They were not figures in a mythical saga to sacrifice. The feeling was almost like a runner's high, and they *were* running, racing to get back to the two squads that had been left to keep the other batch of Belletiener troops bottled up. Lon had to restrain himself to keep from trying to literally make it a race. It would do no good to get to their destination with the men too winded to do anything, or—worse yet—to have them scattered over several blocks because some could not keep up.

A couple of times Lon even stopped for a moment, waving the others on, turning to scan cross streets and into alleys. The unit crossed intersections with caution, two squads moving while the rest took up positions to provide covering fire if that became necessary. Lon would not send his men blindly across the way the Belletiener officer had, into the possibility of a disastrous ambush.

Time had little meaning for Lon. He felt more aware than usual of everything going on around him, but the elapsing of seconds and minutes seemed not to count. There was *now*, and *here*. He no longer thought about how long it might be until the rest of the regiment arrived in Oceanview, or how long it might be before his platoons could be reunited with the rest of the company. He did think about how to deploy his men when they got to those two buildings. During one brief respite, while the platoons were crossing an intersection, he laid out his plans for the platoon sergeants.

"Either of you see any problems with that?" he asked then.

"It should work," Ivar Dendrow said. "But do we need to bother with them at all now, Lieutenant? I mean, another half hour and we should have the whole regiment in the area. We can worry about getting through again, or do whatever else we might be told to do. Do we really need to risk our people to shut down a few more of the enemy?"

Lon hesitated. It was a question he really had not been

considering. He knew the *what* and *how*, but had not worried about the *why*. "Maybe it won't make any difference to the contract," he said slowly, "but the way I figure it, the more confusion and trouble we can cause back here, the less they'll be able to concentrate on the rest of our people. As long as we can do the job smart. Weil, what do you think?"

"I go along with your thinking, Lieutenant," Jorgen said after a silence that was almost long enough to make the other two wonder whether or not he was on-line with them. "Especially now. The more we can put an itch up their backsides, the easier the rest will have coming in and setting up to finish this off."

"I withdraw my question," Dendrow said. "I see your point. I just hope Belletiene gives us time to finish this. If they've still got reinforcements moving in from the south, we could find ourselves in the middle of something I see in my nightmares."

"Colonel Gaffney and the other battalions should be landing within minutes," Lon said. "We get started, Belletiene should have plenty to think about besides us."

It was not necessary to put a line of men completely around the buildings. Squads were positioned where they could cover doors and windows. Snipers were posted to keep the Belletieners from going back and forth between the two buildings. The avenue between them was wide—a perfect killing zone for expert marksmen. At the moment, the Belletiener troops were quiet, doing no shooting, and not showing themselves. The Dirigenters outside held back as well. As long as the enemy did not present a worthwhile target, no one was going to waste ammunition.

"We'll take this building first," Lon told Dendrow, who was next to him in a building just across the street from the target. "Put two squads in through the doors we can see. I want everyone on this side covering them. RPGs in the windows and doors. We get close, a regular drill—hand grenades through each doorway before anyone sticks a neck out. We secure this building, we'll have the other one in a real hurt. Maybe enough that they'll surrender rather than have us take them the hard way.''

''Should we ask the first batch to surrender before we go in?'' Dendrow asked. ''They've been cooped up quite a bit already, with no one come to rescue them.''

''Go ahead. Tell them they've got one chance to come out whole, and don't give them a lot of time.''

Lon listened while Dendrow delivered the ultimatum. He used his helmet radio as a bullhorn—helmets used by DMC officers and noncoms had that capability. Dendrow spoke slowly to make certain that he would be understood. The dialects spoken on Dirigent and Belletiene were different enough to make that caution advisable. Dendrow kept his message simple, with no additions beyond what Lon had told him.

When Ivar finished, both he and Lon looked at the time-lines on their visor displays. Ivar had given the Belletieners one minute to lay down their weapons and start filing out of the building with their hands above their heads.

We don't have enough sleep-patches to put many more of them down, Lon thought. He was startled by the way that idea popped into his head. *We're not set up to watch prisoners, but I'd rather see them surrender and avoid a bloody fight.* Several seconds passed while he assured himself that there were no sinister motives behind the thought. *We don't kill prisoners, ever. It's not right, even without the penalties the Corps has for that.* Under the military discipline of the DMC, murdering prisoners was no different from any other kind of murder. The punishment was ''Death or such lesser sentence as the court-martial convening authority shall deem appropriate.''

The minute expired. No Belletieners emerged from the buildings. There were no messages from them, no reply to the ultimatum. Nolan and Dendrow looked at each other, each seeing only the blank mask of the other's faceplate.

''Get the men in position, Ivar,'' Lon said. ''Move as soon as you're ready. Coordinate with Weil. You call the shots.''

Dendrow nodded once, then started giving orders to his

squad leaders. There was nothing unusual about delegating that authority to a platoon sergeant in the DMC. Lon stayed near the window, looking out from the edge, staring across the street, watching in case—even now—the enemy soldiers decided to give up without pushing the fight to a climax. He had thoughts of going along with one of the squads. But a minute of waiting gave him a chance to calm down enough to stay where he was—where he belonged. He had two platoons to command. Risking himself in the sort of costly fighting that might ensue when third platoon stormed the first building would be inappropriate, a cause for censure, not acclaim. *No grandstanding,* he thought. *You don't have to prove anything to anyone.*

He considered calling Captain Orlis but thought, *Captain's got anything I need to know, he'll call. He might still be too busy for interruptions.*

Two squads from Dendrow's platoon, first and second, moved toward their jumping-off positions. The rest of the men in both platoons got ready to start firing. The preparations did not take long. Lon monitored the radio channels that Dendrow used, listening to the terse conversations between the platoon sergeants, the orders given to the various squads. As well as he could from his restricted viewpoint, Lon also watched as his men got ready. When the shooting started, Lon would take part in that, but from where he was, he would help by providing suppression fire and cover for the men who had to cross the street and enter the first of the two enemy-held buildings.

His earlier euphoria had faded. His concentration was more conscious, reasoned now. He focused on his breathing, working to make certain that he was as steady as possible when the shooting started. In control. He made several quick calls to squad leaders around the perimeter, to remind them to watch for possible enemy reinforcements coming up behind them. *If I can get caught up in one thing and forget other possibilities, then others can,* he told himself. And getting caught from behind unaware could be deadly. The situation could reverse itself with the suddenness of a snake's strike.

"We're ready to go, Lieutenant," Dendrow said.

Lon blinked once before he said, "Go."

He settled into a firing position. He had spoken only to Dendrow. The platoon sergeant would give the order to the squads. Lon waited until he heard it, then brought his rifle up, aimed at an open window, and triggered his first three-shot burst, aiming carefully at the edge of the window opening. Spraying the middle of the gap would be a waste of ammunition. If there was an enemy shooter there, he would be at one side or the other. No return fire came from that window. Lon scanned the openings opposite him, looking for muzzle flashes.

The top floor, the third. He shifted his aim and waited for the next muzzle flash there, then squeezed his trigger. A rifle fell out of the window and bounced off the sill, away from the wall. *One down,* Lon thought. He looked for another target.

Once the two squads of Dirigenters entered the building, none of its defenders bothered shooting *out*. They had to deal with the intruders or face the choice of surrender or death. Grenades exploded as Lon's men moved from room to room, clearing each before they moved on to the next. None of the Belletieners in that building surrendered. The fighting lasted twenty minutes. Then Sergeant Dendrow reported the results. "There are maybe ten wounded Belletieners, twice that number dead. No one gave up who was conscious and able to resist."

"What did it cost us?" Lon asked.

"Two dead, four hurt—two of them pretty badly." Dendrow gave Lon the names. Lon felt his stomach knot up. One of the dead was Balt Hoper, from Girana's squad. That was bad enough. But Carl Hoper, Alpha Company's other lieutenant, was Balt's cousin. "The squad leaders have the personal effects of the dead," Dendrow added softly.

"I'll tell Carl as soon as I can," Lon said. It was not unusual for a family to have a number of members in the Corps, even in the same company. *Close* relations, brothers or fathers and sons, were generally not assigned to the same battalion, and certainly not to the same company. Carl and Balt had not been that closely related. But they had been close.

"What about the other building, Lieutenant?" Dendrow asked. "We still go in after that lot?"

"Make them the same offer. They'll know what happened to their comrades. Maybe it'll make a difference." Lon glanced at the timeline on his helmet display. "Let's wait a few minutes. There's no rush. The rest of the regiment should be on the ground or coming in, so there's not likely to be any help for these Belletieners. If they've got radio contact with their superiors, they'll know that soon enough, I expect." Lon had lost his enthusiasm for rooting out another small band of the enemy. Waiting five minutes might make it unnecessary. He hoped so. But unless the situation changed, he *would* give the order.

"Wait a few minutes, then give this next bunch the same ultimatum we gave the others," Dendrow said, repeating to make sure he had the orders correct.

"That's right. I'll tell you when, Ivar. If we do have to go in again, rotate squads so that the same ones don't have the dirty work. In the meantime, I want you and Weil to put out a few three-man patrols to range out and make sure no one sneaks up." Lon switched channels and gave the same orders to the other platoon sergeant.

Then there was silence. As the assault on the one building had ended, the Belletieners in the other had done some shooting, much of it aimless, as if to vent frustration, but even that had stopped. There were more distant sounds of warfare, muted, too far off to be a threat to Lon's platoons, a subtle background to his thoughts.

Why doesn't the captain call? Lon asked himself. If the other battalions had moved on schedule, they should have arrived by this time. If they were not already engaging the enemy, they should be close to them. Lon did not consider that some disaster had struck. *That* he would have heard about quickly, as long as someone in Alpha Company or battalion headquarters survived. It took self-discipline to avoid calling Captain Orlis, but he would only do that if he faced a serious threat to his platoons, or if the local situation changed drastically. "Later," the captain had told him. Orlis would call.

Then Lon squeezed his eyes tightly shut for an instant. *How dumb can I be?* he wondered. There was one place he *could* call—CIC. The combat information center would be staffed, and following everything that was happening. *I should have called them long ago,* Lon thought. He made the call, and explained why he was not going to his own immediate superior.

"Right, you're the two detached platoons," the voice of a lieutenant in CIC said. "We've been tracking you."

"Look, we've been out of touch for quite a while. Captain Orlis indicated that he was too busy for anything and hasn't called back." Lon went on to describe, in as few words as possible, his situation. "Before I order my men into this other building, I want whatever information I can get."

"You're at least one point six miles from the nearest friendly forces," the CIC lieutenant said. "We don't have any traces on Belletiener forces, other than those you know about, within a mile of you, but I'll give you the standard caution. That doesn't mean they're not there. The other battalions have debarked safely and are moving into position. Colonel Gaffney is preparing a three-pronged attack, coming in from the south and the west while Second Battalion and the Calypsan army press in from the north against the opposition they've been facing. Regimental staff know your location but have said nothing about what you should or shouldn't do."

"How long before our people can get to us?" Lon asked. "It doesn't appear that there are many of the enemy south of us. Not that we've seen, anyway. And this little scuffle here has been going on long enough that they could have moved people in from anywhere if they planned on doing it."

There was a slight pause before the CIC man answered. "If they meet no opposition, elements of Third Battalion could reach your position in . . . thirty to forty minutes. Does that help?''

"It does. Thanks. Unless my situation here changes or I receive different orders, we'll just keep these birds caged. We're getting low on munitions, particularly grenades.''

"Okay, Lieutenant, I'll make a note here. Good luck.''

Lon connected to his platoon sergeants and told them that they would hold off on any attempt to clear the other building, then gave them the news from CIC. "We keep them bottled up, watch for trouble, and hope that our people get here first.''

Neither sergeant tried to change Lon's mind.

17

Captain Orlis called less than five minutes after Lon finished his conversation with CIC. "We've got a bit of a break here, for a few minutes," Orlis said. "Bring me up to date."

If there was one thing a young officer learned quickly in the DMC, it was how to make short, to-the-point reports. Lon gave his commander the essentials, in order, including the numbers of casualties. "One of the dead was Balt Hoper," he added after he had given the captain the more pertinent data.

There was a pause before Orlis asked, "How did it happen?"

Lon told him, just as Tebba Girana had reported it.

"I'll tell Carl," Orlis said.

"Yes, sir. I was going to tell him myself, but I wanted to wait until I could do it in person, if possible."

"He's here now, not twenty feet from me. I'll give him the bad news. That's better than letting it wait."

"Of course," Lon agreed. "I'll talk to him myself when I get a chance."

"Balt was a good man," Orlis said, almost absently.

They all are, Lon thought. *Every one of them.*

Lon was in contact with Major Osiah Kai, 3rd Battalion's executive officer, by radio ten minutes before that battalion's leading element reached him. Lon told the major what the situation was, and Kai told him that they would detail a company to help. "It shouldn't take long," Kai said. "Colonel McGregor suggests you pull your lot together

173

when we get there.'' Lieutenant Colonel Ian McGregor commanded 3rd Battalion. ''You can tag along after us for the time being, take your bit of rest—what you can get on the march.''

''We can use it, sir,'' Lon said. He knew Major Kai slightly. Kai was one of only nine senior officers—majors and above—currently in the Corps who had not been born on Dirigent. His accent was as thickly British as any Lon had ever heard on Earth.

Lon's men were waiting for the scouts from 3rd Battalion, and the corporal leading that squad was brought to Lon.

''Good to see you, Corporal,'' Lon said. ''You know what we've got here?''

''Yes, sir. My lieutenant told us. Our Delta Company will be along in a few minutes to take over.''

Delta Company's commanding officer was another McGregor, although not closely related to the battalion commander. This one was Captain George McGregor. He linked with Lon before his men arrived, to coordinate the relief.

''We're not sure how many of them are inside,'' Lon told the captain. ''Probably not more than twenty or thirty, and they've got to be getting short on ammunition. But I wouldn't want to make book on any of that.''

''No matter. We're geared to handle whatever they've got. I was told you had patrols out. Have you pulled them back in yet?''

''On your side, Captain. I didn't want to pull the rest in too soon.''

''Don't blame you a bit, Lieutenant. But our scouts are even with your position, left and right, and moving past, except right there where your, ah, situation is, so you can start pulling them in now, I should think.''

''I'll give the orders,'' Lon said. ''Then we can make the switchover and I'll leave my 'situation' to you, and welcome to it,'' he added, with what would have to pass for a chuckle.

• • •

Lon felt his thoughts dulling, even as he told his platoon sergeants to pull in the last of the scouts and get ready to hand over responsibility to Delta of the 3rd. At first he tried to fight against the reaction. It was too soon. There was still more fighting ahead, and anything might happen. But the effort was too much. Without some new threat to start the adrenaline pumping again, Lon could not resist. He could not even stifle a gaping yawn, so intense and prolonged that it made his jaw ache.

He sat with his back to the wall, knees pulled up so that he could support his arms with them and rest his head on his arms—off his feet for the first time in longer than he could remember. It was all he could manage to keep his eyes open most of the time. Thinking beyond the next few minutes was impossible. He would hand over responsibility for the Belletieners across the street to Captain McGregor. Then he would gather his men and fall in behind 3rd Battalion as it moved north toward the larger fight. After that . . .

"Lieutenant?"

Although the word came in through Lon's radio, he lifted his head and looked up, not even wondering how he had sensed that Sergeant Dendrow was standing right in front of him.

"What is it, Ivar?" Lon asked, lifting his faceplate.

"D-Three has arrived and is moving into position. We're pulling our people back as their relief shows up."

Lon nodded, then got to his feet slowly. "Good," he said. "Where are you sending our people?"

"Just back of this building, Lieutenant. Me and Weil both."

"Okay, let's go out and see what's happening."

Dendrow had to notice how slowly Lon was moving, as if he were a hundred years old, but he said nothing about it. The platoon sergeant was feeling the same sort of reaction; he just had not had a chance yet to let it take over.

Outside, about half of Lon's men had already assembled. As they arrived, they all sat against a wall, or lay on the ground, exerting no more energy than needed. Few bothered to look up when their lieutenant and a platoon sergeant showed up. Lon felt relief that his men were as spent as he was, but at the same time he was concerned.

"I wish I could tell you that it's time to find a cave and sleep for eight hours," Lon said, switching to a channel that connected him to all of his people, "but I can't. We're going to be tagging along behind 3rd Battalion until we get back to our people. All we've got right now is however long it takes them to secure that building. It might only be ten minutes, so make it count." The rest of the battalion was pausing in its advance, waiting for Delta Company to take care of the enemy holdouts. The battalion commander did not want to leave a gap in the center.

Captain McGregor arrived with one squad. Lon talked with the captain face to face, but that left him feeling almost depressed. McGregor and his men seemed far too rested, too . . . active. *Almost indecent,* Lon thought. It seemed clear that the newcomers had managed some sleep along the way, more than they might have gotten during the brief shuttle ride east.

After McGregor went to conduct his assault, Lon sat back down. He leaned back against the building and closed his eyes, unaware of the muted sigh of relief that escaped his lips. *Ten minutes—it won't be more.* Lon was quickly near sleep, and even the sudden eruption of grenade explosions and rifle fire could not completely reverse the slide. He had not asked the captain how he planned to make his attack, nor had he offered suggestions.

Lon remained conscious of the sounds of the firefight, but his breathing became shallow and regular. He stalled in the trancelike state that precedes slumber, unable to go farther, unwilling to come back out before he had to. It could not be as restful as real sleep—preferably in a soft bed far from any combat—but even ten minutes of this would make it easier to get back up and go on when the time arrived.

A chance to sleep until my eyes won't stay shut any longer drifted through Lon's mind, almost unnoticed. Rapid bursts of automatic rifle fire, grenade explosions, peaks and lulls—all became background, almost a lullaby. It did not occur to Lon that men were dying in direct relation to those sounds.

"Lieutenant?"

Through the curtains of insulation thrown up by his torpid brain, Lon was vaguely aware of the voice, but it was not until the call had been repeated several times that it penetrated. Then it took a seeming eternity for Lon to climb out of dormancy.

"What is it?" Lon asked before he was aware who had spoken. His tongue felt swollen, too large for his mouth. And his eyes had not opened.

"They're ready to move on, sir." Lon finally recognized Ivar Dendrow's voice. At the same time, he became aware that the gunfire and explosions had stopped.

"It's over?" Lon asked as his eyelids finally rose.

"It's over," Dendrow confirmed. "Took a half dozen prisoners in one piece, maybe another half dozen wounded. I haven't heard a body count yet."

"What about McGregor's people?" Lon's mind was finally starting to function again, though slowly.

"One dead, five wounded, one bad enough to need a trauma tube in a hurry. Third Battalion medics are bringing one in."

Lon stretched and allowed himself a drawn-out yawn. "Time for us to get moving?" he asked. He thought about getting up, but tabled the idea for the moment. *Soon enough,* he thought.

"Pretty soon, I expect. McGregor's lead sergeant says we'll be moving out as soon as those medics get here with the trauma tube. I gather they've had orders to make sure we get back to the rest of our people. I suggested that we could stick around with the security detail for the medics, but no go."

"Our men?"

"Most of 'em still out, those who can. I had to let you know what was going on, though. Sorry," Dendrow added.

"Don't be. I'll live." It was time to get to his feet. Lon had to concentrate on that, as if he were just recovering from a wound, freshly out of a trauma tube himself. He knew what that was like. "I feel as if I'm a hundred and forty years old," he said, more to himself than Ivar.

"You're not the only one, Lieutenant."

Lon did more yawning, and stretching. He lifted the face-plate of his helmet, than took water from one of his canteens and splashed it on his face. That helped—minimally. "You get any rest yourself?" he asked.

"About thirty seconds, on my feet," Dendrow said with the start of a grin. He was too tired for the entire expression to make it to his face. "I've had a lot of practice. I let Weil take both our turns. After all, he's older than me."

Slowly, a smile worked its way onto Lon's face. "Yeah, by what, six months?"

"Who counts?"

Lon started moving around, even did a couple of knee bends, trying to pump his mind up to full speed and shake the sleepiness from his body.

"I'll wake Weil." *If he's really asleep,* Lon thought. Jorgen was as dedicated as Dendrow. "Then we'd better start rousting the men from their dreams of the Purple Harridan. I don't want sleepwalkers when we start moving."

It was another twenty minutes before Delta of the 3rd was ready to move. Lon had ordered his men to get in a quick meal while they were waiting. Besides the need for nourishment, eating would help get everyone's mind functioning. Lon ate a meal himself, and took a couple of minutes to talk with one of the lieutenants from Delta, to find out what news had come through in the last forty minutes. There wasn't much. First Battalion had started meeting enemy resistance. Fourth Battalion was still looking for the enemy, as was 3rd. Only 2nd Battalion, Lon's, remained heavily engaged, along with the Calypsan defenders, and they appeared to finally be having some effect on the Belletiener main force.

Delta left two squads with the wounded, the medics, and the prisoners, bolstering the security detail that had come forward with the medical orderlies. Lon's platoons moved in behind the bulk of Delta as it started north with the rest of 3rd Battalion.

"Just because we're only tagging along, don't start thinking that you don't have to keep your eyes and ears open," Ivar Dendrow told his platoon. "The Belletieners can't be expected to know we're not meant to be fighting just this minute."

Lon smiled as he switched channels and heard part of a similar spiel from Weil Jorgen to fourth platoon; Jorgen managed to slip in the word "supernumeraries." There was no back talk on either channel. Lon was willing to chalk that up to professional sound discipline, but conceded that it might simply mean that the men were too tired to even groan at something they could figure out for themselves.

This operation shouldn't take too much longer, Lon told himself as he walked along with third platoon's lead squad, three hundred yards behind the skirmish line of 3rd Battalion. *We've clearly got the numbers on the Belletieners now, and air cover to boot.* That consolation, deserved or not, made the job of walking a little easier to bear.

The pace was not difficult, and there were frequent stops—though rarely for more than two or three minutes. The skirmish line moved slowly, checking each building they passed, making careful sweeps of parks and other open areas. Lon's men had been able to discard the captured weapons they had taken, so they were not carrying as much weight as they had been. Third Battalion had brought along extra ammunition for the Dirigenters' rifles, along with grenades.

In the first hour, there were only a few scattered contacts with enemy patrols. Reports mentioned that the Belletieners appeared to be pulling into a more compact defensive perimeter, close to their northern line.

"It looks as if they're still trying to move toward the government center," Captain McGregor told Lon during one of several brief conversations. "Instead of pulling away from the heaviest fighting, they're moving toward it. I don't know if that's fanaticism, or if they're just more frightened of failure than they are of us."

Early in the second hour, signs of the major fighting to the north were clearly visible, and audible. Two DMC Shrikes made strafing runs from west to east, using only cannon, not rockets or bombs. Lon made the easy guess that the aircraft had been instructed to avoid damaging buildings if possible, to just go after men who were outside. Calypso would want to keep its capital as nearly intact as possible.

Twenty minutes after that, 3rd Battalion finally met stiff enemy resistance. They had reached the defensive zone around the Belletiener perimeter.

Lon made sure that his men were out of any likely line of fire, resting while they could. For the time being, this was not their fight. "If it looks like this will be over quickly, we'll let it slide," he told his platoon sergeants. "Give the men a little more time. But if it looks as if it's going to go on any length of time, I'll ask if there's anything we can do."

"Unless the Belletieners roll over in a hurry, you probably won't have to ask, Lieutenant," Ivar said. "Colonel McGregor will find something for us to do, and clear it with Captain Orlis or Colonel Flowers, probably before they say anything to you."

The three men were together, squatting next to the stone wall of a three-story building, between the two platoons. Weil was chewing on a not quite tasteless chocolate energy bar. Lon and Ivar were concentrating on water, taking small sips to make it last. Lon had also splashed a little water on his face, trying to stay moderately alert.

"Double-check the men who were wounded," Lon said. "Make sure no one's trying to cover up something that needs a medical orderly." He shook his head. "You know what needs doing."

"I guess we've been keeping an eye on them, Lieutenant," Weil said after washing down the last of his chocolate with a single long drink of water. "Something to help keep our minds from rusting up on the march." Ivar nodded.

"I know," Lon said. "We all need a little extended

sleep, or we're going to be in a fog. There's only so much a stim-patch can do.'' Lon had used two stimulant patches himself in the past eight hours, but had not left either on for long. He was prone to side-effects from them, mostly jitters in his hands and arms—which could affect his marksmanship.

He looked around. Many of the men looked almost co-matose, sitting or squatting, mostly with their backs to the building's wall, too tired to even fall over, Lon thought. When a stim-patch wore off, the reaction could be extreme.

''I want you two to get a little rest as well,'' Lon told the sergeants. ''I'm okay for a while. I get too dopey to stay awake, I'll call one of you.''

Weil and Ivar got up and moved toward their platoons, then found new places to sit. Lon stood and walked a few steps back and forth, working to keep his legs from getting stiff. He had not ordered any sentries. There were men from Delta of the 3rd nearby. They had one platoon held back as company reserve. The battalion's medical orderlies were set up not far away, with four trauma tubes in use and several other soldiers with minor injuries being treated. Colonel McGregor's command post was a block west. There were more soldiers there.

Lon set up one of his auxiliary radio channels to monitor the talk among Delta's officers and noncoms, listening to their descriptions of the battle—terse orders and warnings, occasional comments. A little swearing. He recognized a few of the voices, but not nearly all. It was sometimes dif-ficult to follow what the others were saying. He could not see what they were seeing, and he was too tired to waste energy imagining what the soldiers of Delta were experi-encing.

After a few minutes, Lon sat down, his back to the wall. He had the faceplate of his helmet down so he could see what was going on around him. He worked to keep his eyes open, listening to the talk on the radio . . . but not always hearing it. He never *quite* fell asleep, but his mind was little more active than it would have been in the deepest stages of slumber, and his heart rate and respiration were depressed. Still, his eyes remained more or less open, and he was vaguely aware of the radio traffic. He became less and less aware of the sounds of battle, even though the front line was little more than two hundred yards away, only a couple of buildings and streets to the north. Fear was no longer a concept his mind could recognize.

Lon managed forty-five minutes of this nirvanic release before he heard his name called. "Yes?" he said while he tried to shake the stupor from his brain. He was not even certain who was talking.

"George McGregor," the voice said. Lon blinked several times and looked to see if the captain was close. He was not.

"What is it, Captain?" Lon asked, his voice thick with near-sleep.

"I really hate to do this to you, but we've got a bit of a possibility here and we need a few more men to exploit it. I've already checked with my colonel, and he checked with yours."

"Where do you want us?" Lon asked.

"I'm on my way to you now. I'll give you the details while we're moving."

18

When Captain McGregor arrived, Lon's men were still getting to their feet. Many seemed almost zombielike in their movements. *About the way I feel,* Lon thought. But the prospect of action had his mind cycling up to full alertness.

"What's up, Captain?" Lon asked.

"A chance to drive a wedge through a weak spot in the Belletiener line." McGregor shrugged. "If it doesn't close up before we can get enough people in position to push through."

Lon nodded. "That might tip the scales, get this whole bloody mess over with in a hurry."

"If we're lucky," McGregor said. "I'm not counting on it, but we've got to try. Your men up to a little work?"

Both officers were scanning Lon's men. "If they're not this second, they will be by the time we get in place," Lon said. "We're all a little groggy, but walking will clear the cobwebs."

"This is going to be something of a cobble, I'm afraid. Besides my company and your two platoons, it's a matter of grabbing a squad from here and there, anyone we can assemble in a hurry. My colonel's even putting his headquarters security squad in. We should have about three hundred and fifty men for the push, if the enemy hasn't closed the hole."

While Lon's platoon sergeants were forming up their men, several squads from 3rd Battalion approached, one of them moving at a jog, coming from the east. The various squad leaders reported to Captain McGregor, and he had them move with Lon and his platoons.

"I'll put these men under your tactical control," McGregor told Lon. "I'll have my company, a couple of other squads, and overall command of the operation."

"Just tell me what you want us to do," Lon asked as they started moving north. The columns of men stayed close to walls, moving in a crouch, weapons at the ready. Ahead, Lon could see flames. At least one building was on fire.

McGregor, walking at Lon's side, pointed toward the blaze. "I don't know how that started. There was an explosion inside. Either the Calypsans had something stored there that went off, or the Belletieners had an accident with explosives. The wall of the west end of the building blew out, and flames spread to the next building. We think that the enemy abandoned the second building, and we're working to make certain that they can't get back in. The idea is to move across between those buildings as quickly as the flames die down, to sever the enemy line. That happens, we can pull in more troops to try and roll them up."

"One of the other battalions moving men around?" Lon asked.

"First Battalion is freeing up a company to slide around from the east," McGregor said. "It's going to take forty-five minutes for them to arrive, maybe an hour, so—if we do get in—we'll have to hold on that long."

Lon grunted. "Could be worse, Captain. We had to wait a lot longer for you people to get here from the west."

Lon followed McGregor into one of the buildings that was part of 3rd Battalion's front line, across the street from the building that the Belletieners had evacuated. Some smoke came from the east end of that building, but there was no longer any indication of fire inside. To the left, Lon could see the building that was still burning. The fire was contained inside for the most part. Some greenery was smoldering along the side where the wall had blown out. It looked as bright as day out there, though. Any men crossing the street would be clearly silhouetted, visible for a considerable distance.

"On either end, we're pouring everything we've got across to keep the enemy from closing the hole," McGregor said. The two men were using radio even though they were next to each other. It was easier to hear over the noise of battle.

"How long's that been burning?" Lon asked.

"Maybe forty minutes," McGregor said. "We put this together in one hell of a hurry." He paused, then added. "Had to. It ought to burn itself out fairly soon, though. Most of these buildings don't have a lot of combustibles in them. Plascrete and metal framing. I'm a bit surprised that it hasn't fizzled out already."

"How do you figure to handle the crossing?"

"Basically, put up all the firepower we can, then run like hell. It's eighty yards from the last cover on this side to the corner of that building over there."

Lon blinked, a pause long enough to let him censor the first comment that came to mind: *Could be a slaughter.* If the Belletieners *were* waiting, it would be a frontal attack, and it could be suicidal.

"Just how confident are you that the enemy's cleared out of that building, and not waiting perhaps just beyond it, where they can cover this gap we're going to cross?" Lon asked then.

"Not one hundred percent, obviously," McGregor said. "I thought about putting one squad over first, but the colonel vetoed that, said it might do nothing more than give the enemy information, warn them that something's coming."

"Six of one, half a dozen of the other," Lon said.

"We'll cross in two groups," McGregor said. "You take your platoons and the extra squads first, try to get over there before the enemy knows what's up. Then I'll bring the rest over as soon as you get over. That way we can cover each other."

Lon nodded. "Sounds as good as anything." Going first did not worry him. It was probably the safer position. There was a chance that they could be most of the way across before the enemy responded. It was Captain McGregor and his men who would likely face more enemy fire.

"Any suggestions? I'm wide open. I'd like to see something a little less hairy myself."

"I wish I did, Captain. But if it had been me, I probably would have sent the patrol over first and given the whole thing away too soon, if I'd even thought of a way to do it in the first place. We'll do what we can."

"We'd better get in place. That thing over there could blink out in a hurry. It shouldn't be long."

"I hope not," Lon said. "I'd rather not have too much time to worry about it. Better to get it done."

Lon switched channels and passed on the details of the operation to his platoon sergeants and the squad leaders—his and the three who had been attached to his command.

"What happens after we all get across?" Ivar Dendrow asked.

"I'll let you know as soon as I find out," Lon said. "Depends how the enemy reacts. The main idea is we hold the gap until reinforcements come."

Lon told the noncoms what was coming. Squad leaders told their men. Everyone moved into position, ready for a mad sprint across the avenue, into the gap between the two buildings. By the time Lon got to where his men were waiting, he could see that the fire was dying out rapidly.

"This may be out of order, Lieutenant," Jorgen said on their private channel, "but I've heard smarter ideas. Seems we're taking an awful lot on faith, and not enough hard intelligence."

Lon agreed, but this was not the time to voice doubts. "It's a chance to get this over with in a hurry, Weil, a chance to keep down the number of casualties overall. When the shooting starts, make sure we get our people across that street in record time, before Belletiene has a chance to react. We'll be getting the order to move in a minute or two."

Jorgen simply clicked his transmitter in acknowledgment.

Lon measured his breathing, forcing a steady pace, deep breaths, oxygenating his lungs before the race. It could not be simply a mad dash for the goal line—not for Lon. He would have to hang back a little, stay near the rear of his men, ready to help stragglers. Or wounded. There were times for a leader to lead from the front, but this was not one of them.

He had put a fresh magazine in his rifle, and checked to make certain that his pistol was loaded and ready. To his own surprise, Lon found that he was not particularly nervous about this operation. *It is an audacious plan,* he thought. *Maybe that's its saving grace. We might pull it off, be the spearhead on the telling assault.* People would remember that, in the Corps. It would tell to his advantage for years. If it worked.

"Your men ready?" Captain McGregor asked.

"We're ready," Lon replied.

"The covering fire will start in thirty seconds. I'll give you the word to move ten seconds after that, just long enough to see that no one opens up from right in front of you, where we don't think they are."

Nice to know you're giving some thought to the intelligence being wrong, Lon thought. He passed the alert to his noncoms, then watched the time, giving more of his attention to that than to the empty space across the avenue between the two buildings, or to the building to the left, the one that Captain McGregor believed had been vacated by the enemy.

The barrage of small arms fire started exactly on schedule, and then Lon focused on the target area, looking for any sign of enemy activity, muzzle flashes or movement. He had seen nothing by the time McGregor gave the one-word command. "Go!"

"Hit it!" Lon said, on his all-hands channel. He got to his feet with the men closest to him. Squad by squad, his men raced toward cover on the far side of the avenue. There was not room or time for normal separation between men, and this was not a fire-and-maneuver operation with half of the men moving while the rest laid down covering fire. It was everyone going at once, moving as quickly as they could without fragmenting ranks.

For the first few paces, Lon managed no more than a walk. He scanned the front, looking for signs of enemy activity and watching for any of his men who might have trouble. Girana's squad was closest, the men in a shallow wedge in front of him. As the squads in front of them pulled away, Girana's men also picked up their pace, and Lon stayed virtually in step.

Only a few flickering embers remained in the building that had housed the explosion, though the building glowed in infrared. The heat of the fire would remain for some time. *That might help us, once we get across,* Lon thought. With that glow behind them, his men would have greater protection from thermal imaging. They would be harder to detect with normal night-vision gear.

Lon nearly tripped over the curb on the north side of the street. He had not been watching where his feet went. He stumbled, but caught his balance and kept going forward. The first squads were entering the building on the left. Other squads were moving to set up positions north of the buildings and cover the eastern approaches.

Just past the nearest corner of the building on the left, Lon stopped. Girana halted his squad, directing them to various points of cover. Lon looked around for a few seconds, noting where his other squads had gone, then called Captain McGregor.

"We're across," Lon announced. "No trouble. No casualties. I've got my people in position. Whenever you're ready."

"We're on our way . . . *now*," McGregor replied.

McGregor's company started running across the street. The first platoon was halfway across when a grenade exploded in the street, a little to the west. It was close enough to send some shrapnel into the nearest Dirigenters, but only one man fell, and the next two men picked him up by the shoulders and dragged him on with them to cover. Several other grenades exploded in the street, but only that first one was close enough to cause casualties. Grenades could be launched from cover, over buildings. Riflemen would have to expose themselves to get shots off at the men crossing the street.

So far, so good, Lon thought as the first of McGregor's men pulled up in the area between the two buildings. A medical orderly went to the man who had been dragged across after being hit. Lon went to him.

"He'll live," the medic said, looking up at Lon for just an instant before he resumed tending the wounded man. "But he'll recover a lot faster if we can get him into a trauma tube."

Lon simply nodded, then moved back out of the way. The next wave of men from Delta Company was coming across.

"It went better than I expected," Captain McGregor said once the last of his men were across. There had been a total of six casualties, but the other five wounds had been minor, almost insignificant. Only the one man needed a trauma tube.

"You were right about catching them off guard," Lon said. "They still haven't started to hit back. We've pushed right to the end of that building." He pointed to the structure that had burned. "And across to the next street."

McGregor had not specified deployments. That had been left, temporarily, to Lon's judgment. "Might as well grab as much as we can hold," the captain said

"As long as nothing holds up that company from 1st Battalion," Lon replied.

"They're on schedule, as of five minutes ago. I'm going to see how much we can hurry them." McGregor switched radio channels, and Lon could not hear his call. "Twenty minutes," McGregor said when he returned to the channel he had been sharing with Lon. "They'll be in position to come across behind us in twenty minutes. Now, I need to get in somewhere where I can check our deployment and see what we can do next."

• • •

The two officers separated, but remained in contact by radio. Lon had focused his men on the left half of the salient, the building that had been abandoned by the Belletieners, leaving McGregor's company to the right and across the center. While the captain checked the deployments, Lon moved into the building where half of his men had taken up defensive positions. The rest were outside, along the west and north of the structure, digging in as quickly as they could.

"I don't believe we got over here so easily," Tebba said. He remained with Lon, along with one fire team from his squad.

"Things might get rough in a hurry though, Tebba," Lon said. "Maybe we caught them napping, but they know we're here, and they've got to try to kick us back out. As long as we hold this gap, we're a knife at their throats."

"Well, let's cut them and have done with it," Tebba said. Lon did not respond.

They climbed to the second floor and went to the west end. That gave Lon a view of the enemy positions in the next block. He could see the enemy moving troops. He relayed that to Captain McGregor. "Could start any second now," Lon said.

"On the other side too," McGregor said. "You handle your end. I'll deal with this side. Good luck, Nolan."

"Yeah, you too, Captain."

Then the shooting started.

Belletiene attacked Lon's half of the salient, pushing three companies of infantry forward while more stayed behind and provided heavy covering fire. In the middle, the advancing soldiers leapfrogged each other, trying to suppress return fire from the Dirigenters. But Lon's defenses were stacked, men flat on the ground and on each of the three levels of the buildings. There was no cover for the men coming at them. They kept coming.

Lon moved to a window and stood at the side, using his rifle to join in the fight. He could not concentrate exclusively on that, though. His primary responsibility was to command. After a moment, he moved back away from the window and gestured for Tebba to follow. They went up to the top floor and Lon looked out to the north, toward that part of the attack.

"If we can get up on the roof, I can watch it all at once," Lon said, moving close enough to speak to Tebba without using the radio. "You seen anything that looks like roof access?"

Tebba shook his head. "Not inside. There's a ladder on the outside to the roof, but that's on the north wall, and I don't think this is the time to try that."

An explosion rocked the building. It was powerful enough to almost throw Lon and Tebba to the ground.

"What the hell was that?" Lon asked, shouting over a ringing in his ears.

"Cheez," Tebba said. "They must be using rockets against us. That was something meant for a tank or an airplane."

Lon switched to a channel that connected him to all of his noncoms. "What was that explosion?" he asked, already moving toward the stairs. There was nothing visible on the third floor. It must have hit lower.

"We've got a hole in the west wall, Lieutenant," Ivar Dendrow reported. "We've got casualties there, a good part of fourth squad is down. I don't know how serious yet."

"What about you?" Lon demanded. "You don't sound too good yourself."

"I'll live," Dendrow said.

Lon and his escort kept going past the second floor landing down to the first. Most of the first floor had been one large room, with only a few small partitioned offices along the north side. That main room was now filled with smoke, but Lon could see the gaping hole at the far end of it. Men were being carried back away from the opening, out into the foyer near the stairs.

"Tebba, you'd better get down there." Lon gestured to include the members of Girana's squad with them. "Help plug that gap until we get things sorted out. I'll be along in a minute."

Girana nodded and started down the length of the room with his men. Lon stayed in the foyer, looking at the casualties who were being lined up in two rows. Two men were clearly dead. They had been laid off to the side, by themselves. Lon could not tell who they were. He started to move closer, but saw someone staggering toward him, out of the densest smoke, trailing one leg behind the other, supporting himself with his rifle. Lon went to help. The wounded man was Ivar Dendrow.

"We got hit bad, Lieutenant," Dendrow said while Lon half carried him to where the other wounded were. "I think we've lost half of fourth squad, dead or too badly wounded to keep on."

"Don't worry about that now, Ivar," Lon said. "I'll get a medical orderly for you."

Dendrow did not respond. Lon looked to make sure that the platoon sergeant was still alive, still conscious. He called for help by radio while he worked to put bandages over the most obvious of Dendrow's wounds. His left arm and leg, his entire left side, was bloody. The side of his helmet was cracked.

You're going to need a trauma tube, Lon thought. He looked around at the other wounded. Dendrow was not the only one who was going to need time in a tube to recover from this.

A medical orderly came over, knelt next to the platoon sergeant, and started examining him. Lon waited for a few seconds, then got up and stepped across, looking toward the hole that had been blown in the far wall. The building had holes in both ends now, the first remaining from the earlier explosion in the building next door.

The smoke was beginning to clear, finally. Lon started working his way toward the east end. He had to be careful. There were bullets flying, coming in the hole. He stayed low and moved to his right, along the series of cubicles on the north side. The doors were all open—those that had not been blown off—and Lon glanced in each one, looking out the window at what was going on along the north side of the building. The fighting was continuing, but Lon saw no evidence that the Belletiener force was getting too close.

Tebba Girana and the men he had brought with him had moved to the hole in the end wall. Lon moved to the side, finding a spot where he could look out to the right, past the corner of the building—the weak spot in the defenses. The building had no windows right on the corner, so there was a narrow angle that was not as well covered by fire zones as the rest of the perimeter. Only a squad of men outside, on the ground, had that angle directly in view.

"I think it's covered okay, Lieutenant," Tebba said when he saw where Lon was looking. "The men are mostly at one side of a window or the other. That gives them a chance to see anything happening along there."

Lon nodded. "Ivar is out of action, wounded," he said. "You're senior squad leader in the platoon, so that means you sub for him until he's fit for duty again."

"Yes, sir."

Lon told the other squad leaders of the temporary arrangement, to make certain that there would be no questions at a delicate time.

"Here they come!" an anonymous voice said. Lon thought that it had to be one of the men from the squads that had been attached to his command. It was someone whose voice he did not recognize. "On the west."

Lon moved closer to the hole in the wall, bringing his rifle up as he did. It appeared that Belletiene was going to make a solid run at them, a frontal assault by two or three companies of infantry, with more supporting them from behind. Lon passed the news to Captain McGregor.

"They're coming in from the north too," McGregor said, "on the eastern half of our line. You'll have to hold with what you've got. Still another fifteen minutes or more before our reinforcements arrive."

"We'll do our best," Lon said before changing channels to talk to his squad leaders. He gave orders to move some of the men upstairs over to the west side of the building, and had another squad come into the building to reinforce the men on the ground floor. That squad could scarcely find positions to fire at the enemy. Lon wanted them close in case the Belletiener assault made it to the wall.

He looked around. If a grenade came through that hole and exploded inside the room, the results would be devastating, but there was no help for that. There was no time to move the men outside, and no time for them to dig slit trenches if they could.

The Belletiener attack faltered fifty yards from the Dirigenters who *were* outside. The enemy skirmish line dropped to the ground, grabbing what minimal cover they could find on the manicured lawn. But within fifteen seconds a second line of Belletieners came forward past the men on the ground. And a third line came along twenty yards behind them.

"I don't think they're gonna back off, Lieutenant," Tebba said. "Someone's putting the spurs to them. They're gonna keep coming as long as any of them can move."

"I think you're right, Tebba. Let's make sure not too many of them can move this far."

The second skirmish line went to ground fifteen yards in front of the first. The prone soldiers continued to fire, and continued to suffer losses. The third line moved past. More men came up from behind, and the first line that had gone to ground got up—those who still could—and resumed its advance.

Lon's men were firing at point-blank range. It was impossible to miss the men running on at them. But they kept coming, and men were falling on the Dirigent side of the line as well. "Fix bayonets," Lon ordered on his all-hands channel.

Some of the men had already taken that precaution on their own. The rest hurried to comply.

Belletieners started trying to climb into the building. The first were cut down by bullets, some fired from no more than three feet away. But more kept coming, a suicidal surge. The Dirigenters on the outside were in hand-to-hand fighting, and were being pushed aside.

The last squad that Lon had ordered into the ground floor of the building came forward to meet the enemy. Ten Dirigenters moved forward toward the gap, their rifles firing single shots now, or short bursts, as they attempted to throw back—or destroy—the enemy assault. Lon moved into the gap with them, thinking only of ending the threat as quickly as possible. As long as the enemy could be kept out, Lon thought that his men would be able to hold. He heard reports from outside, and knew that the men out there were being hit even harder.

But the line was holding.

Less than three minutes after the first Belletiener had touched the outer wall, the immediate fight was over. The enemy had suffered dozens of men killed, and had more wounded. Few of the enemy had surrendered. The comparative silence left a hollow ringing in Lon's ears. He stood dumbly, looking around at the bodies, his men and the enemy, too stunned to do much else.

A sudden cramp in his stomach brought him out of the daze. He blinked several times, then switched to his noncoms' channel. "I want reports on our casualties as quickly as you can give them to me," he said. "Keep your eyes open. This may not be over."

19

The company from 1st Battalion came and went. The men stopped in the pocket that Lon's platoons and Captain McGregor's company had defended only long enough to let their commanding officer ascertain the situation. Then they moved on, pushing north. "We're to try to split the enemy completely in half," the company's captain explained, taking only a few seconds to talk to Lon and George McGregor. Then he was off with his men.

"It looks like this might all be over with by morning," McGregor told Lon when the two talked over a private channel. "Things are popping all around the perimeter now, from what I've been hearing."

"So what are we supposed to do?" Lon asked.

"Treat our wounded, identify the dead, and pull ourselves together." McGregor's voice sounded as leaden as Lon felt. "If our people keep tightening the noose around the enemy, they can do without us for a bit."

"Yeah, well, I've got men to see to, Captain. I know you do too," Lon said. There was a taste of bile in his mouth, and a knot in his stomach. It was the taste he noticed most.

The wounded were being treated. Medical orderlies triaged the wounded, making certain that those in most desperate need of a trauma tube were transported to where the tubes were set up, then helped care for the wounded who could wait for tubes. Relays of men toted the wounded to 3rd Battalion's medical aid station. The rest of the casualties, those with minor wounds, were mostly being cared for by their squad mates.

Lon checked in with each squad leader or assistant. Heyes Wurd, who had third platoon's first squad, was among the dead. Third squad's Corporal Ben Frehr had been wounded, and already carried across to get his turn in a trauma tube. By the time Lon had talked to the men in all of his squads, the knot in his stomach had become a steel claw. Third platoon had seven men dead and a dozen wounded. Fourth platoon's numbers were five dead and fifteen wounded. The story was much the same in the squads that had been attached to Lon's command—bad.

The Belletiener wounded were being treated by the prisoners, under guard. The number of dead Belletieners was revised upward several times, as wounded died of their injuries. Prisoners would be given turns in trauma tubes, but not at risk to Dirigenters. "We take care of our people first," one DMC corporal told a prisoner who wanted a wounded friend taken immediately to a trauma tube. Lon overheard the exchange but did not contradict the corporal. *"If we can get a man to a trauma tube alive, he's got nineteen chances in twenty to stay alive,"* the claim was, *"and if he survives the first two minutes in the tube, his chances are virtually one hundred percent."*

Major Kai, 3rd Battalion's second in command, came over to look at the site of the battle and talk to the officers who had led the fight. He asked questions and listened to Lon's sometimes disjointed answers. He made commendatory remarks that Lon scarcely heard.

"As soon as we get our lines tied together north of you," Kai said finally, "we'll pull your people back to battalion headquarters and give you a chance to rest and regroup. You boys have taken a licking, but you did good. You did what we needed you to do."

"I hope it was worth it," Lon said, privately certain that it could not be, not even if the rest of the Belletieners suddenly decided to surrender. Or drop dead. "I lost more than ten percent of my men killed."

"I know it's hard, Lieutenant," Major Kai said. "I've been through it too. But your lads may have saved a great many other lives tonight."

It was another fifteen minutes before Lon received the order to pull his men back to 3rd Battalion headquarters, which had moved closer to the medical aid station. Captain McGregor's company moved there as well. It too had taken serious casualties. McGregor was wounded, had lost part of his left hand, but he had stayed with his men until all of them could pull back. Once they reached the aid station, his lead sergeant half hauled the captain to help.

Lon got his men, the ones who were still fit for duty, settled, then went to check on the wounded. He talked to the ones who were conscious and asked the orderlies about each of the others—when he could find a medic willing to take a few seconds to answer a question.

When Lon got back to his platoons, he almost fell, his muscles and joints going limp as he started to sit—a reaction, part exhaustion, part delayed fear . . . and disgust. He took a moment to steady himself, then pulled his helmet off and dropped it at his side. He leaned forward, arms on his thighs, head hanging as far as it would go. Now, his mind was almost blank. There was simply too much to think about, too much to regret.

"There's only one constant about our business," Lieutenant Arlan Taiters, the officer who had mentored Lon through his cadet stage in the DMC, had told him. *"Men die in battle. You've got to be able to deal with that, or you don't have any place in the Corps, not as an officer, not as an enlisted man."* Taiters himself had died not long after that. It was his two platoons that Lon had inherited when he received his commission. Lon thought about him, when his mind started to function again. Taiters had died in a confrontation not all that different from the one that Lon and his men had just experienced.

"You okay, Lieutenant?" Tebba Girana asked.

Lon looked up. Tebba was just then squatting in front of him. The corporal had his faceplate up.

"Tired," Lon said. "And thinking about the men we lost." He shook his head. "And remembering Arlan Taiters."

"Sometimes I have nightmares," Tebba said, very softly.

"I see all of the men I've known who got killed. Been a lot of them in the fifteen years I've been in the Corps. But that's always at home, back on Dirigent. It's not good to dwell on them on contract. Can't help them, and don't help the men I'm supposed to take care of now."

"I know, Tebba. I know." Lon let out a breath. "I'll be okay in a minute or two. Just gotta clean out the cobwebs, and the memories are tangled up in them."

"Sergeant Dendrow's gonna have to go in a tube, but he's waiting for the more seriously wounded guys first. Looks like it might be mid-morning before he's ready for duty."

Lon nodded. "I talked to him a few minutes ago. He tried to tell me a half dozen things that I needed to do before I could shut him up and tell him that we're coping, to just rest and take care of himself."

"Yeah, he gave me a hard time too," Tebba said. "I finally had to just walk away from him so's he would shut up."

"We need to find a good water supply," Lon said after a moment. "Get the canteens filled, try to get a little extra so men can douse themselves, get a little of the stench off."

"Weil and I are already working at it, Lieutenant. Phip and Janno found some pails in one of the buildings. And the water's on in most of them. I'll bring a bucket around for you, soon as it all gets here."

Lon shook his head. "Not till everyone else is taken care of, Tebba."

"Don't worry about that sort of nonsense now, Lieutenant," Tebba said. "We'll get everybody taken care of, more or less at once. It's only 'women and children first,' that I recall, and we don't have any of those here."

Lon had a call from Captain Orlis. The rest of the company was still in action. "I know you took a beating, Nolan, but I hear that you did a great job," Orlis said. "You and your men stay put. Try to get some sleep. We'll worry about getting you back in the morning."

Lon got his men moved into a building. Shelter, running

water, and toilets. The building housed professional offices, a half dozen separate units. Many of the windows had been blown or shot out, but that scarcely mattered. None of Lon's men were in any hurry to carp about details, even though it meant that they could hear the distant sounds of fighting—gunfire and grenade explosions. It was infinitely better than sleeping outside. There were no complaints, no bad jokes.

Not a good sign, Lon thought, but he shared the same apathy. "A griping soldier is, basically, a happy soldier," one of Lon's instructors at the North American Military Academy had been fond of saying. "It's when he stops griping that you have to be most concerned about his morale." *Morale isn't supposed to be a problem in the Corps,* Lon thought. *We're professionals, career soldiers. This is what we chose to do.* He sighed. They had good reason to be quiet. Too many men had died. If the men did not snap back from it after a night's sleep, then there might be something for Lon to worry about.

The room Lon selected for himself was on the second floor, in a corner. There was a sofa covered with what might have been real leather, soft and almost long enough for him to stretch out fully. Tebba and part of his squad were in the other two rooms of the office suite, with the rest of third platoon distributed around the second floor; fourth platoon was below, on the ground floor.

Lon stripped off his helmet, pack, harness, and web belt, which made him more than forty pounds lighter. *I could almost float away, if I wasn't so dead tired,* he thought. He sat on the sofa and let his shoulders slump forward. Sleep held great attraction, but Lon could not simply collapse. He tried to think coherently, tried to make certain that he was not forgetting anything essential. Third Battalion headquarters and the technicians at the aid station knew where Lon and his men were. They would not be "lost," and the men who were released by the medics would be able to find them. Lon had not set up any schedule of sentries; that might be a mistake, but he thought not. They were away from the fighting, with enough active soldiers around to give warning of any trouble.

"I need sleep," Lon muttered. But he got to his feet and shuffled across to the private restroom that the office boasted—the other reason (aside from the sofa) that he had selected it. He could take a couple of minutes to wash some of the grime away.

When he finished his toilet, Lon returned to the sofa. For several minutes he just sat on it. Then, finally, he took off his boots and lay down. His feet hurt. They were moderately swollen. Lon was too tired to appreciate the softness of his bed. Almost immediately, he was asleep.

Lon came awake with a start. He lay absolutely motionless, trying to determine what had brought him out of sleep so abruptly. He needed time to realize that what was "wrong" was silence. The guns had stopped firing. There were no explosions. He did not even hear men talking below his window.

It was still dark. That window was just a rectangular space that was not quite as dark as the wall that framed it. Lon was cautious getting up, trying to be as silent as the world around him. He got his helmet and put it on, giving himself its night-vision capability. Then he went to the window to look out. Several large tents had been erected where the medical orderlies and technicians had been treating the wounded earlier. Lon saw four men standing guard at the perimeter of the square. *Standing,* Lon thought. The men were not behind cover looking out over their rifle barrels.

The fighting must be over, Lon decided. *The enemy must have surrendered.* Otherwise, the guards would have been more cautious. They would not be standing the way they were, as if they were in front of Corps Headquarters on Dirigent.

Lon looked at the time on his helmet display. It was a few minutes past five-thirty in the morning, local time. It would be light soon.

I wonder if anyone's been trying to contact me, he thought. With his helmet on the floor next to the sofa, there was a good chance that he would not have heard a radio call. Then he realized that if anyone had tried to contact him and he had not answered the radio, someone would have been sent to wake him. *Enough people know where I am.* He toyed with the idea of calling Captain Orlis, but decided against it. Orlis might be sleeping, needing his own rest after a long day and night of fighting.

"It can wait," Lon said softly, keeping his voice down as though he were afraid of waking someone—even though there was a closed door between him and anyone else. He continued to stand by the window, observing the minimal activity below. Two men came out of one of the tents, went over to one of the guards, and apparently conversed with him briefly before going on out of sight, in the direction the guard had just pointed—wounded men looking to rejoin their unit after completing their treatment.

"I wonder if our wounded are back yet." Lon went back to the sofa, sat, and pulled on his boots. He did not consider lying down and trying to go back to sleep. Even though he had had little more than an hour, he was no longer sleepy. His mind was alert, and until he knew for certain what was going on, he would be unable to shut off his thoughts enough for slumber.

Lon was uncertain what to do next. His impulse was to put on the rest of his gear and go prowling through the building, maybe go out to the medical tents to find someone who might be able to tell him what had happened. But he did not want to wake any of his men unless it became necessary. They needed to get as much sleep as they could, while they could. *I don't know that it's over,* Lon reminded himself. There might still be units of Belletiener troops in The Cliffs or elsewhere.

As much to fill time as to assuage hunger, Lon opened a meal pack and ate. He started to remember the night before, the fighting, the deaths. He would have to write up an after-action report, and the sooner he fixed the details in his mind, the less likely he would be to omit anything when it was time for the formal report. The dead. The seriously wounded. Names. He recalled the faces that went with the names, and he remembered more. Especially about the dead. *His* dead.

I hope we don't have to spend the whole six months here, Lon thought at about the time that he finished his breakfast. *We've had our share of Calypso. Let Second Regiment fill out the time when they get here, if the locals still want help around to prevent another attack. Let us go home and lick our wounds.* On the trip out, some of the men had talked about the joys of spending six months in a "tropical paradise" with nothing to do but wait around in case there was an invasion, maybe spend time training more Calypsan soldiers. But paradise had turned sour.

He went back to the window, and was surprised to see that it had started to rain—a gentle shower, fit for a storybook spring day. The sky was a little lighter with approaching daylight, but the overcast seemed determined to retard the dawn. *At least it'll give the men something safe to bitch about when they get up,* Lon thought. He shook his head. It was time to do something more constructive than standing around and staring.

After putting on his gear, Lon picked up his rifle and left the room. He moved quietly through the outer room of the suite, hoping to avoid waking anyone, but Tebba either woke or was already awake. He got up and followed Lon out into the corridor.

"I'm going to go see if I can find out what the situation is," Lon said, lifting his visor and speaking softly. Tebba was carrying his helmet. "The shooting has stopped."

Girana nodded. "Yeah, I noticed. More'n an hour ago it was." He shrugged. "At least, that's when I woke and noticed it was quiet."

"That's what woke me too," Lon said. "Sleep through all the racket, then wake when it gets quiet."

"You figure that Belletiene surrendered?" Tebba asked.

"Something like that. The troops here, anyway. Hard telling if there's any contact with their government."

"I didn't even think about that. All I had in mind was the bunch here fighting us. That *is* all we gotta worry about, isn't it, Lieutenant?"

"I don't know, Tebba," Lon said. "For the moment anyway. But if their government isn't ready to come to terms that Calypso will accept, maybe not. We could still have to wait out the full six months of our tour, maybe face more of them somewhere down the road. It's all guesswork. I might know more after I get a chance to talk to Captain Orlis. Whenever that is. Right now, I'm going to drift over to the aid station, or maybe 3rd Battalion headquarters, and see if I can find out what's what."

"You want me to tag along?"

"No need. Stick around here. Is Ivar back yet?"

"No. He would have looked you up right away, and tripped over me in the process. Shouldn't be long, though, I think. By now they must have most of the wounded cycled through the tubes."

If anyone else woke while Lon was working his way through to one of the building's exits, they did not bother to get up or say anything. Lon stood in the doorway for a couple of minutes, feeling the soft, damp breeze coming from the east, getting a little drizzle on his faceplate. He lifted that and let the air and the water hit him in the face. There was a fishy smell to the air, to the rain.

It's only dead fish smell like that, he thought, remembering one summer when all of the fish had died in one of the nearby streams—back in eastern North America on Earth. After a couple of days the stench downwind had been intense, much worse than the hint of fishiness here. He did not recall what had caused that die-off. At eleven years of age, such things had not concerned him for long.

Lon pulled his visor back down before he stepped out of the covered doorway and walked to 3rd Battalion's headquarters. That was in another building, for now. If the fighting was over, Colonel McGregor and his staff would almost certainly be displaced by the building's regular occupants. Lon was surprised that the battalion's medical section had bothered to erect tents rather than make use of one or more of the vacant structures.

There was little activity at the headquarters. Two enlisted

men were busy on complinks. Major Kai was sitting at a desk at the rear of the room, leaning back, his eyes closed. But he apparently heard Lon enter. He sat up, then stood and walked over toward Lon, who had lifted his faceplate.

"Lieutenant Nolan," Kai said, nodding to him. "I figured you'd still be sleeping."

"The silence woke me, Major," Lon said with a self-conscious grin. "I came over to see what's going on."

"Not a whole lot, as you can see," Kai said.

"Is the fighting over?"

"The general commanding the invasion force surrendered his command less than two hours ago," Kai said. "The Calypsans and our people are still collecting prisoners and seeing to the wounded on both sides. For the rest of us, we've been given the word to stand down—provisionally. Colonel Gaffney has scheduled a regimental officers' call for noon. No word yet on where it will be."

"What about my platoons? Do we stay here or pack up and rejoin our company?"

"No hurry, Lieutenant. You might as well let them sleep for a couple more hours before you worry about trekking off to find the rest of your lads. No one's yelling for you, so as long as you don't make noise, you should have plenty of time. You might even try getting a little more sleep yourself."

Lon shrugged. "I need to check on my wounded, see how long it'll be before the last are released by the medics, and make certain none of them are going to be shipped up to *Long Snake* for rehab or extended treatment."

"Come over to my desk. I can give you some of that information here." Kai led the way. When he sat down, he pulled his portable complink closer and keyed in a request.

"Here's what I have, Lieutenant," he said then, turning the unit so that Lon could see the screen. "Two of your boys are going to be returned to ship for regeneration or rehabilitation. Your platoon sergeant, Dendrow, nearly lost an arm. He's going to be off the duty list for a month for tissue regeneration and therapy. I talked with him for a couple of minutes. I didn't get to talk to the other one."

The other man being sent back up to the ship was Loe Gavish from fourth platoon's first squad. "When will they be shipped out, Major?" Lon asked.

"Any minute now, I suspect," Kai said. "All of the wounded who need further treatment were collected nearly an hour ago, taken over toward the beach. A shuttle should be coming in for the pickup right about now."

"No chance for me to talk to my two men before they go, is that what you're saying?"

"I'm afraid that's the way it is, Lieutenant. Sorry. I didn't think to have you notified. Perhaps I should have."

"I guess it doesn't matter, Major. I should have taken the time to see them on my own, earlier. I was afraid the medics would chase me out, though."

Major Kai chuckled. "Very likely. One of the technicians even gave Colonel McGregor an earful. But if you go over there now, you'll probably be able to speak to the rest of your wounded. Things have quieted down considerably, especially since there are no new wounded coming in."

20

Intermittent light showers, rarely more than a drizzle, persisted through the morning. There were few complaints. Most of the comments that Lon heard were of the ''I hope it stays like this and keeps the temperature down'' variety. That was unlikely. The reports Lon got from CIC aboard *Star Dragon* suggested that the rain would end around midday and that the clouds would move out to sea shortly after that.

At eight o'clock Lon received a call from Matt Orlis. The captain asked for more details on how Lon's platoons had fared, then suggested that they move north to rendezvous with the other half of Alpha Company before the regimental officers' call. ''That should give you time to collect the rest of your men from the medics,'' Orlis said, and Lon confirmed that it would be. The last were scheduled to be returned to duty by 1000 hours—except for those who had been evacuated to the ship.

During the next two hours, Lon talked with each of his remaining noncoms, getting more detailed information on the activities of each squad during the final fight of the previous night . . . and how many casualties had been suffered. Everything was recorded, both for his personal record and as part of the official archives for the regiment.

Tebba Girana was told that he would continue as interim platoon sergeant until Ivar Dendrow returned to duty. Lance Corporal Dav Grott would take over second squad temporarily. In third platoon's first squad, Lance Corporal Jez Aivish succeeded Heyes Wurd as squad leader. There were also a couple of temporary changes in fourth platoon that

Lon had to confirm with Captain Orlis—who accepted all of Lon's recommendations.

The two platoons hiked north and east, then north again to rejoin the rest of 2nd Battalion. It was no drill field march, but the men were formed up in double columns and kept fairly regular order. Weapons were slung now, chambers empty, safeties on. The battle was over.

Civilian work crews were already in Oceanview cleaning up after the fight. Damaged buildings were being surveyed. Trucks were hauling away debris. Maintenance crews were replacing broken windows and doors. In the area that had seen the most prolonged fighting, the damage would take weeks—or months—to repair. Several imposing buildings had been gutted by fire or explosions and might have to be torn down and replaced. Others would need to be completely restored inside.

The bodies had already been removed.

Most of the Dirigenters had been moved out of the city proper, out past the ring of residential blocks. Second Battalion was near the shore, just inside the arc of native forest that served as a buffer between the capital and the rest of Calypso. The last stretch of the hike for Lon and his men was along the beach. They could look up and to the left and see Government House and the other major buildings at the heart of the city. The Belletieners had never reached them.

"Any word on how badly the enemy was tore up?" Weil Jorgen asked Lon during a five-minute break on the beach.

"Not that I've heard," Lon said. "The only thing Captain Orlis mentioned was that there are more than a thousand prisoners, here and in the mining region. I'm not sure if anyone has totals on their dead and wounded yet."

"Who's guarding the prisoners, us or the locals?"

"Some of each, I guess. Colonel Gaffney didn't leave any of our people out west, so the Calypsans have to be guarding the Belletieners captured there. Here, well, Third Battalion was riding herd on about two hundred of the enemy when we left."

"You know what I was getting at, Lieutenant," Weil said.

"I know," Lon said. "I don't think that the prisoners are in that much danger from the locals. Not as long as we're here, at least. Massacring captives would violate the contract."

Lon turned so that he was looking out to sea. There was nothing man-made on the water, no indication that this world had ever been settled as long as he kept his back to the city. *I wonder what the first people who saw this thought,* he asked himself. *What was this world like back at the beginning?* It was a new kind of question for him, not just concerning Calypso but also the few other worlds in his experience. "I wonder what it would be like to be the first human to set foot on a new world," he mumbled. Then he shook his head and got to his feet. It was not something he expected to ever find out firsthand.

"Time to get moving," Lon said after switching on his transmitter and selecting the channel that connected him to his noncoms. "They're getting lonely without us."

It was a long but gentle climb up from the beach, first over coarse sand and poverty grasses, then onto more uniform turf, soft sod that felt almost springy underfoot, like an exercise mat. At the end of the bay, paths had been carved into one bluff face to provide easy access. The lane was wide and the grade gradual enough for a small ground-effect vehicle. But the climb could be felt in leg muscles. Walking through sand and up the slope was especially tiring for men who had spent too much of the past two days active.

Everyone was anxious for another rest once the platoons got to the top, but Lon kept them going until they got to the bivouac area where the other platoons of Alpha Company had already set up tents. Tents had also been erected for Lon's platoons. The discovery of that fact almost brought a cheer from the men.

Captain Orlis came out to meet them. He spoke to the platoons as a whole first, and then, after the men had been dismissed to the charge of their noncoms, Orlis took Lon aside. "I know you've had a rough time, Nolan, but you and your men performed admirably. I've heard that from Colonel Flowers and from Colonel McGregor."

Lon blinked twice, slowly, before he replied. "We tried. But all the praise in the galaxy can't bring back the men who were killed. I know," he continued, holding up a hand to forestall any comment from the captain. "It's part of what we do, who we are, but that doesn't make it any easier."

"I know that, Nolan. It never gets easier to lose men, comrades, even friends. If it does get easy, then you don't belong in this line of work. Take a few minutes to get squared away. You'll be sharing a tent with Carl Hoper. We'll be leaving for the officers' call in about twenty minutes."

Hoper. "I've still got to talk to him about Balt," Lon said. "That won't be easy either."

"He already knows that Balt was killed, Lon," Orlis said. Lon was surprised by the use of his first name. It was unusual for the captain.

Carl Hoper was sitting on his bedroll in the tent. He looked up when Lon came in, then stood. When the two men came face to face, all Lon could say was "I'm sorry, Carl. Balt was a good man. It hurts to lose him."

"It happens," Carl said. "We all know that going in." He was obviously holding himself under tight control. It showed in his voice. The pain was visible in his eyes. "Later, maybe on the ship going home, you can tell me the details. Not now," he added before Lon could interrupt. "It's too soon now. I need a little time."

The regimental officers' call was held a half mile from where Alpha Company was camped, in the open near Colonel Gaffney's temporary headquarters. Third Battalion's officers were the last to arrive. They had the farthest to come, but when they did show up, it was by floater. Someone had called for two taxicabs. That entrance generated a few laughs.

Lon did a lot of looking around. He knew, at least casually, every officer in the regiment. Not fully conscious of what he was doing, he was trying to see if anyone was missing, if there had been casualties among the officers. The few minutes that Lon had were not sufficient, though. Colonel Gaffney and his staff officers arrived, and the colonel started the meeting.

"This isn't the time for a full critique of the fight," he said, "but I will give you the hard figures I have. The regiment's casualties numbered one hundred and ninety-four dead, sixty-three wounded badly enough for extended periods of regeneration and rehabilitation. Three hundred have gone through trauma tube sessions and been returned to duty. I don't have what I consider to be accurate figures on the casualties suffered by the Calypsans. Their commanders are being . . . reticent about those. The commander of the Belletiener expeditionary force is being similarly tight-lipped. All we know for certain about their losses is that we have nearly eleven hundred prisoners and that more than eight hundred Belletiener dead have been buried. The number of dead might be considerably greater, since we have no data on their losses before we arrived." Gaffney paused for an instant, then continued.

"That's what we've been through. The enemy commander here surrendered without condition, and ordered his men to cease hostilities and surrender to either our people or the Calypsan army. The prisoners taken here on the coast are being held in four separate groups, scattered around the outskirts of Oceanview, until some determination is made about what to do with them on a more permanent basis — theoretically, until they can be repatriated. For the moment, at least, any negotiations will be between Calypso and Belletiene. We will become involved only by request. Unless there are difficulties. I did send one message to the government of Belletiene, telling them that their commander here had been defeated and had surrendered his command, and suggesting that they contact the government of Calypso to arrange a formal end to hostilities. There has been no reply, not even a formal acknowledgment." Gaffney paused again, this time for considerably longer than before.

"I don't know what the long-term status of the contract is for us. That depends in part, I suppose, on whether the two governments involved can come to some agreement. Temporarily, we will be staying close to Oceanview, but not right in it. Third Battalion is the only one still in local, uh, housing, and they will be moving to quarters similar to those the rest of us are in this afternoon. The government of Calypso is in quite a hurry to get conditions back to normal. You may have noticed that they're already hard at work repairing the damage to their capital. For at least the next couple of days, we should have nothing special to do except guard prisoners. Each company will take its turn in providing men for that. Otherwise, give your men a chance to rest and recuperate. Do the necessary things. Several shuttle convoys will bring down additional supplies to make things a little easier. I'll keep you posted."

"Were any officers killed?" Lon asked Captain Orlis after the officers' call had been dismissed and they had started back toward their camp. "With as many dead as we suffered . . ."

"Five," Orlis replied. He listed the names. They included one major, 1st Battalion's executive officer; one captain from 4th; and three lieutenants. The only dead officer from 2nd Battalion was Lieutenant Juan Gutierrez from Bravo Company. "We lost too many men," Orlis said. "Fighting from building to building in a town is bad enough, but to have to do it the hard way, without being able to call in heavy firepower to just flatten buildings, that's asking too much."

Lon turned to look at the captain, surprised at the hint of emotion in his voice, and the implied criticism in his words. *I guess you meant it when you said it never gets easy,* Lon thought. But Orlis was normally much more guarded in what he said.

"At least it's over, Captain," Lon said. *We won.*

"I hope it's over," Orlis said. "That depends on some

sort of settlement between the two worlds. And *that* depends on how rational their leaders are.''

It was the first time that Lon had swum in an ocean. A company at a time, 2nd Battalion went to the beach for an hour of recreation. Since the battalion's bivouac lacked showers, the rotation gave everyone a needed chance for personal hygiene.

"It's a good thing that Colonel Flowers has a very orderly mind," Tebba said to Lon as the first men started moving out into the water. "That puts Alpha Company first. We get a chance at the ocean before the rest of the battalion gets it so dirty that it's all mud for the first mile."

Lon laughed softly. His earlier dolor had lifted somewhat. He was ready for an excuse to laugh. "We'll give it a good start ourselves."

"They got any nasty critters in this ocean that we need to watch out for?" Tebba asked.

"Nothing was said. The locals use the beaches regularly, and push them for tourists. It must be more or less safe."

"More or less," Tebba said, his voice falling away with the words. He looked around. "I'll tell the men to stick together, at least two or three. Just in case."

Within minutes, virtually everyone was in the water. No man could get through recruit training on Dirigent without learning to swim, if he did not already know how. One of the tests that each trainee went through before he was allowed to graduate from boot camp was to swim fifty yards in battledress and boots. It was a serious challenge for all but the strongest swimmers.

Lon waded out until the gentle surge crested against his chest, thirty yards from shore, then leaned forward and started swimming away from the beach. The bottom was white sand, and sloped gently. The water was almost as clear as glass. Lon used a regular crawling stroke, pulling himself along as if he were in a pool on Dirigent, counting fifty strokes before he rolled onto his back and looked toward shore, to see how far out he was. Then he turned to the right and swam another fifty strokes before heading toward land again.

Swimming was a tonic for Lon. Concentrating on what he was doing made it easy to push everything else out of his mind—the tension of combat, even the men he had lost. As he neared groups of his men, he turned and swam farther from shore again, occasionally diving to estimate the depth of the water, or to look at some creature. He saw several brightly colored fishes, red and orange and an iridescent blue-green. He also saw a salmon-colored animal that looked as if it might be akin to lobsters scuttling across the sand, its body protected by a variety of knoblike projections. None of the sea life seemed inclined to molest him. All seemed happy to head in the opposite direction, away from the large intruder.

Lon finally headed back toward the beach. Many of his men had already emerged from the water, to lie in the sun or gather and talk. His platoons had stayed apart from Carl Hoper's platoons in the water, and on shore they gathered in separate cliques. There were no overt signs of rivalry between the groups—not on a strange world so soon after a costly fight. Back on Dirigent, in training or on field exercises, that might be different, with the platoons openly competing against each other.

As Lon waded out of the sea, the last of his men who were still in the water started toward the beach as well. Squad leaders checked to make sure that everyone was accounted for. Lon went to where he had dropped his clothes and helmet. He checked the time. Alpha Company's hour was almost up.

"Let's get started," Lon said, calling out toward the largest group of his men. "Bravo will be coming over the ridge any minute now." Captain Orlis and Company Lead Sergeant Jim Ziegler had not made the trek to the beach with the rest. Lon assumed that they would find a chance to get there, sooner or later, if they were unable to make more *civilized* arrangements for getting clean.

Towels were in short supply, but the sun and the heat-reflecting sand served to dry everyone quickly. The men dressed, with some joking among them. Lon nodded to himself. His men were professional enough to bounce back from just about anything. Another couple of days and they would be back to something approaching normal. Their dead comrades would not be forgotten, but the pain of loss would ebb.

Carl Hoper's platoons were the first to start hiking up the slope back toward camp. Lon's men were not far behind, but took a separate track. Neither lieutenant attempted to put his men in military formation, but the result was still not far from it. Veterans tended to group that way, and usually fell in step automatically. Even when they were on pass in Dirigent City, it was not unusual to see a group of off-duty soldiers walking in step along the street, as if they were on parade. Until one of them noticed and said something. Then, as often as not, they would consciously try to avoid it. For a time.

They ran into Bravo Company at the top of the rise. There was some joking back and forth between the new arrivals and the men who were leaving the beach, and questions about what the water was like. The two companies did not mix, or stop. Alpha did receive one piece of encouraging news. There would be a hot meal waiting—a change from the self-heating meal packs they had been living on since landing on Calypso. It was one more boost for morale.

"All we need now is word that we're heading home," Tebba told Lon. "Let Second Regiment hold the Calypsans' hands until they get over their scare of invasion."

"Do me a favor, Tebba," Lon said. "Don't go talking like that around the men. All we need is to start rumors, get their hopes up too soon."

"You know me, Lieutenant. I don't start rumors unless I'm ordered to." They both managed a chuckle over that.

Supper was not just a *hot* meal—it was also, by general consensus, extremely good. Their hosts had the dinner catered, served in each company's camp area. The Calypsan army had hired civilian chefs from The Cliffs' best tourist hotels. There was plenty of food, and most seemed naturally grown or raised rather than produced by nanotech replicators. The only thing missing, from the viewpoint of most of the men, was alcohol, and the Calypsan fruit drinks that served in place were *almost* an acceptable substitute. They talked about liquor, and wondered about the chances of getting passes to go into The Cliffs to see what the bars and hotels there offered for tourists.

"Nothing's been said about anything of the sort," Lon reminded Phip and his comrades in Tebba's squad. "Don't get your hopes up. That thirst of yours may well have to wait until we get back home, and that might still be six months from now."

"If I've got to wait six months to have a good nip, I might drink Dirigent City dry the first night," Phip said, a mock threat. "It would be a lot more prudent to give us all a chance to wet our whistles now and then while we're here, keep us from going amok when we get home. You don't want disciplinary hearings the second day we're back in barracks because we got drunk and disorderly, do you, Lieutenant?"

"I'll make sure we lay in a good supply of killjoy-patches," Lon said.

It was, overall, a pleasant evening. Between the afternoon's swim and the ample supper, Lon felt more relaxed than he had been since first hearing the news of the Calypso contract. When he finally got to bed, on an airpad in a sleeping bag, he fell asleep almost instantly. His slumber was deep, undisturbed by dreams—especially nightmares. That sleep lasted little more than four hours, though. Lon and Carl Hoper were wakened by Captain Orlis's orderly just after two in the morning.

"Captain wants you both, right now, sirs," the orderly said once the two lieutenants were awake. "There's trouble, I think."

"What kind of trouble?" Hoper asked while Lon was trying to control a yawn that threatened to dislocate his jaw.

The orderly shook his head. "I don't know for sure,

Lieutenant. He had a call from battalion headquarters. He looked worried when he sent me to fetch you.''

It did not take Lon and Carl long to dress. They carried their helmets as they followed the orderly to Captain Orlis's tent. Orlis was sitting outside it. A small lamp provided enough illumination for conversation.

''It's not over,'' Orlis said when his lieutenants arrived. ''Sit down.'' There were no chairs or stools, so Carl and Lon sat on the ground, as Orlis had.

''What is it, Captain?'' Lon asked.

''It looks as if Belletiene isn't ready to let go,'' Orlis said. ''CIC has spotted at least seven ships on course for Calypso from Belletiene, and they haven't answered any of our queries. We can't be certain yet, but it looks like they're sending another invasion force.''

21

The fleet traveling from Belletiene to Calypso was visible to the detection systems of the Dirigent ships the entire time they were en route. The trip would take slightly more than three days.

On Calypso, preparations were made based on the assumption that it was indeed a second invasion force—since none of the approaching ships was answering queries. After consultation with local military and governmental leaders, Colonel Gaffney dispatched a message rocket to Dirigent, detailing the supposition that they were about to face a second enemy army, perhaps as much as twice the size of the force that had been present when the regiment landed. Gaffney expressed his ''hope'' that 2nd Regiment had already been dispatched as planned.

Colonel Gaffney shared all of that information with his officers, the afternoon after the Belletiener fleet had been spotted. ''But, as you know,'' he continued, ''even if the Council of Regiments dispatched those reinforcements immediately on receipt of my message that the invasion had occurred before we arrived, we're looking at a minimum of another twenty-five days before help can arrive.'' The requirements of interstellar passages made that time immutable. ''Until then, we're on our own, us and the Calypsans.'' The only good news was the colonel's reminder that they had warships and a squadron of Shrikes to meet the invaders. With a little luck, the enemy would not be able to land everyone they might bring, and every ship or shuttle shot down would improve the odds for the men on the ground.

Gaffney detailed the preparations that the regiment, and the Calypsan army, would make. There was no time to recruit and train civilians to bolster the ranks of the defenders, but civilians would be enlisted to provide information on enemy movements. The local army and the mercenaries would concentrate their efforts on the defense of Oceanview and The Cliffs, with the Dirigenters ready to use shuttles to transfer men in case the enemy chose to attack elsewhere first. Supplies and vehicles would be gathered and positioned at a number of points, just in case. Dirigenters were being detailed to help choose defensive strong points around the two cities.

"Since we can't know where the enemy might land, there are limits to what we can do to prepare," Gaffney said. "We can set up our perimeter around Oceanview and man a few key points on the outskirts of The Cliffs, but that's about the limit. We'll have to react when they arrive." Packing up and leaving for Dirigent before the new Belletiener army could arrive was not mentioned. The Corps had accepted a contract. It would be honored.

Seven ships, then three more. The second group was moving faster than the first and would, according to CIC's calculations, rendezvous with the first group just before they reached Calypso. The faster vessels were assumed to be warships sent to cover the landings and deal with the Dirigenters' fleet. The ETA for the combined fleet was honed. The earliest minute that the Belletieners could reach orbit was noted and circulated. Preparations needed to be complete by that time.

When that time came, at three o'clock in the afternoon, Oceanview time, the soldiers were still working, assisted by civilian laborers. The Belletiener ships had slowed earlier than expected. They would not be in position until slightly before sunset.

"They want the night for cover, the same way we would," Weil Jorgen commented to Lon. "They'll come in when it's full dark."

Lon shrugged. "It doesn't matter. We'll have a few

minutes warning when they launch their landers.''

''I figure they'll drop far enough from us that they don't have to worry about us on the ground until they're set,'' Jorgen said. ''The way we'd do it. They've got to have enough smarts not to come down right in the middle of us.''

''Always give the other guy credit for being at least as smart as you are,'' Lon said, almost a quote from a half dozen instructors and mentors he had had over the years. ''Even then, there's always the chance you're underestimating him.''

''You seen any data on how many soldiers Belletiene has?'' Weil asked. ''I don't mean just what we've seen and this new bunch. I mean, how many times could they throw a force against Calypso before they run out?''

''I haven't got a clue, Weil. I'm surprised they could throw a second army against Calypso with the first all killed or captured.''

''That's another thing that bothers me. Keeping all those prisoners secure in the face of new fighting is going to be tricky as hell. Dangerous.''

''We can't just line them up against a wall and shoot them, or let Calypso do it.''

''I know, Lieutenant, but that would make life a lot simpler for us the next few days.''

Regimental headquarters provided a continuous feed from CIC as the new armada from Belletiene approached and the battle in space was joined. Only rarely was there a burst of light that could be seen from the ground to mark the fight. Most of the battle in space was well to the west of Oceanview. To Lon's surprise, the fight was almost equal. Belletiene had fewer fighters, but their capital ships were well armed, and the crews knew their business. The regiment's transports had been moved out of harm's way prior to the arrival of the enemy. The escorts moved to engage the invaders farther from the surface, in an attempt to keep them from launching shuttles to land troops. That was only partially successful. The Belletiener ships kept coming. Fighters were launched, then shuttles. A few shuttles were destroyed, but—to Lon's pragmatic thinking—too few. The bulk of the landers came on, protected by rocket and beamer fire from the ships that had launched them, and by the aerospace fighters that came in with them. Then, finally, it was possible for CIC to plot where the shuttles were likely to land—south and southwest of The Cliffs, more than ten miles from where the bulk of the defenses were.

"There may be more troops that haven't been launched yet," a message from CIC said. "It's possible that there are as many as two thousand more soldiers available." That possibility limited the response of the Calypsan government and Colonel Gaffney. Not all of the available defenders could be moved south to meet this first wave—if that was what it was—of the new invasion.

"Our Third and Fourth Battalions are being hurried south, along with one battalion of the Calypsan army," Lon told his noncoms as soon as he had been briefed. "That should make the numbers there about equal. The rest of us are going to have to adjust to cover more of the perimeter up here."

"Anything more on whether or not there are more troops waiting to come in?" Tebba Girana asked.

"It looks as if the Belletiener fleet is going to make a tight orbit. If they're planning on launching another strike tonight, it could come in as little as ninety minutes," Lon said. "But that's guesswork. If they do have additional soldiers up there, nothing says they have to commit them right away. They might hold them back for hours, waiting to see how the fight develops. We deal with what we know about, and wait for them to show their hand."

"My guess," Weil said, not quite interrupting, "is that they'll want to put those extra soldiers, if they exist, on the ground as quickly as possible, because they're going to be in as much danger up there as they would be down here. And losing troops before they get dirtside is one hell of a waste."

"Let's hope for a lot of waste," Wil Nace said. "The

more our sky-guys space, the fewer we have to worry about."

On the ground, the waiting continued. Alpha Company spread its men to cover a slightly larger segment of the defenses for Oceanview. They were on the north side of the capital, as far from the expected landing zones of the new invaders as anyone.

Belletiene landed without opposition on the ground, though they were dogged all the way in by Dirigenter fighters. Lon saw one flaming craft arc across the southern horizon, but there was no way for him to determine whether it was friend or foe.

They're going to have time to get organized on the ground before any of our people get close enough to engage, Lon thought. He felt a growing anxiety even though the fighting would be far away from him and his men. Battle had been joined again, with too many uncertainties.

The Belletiener fleet completed its orbit of Calypso. More shuttles were launched, also with fighter cover. Lon waited for word as to where these landers might be aimed. It was another twenty minutes before the news came from CIC. They were headed north of Oceanview, possibly to an area within five miles of Lon's platoons.

Lon took in a deep but fluttering breath and held it. *Our turn,* he told himself.

22

Lon anticipated orders for the regiment to move to intercept the enemy, but they did not come. "We're staying here," Captain Orlis told him. "Our instructions are to make certain that the invaders do not get into Oceanview. As long as they want to muck about in the forest, we let them. Our fighters will continue to hit them, as they can. And keep us posted on their movement."

"Aren't we even going to put out patrols to slow them down?" Lon asked.

Orlis's no was too terse, too contained. "We man the line and wait for them to come to us."

That's foolish, Lon thought, but he did not say it. The order had to have come from Colonel Gaffney, probably under pressure from the Calypsan government. *We're not meant to be static. It's all about mobility.*

It would have been too much to hope for that the Shrikes would knock all of the enemy shuttles out of the sky, or even half. *But it would be nice,* Lon told himself, *like winning a tontine.* The Dirigenters left to guard the capital were near the outer edge of the native forest left around the city on all sides but the east, where they would have clear fields of fire. A series of fallbacks had also been readied. The risk in that scheme had been that the invaders would guess correctly about the disposition of troops and make their landings in the heart of Oceanview, which was guarded by only a few platoons —though heavily equipped with surface-to-air missiles. They might have shot down a few shuttles, but would have been insufficient to deal with the troops who managed to land safely.

"We wait," Lon whispered on a radio linkup with Tebba and Weil. The sounds of fighting were audible, dogfights between Dirigenter and Belletiener fighters, the rapid-fire cannon as the Shrikes strafed enemy troops who made it to the ground, and the explosion of missiles. Except for the cannon fire, it was rather like listening to a distant thunderstorm. The flashes were similar enough to lightning hidden by clouds to complete the illusion. It ended almost as quickly as a summer thunderstorm as well. The combatants had to burn for orbit to rendezvous with their motherships—for ammunition and fuel, if nothing else.

"How soon do you think they'll get here, Lieutenant?" Phip Steesen asked when Lon stopped for a few minutes near that squad. Lon had started making the rounds, pausing to talk with each group of men.

Lon shrugged. "If they push hard, they could be here in an hour, Phip." There was no humor in the short laugh—almost a grunt—he used for punctuation. "If their luck was good and they didn't get slowed down by the mines and booby traps we set." Explosives had been brought down from the ships soon after the new Belletiener fleet had been spotted, and the Calypsans had also uncrated much of their remaining stockpiles.

"Any word on how many of them made it to the ground?" Lance Corporal Dav Grott asked.

"The last estimate I heard was three thousand on our end of it." Lon paused. "Give or take five hundred."

"Which means they don't have any idea?" Dav suggested.

"That's about the size of it. And maybe the same number, with the same margin of error, on the other end, down past The Cliffs," Lon said.

"Puts us on the short end of the numbers, doesn't it—even allowing for the Calypsans?"

"Not by all that much," Lon said. "Even if there are seven thousand of the enemy this time, that's not much worse than seven-to-five, and we're the defenders. That should make up the difference, not even allowing for the fact that we're supposed to be the super-professionals. And if the estimates are off all the way in the other direction, the numbers would be about even.''

"I'd feel a lot better with the numbers working in our favor," Dav said. "A whole lot better."

"This is our business, Dav."

Lon knew that he had time for the moments of byplay during his tour. He was receiving updates from CIC, and there were electronic snoops out in front of the lines, up to five hundred yards away. And there was always a chance that the enemy would not head directly at the few hundred yards of perimeter that Alpha Company of the 2nd Battalion was guarding.

That chance became slimmer in a hurry, though.

"Almost enough to make a man paranoid," Tebba said when they received more definite information on the course the Belletieners were taking. "That whole army is coming straight toward us. Straight toward me is how it feels," he added, shaking his head.

"I know what you mean," Lon replied. He had shared the news of the enemy's approach with his men immediately. The Belletieners were more than two miles away, far enough that a change of course was not impossible but Lon planned for the worst. A force the size of a complete Dirigenter regiment might try to poke through precisely the section of the perimeter he was responsible for. "Give us a chance to show what we can do."

Tebba snorted at the bravado. "Gonna have to keep you away from those adventure vids, Lieutenant," he said. "You're starting to sound like some Galactic Ranger."

Lon laughed. He could feel his tension growing, and any release was welcome. It made the waiting easier to bear. "My secret is out," he said, his voice no more than a whisper, even amplified by Tebba's earphones.

It was three in the morning when the point squads of the Belletieners came within range of the first snoops. Five hundred yards. "Get everyone down and in position," Lon told his noncoms. A couple of minutes later, he heard an explosion and saw the brief flash of flame as one of the land mines went off. *Four hundred yards off,* he thought. That was where the first line of explosives had been planted.

Lon was in his slit trench, on his knees watching the far side of the clearing, with the visor of his helmet set to maximum magnification. For the last 150 yards, the enemy would be in the open, easy targets if they were foolish enough to try a frontal assault over that much open ground. An attack like that, against a trained force of defenders with automatic weapons, would be almost suicidal, without some advantage—such as tanks or close-air support. Heroism alone would not do it.

They have to know we're here, Lon thought. *We haven't been observing full electronic silence, and they had to expect that the capital would be defended.*

"Be on the watch for enemy aircraft," Lon warned. There had been nothing from CIC, regiment, or battalion, but the Belletieners had to have *something* planned.

Captain Orlis called Lon and Carl Hoper. "They must be setting up in that next patch of woods," he told the two lieutenants. "I think we've got a few minutes before anything happens. Their ships have launched fighters again. If they're coming our way, it will take them fifteen minutes to get here."

More waiting, Lon thought. The palms of his hands started to sweat. He dried them off quickly, wishing he had something to stop the perspiration completely. Someone might notice, and realize that he was . . . nervous.

Fifteen minutes passed. It was another two minutes before Lon heard the sounds of aircraft coming in at transonic speeds. Lon felt his shoulders tighten. He had been in a prone firing position, on his elbows, looking over the end of his trench. At the sound of aircraft, he went completely flat, waiting for the first sounds of attack. But the fighters did not attack the perimeter. The aircraft—Lon thought that there had to be at least six—kept going toward the center of Oceanview. Seconds later, Lon heard the first explosions, south of his position.

"There's no one there for them to hit," Tebba said on

his channel to Lon. "They must be trying to destroy Government House since they haven't been able to capture it."

"Something," Lon said. "Maybe they think that will draw men away from the perimeter and make it easier for their infantry."

"Will it?" Tebba asked.

"I doubt it," Lon said. *I hope not.* The tactic would not get a professional military leader like Colonel Gaffney to change his dispositions, but Gaffney might not have the final say. The Calypsans were so concerned about the safety of their capital that they might insist, or might pull their own troops back to protect the government buildings, leaving the mercenaries on the front line even more shorthanded than they already were.

The Belletiener attack on the government district did not go completely unopposed. There were still a few teams of Calypsan soldiers there with surface-to-air rockets, and Dirigenter fighters came in from above to challenge the move. But there were too few interceptors in the air, and the men on the ground had minimal success with their shoulder-launched missiles. The Belletiener pilots mostly stayed high enough to give themselves time to escape any rocket coming up from the surface.

Then, abruptly, the Belletieners changed their target, veering away from the center of Oceanview to attack the defensive perimeter. The Dirigenters had little warning. The enemy fighters were operating at speeds that meant that only a few seconds elapsed from the change of course until the fighters were making their strafing and rocket runs along the line of defenders. For the most part, there was nothing that Lon and his men could do but press themselves into the dirt near a side of their slit trenches, presenting as small a target as possible.

Each platoon of mercenaries had two rocket launchers. Those were loaded and ready for use, but the response was only minimally successful. The enemy fighters were past and climbing out of range too quickly. Only one enemy fighter exploded, then cartwheeled to the ground in pieces. By the time it hit—far to the west—the defenders were just starting to lift their heads to check for casualties among their comrades. Several men had been wounded and needed treatment. Luckily, there had been no fatalities in Lon's platoons.

"Keep an eye out for the enemy on the ground!" Lon warned on his all-hands circuit. "If they're coming, this could be the time."

The Belletiener infantry *was* coming, or, at least, they had started to shoot. They were too far off yet for accurate fire from rocket-propelled grenades, but their rifles opened up, aiming for men who were attempting to assist wounded comrades. Then Lon heard the *whoosh* of rockets, looked up, and saw the trails of small missiles coming in. He yelled a warning over his radio. Three rockets passed over the heads of Lon's men and exploded behind them—when they struck something. The missiles were not designed as anti-personnel weapons; they were meant for tanks or aircraft, with armor-piercing warheads.

"Just as soon have them waste those like this," Tebba said on his link to Lon. "Can't do us much harm, and every one of those rockets they shoot our way means one less they've got to shoot at our fly-guys."

"Until they get lucky and have one of them explode near enough to hit someone," Lon said, more coldly than he had intended. "There's enough shrapnel in those to kill a squad."

For several minutes there was nothing but static fighting, long-range sniping, almost exclusively by Belletieners. Lon had given only his men with beamers clearance to fire if they had a solid target. Then Weil Jorgen called. "Looks like they're starting to move, Lieutenant. It looks as if they're aiming to cut the line to our right, either through our first and second platoons or where Bravo is."

Lon shifted his weight onto his left side to look to the right without exposing himself to enemy fire. There did seem to be a heavier concentration of that fire in that direction, but he was no more certain of exactly how far over it was than Jorgen was. There was too much space between adjoining units. They were spread thin.

"I see what you mean, Weil," Lon said. "But even if the point of the thrust is there, they're sure to broaden it, and that means they'll be coming against us soon enough."

"If they're not just probing for weak spots," Jorgen replied. "If that's what's going on, there could be a lot of false starts before they find a route they like."

"I don't think that's what they're doing. They've got about everyone they brought massed. It looks as if they've decided where they're going to attack, regardless of the defenses."

"There's about ninety yards open between us and Bravo Company," Weil said. "Could be that's where they're going."

Just have to make sure the perimeter holds, Lon thought—knowing that would be impossible if the enemy threw three thousand men against it. If the enemy broke the line, they would limit the ability of the defenders to respond. But a ninety-yard gap was not excessive. The enfilading fire zones on either side overlapped through most of the distance the enemy had to cross.

"Be smart with ammo," Lon said on his all-hands circuit. *One Belletiener, one bullet would be nice.* "There are a lot of them out there." When the perimeter was established, extra stocks of rifle ammunition and grenades had been distributed to each unit. But there could never be enough for peace of mind.

The Belletieners started their assault. Lon could not fault the fire-and-maneuver tactics the enemy used. It made their advance extremely slow, but it was the only hope they had—other than a suicidal run across the broad kill zone. While two or three platoons advanced, crawling when they could, the rest of the Belletieners kept up heavy suppressive fire.

"When you've got targets, fire," Lon ordered his platoons after receiving the same order from Captain Orlis. But they were at the periphery of the fight. They were receiving incoming fire, but there were few clear targets for Lon's men, and those were at extreme range. Lon did not do any shooting. For the time being, his energies were better directed at observation—careful not to expose himself any more than necessary to enemy sniper fire.

By monitoring the common channel used by the lieutenants and captains in the battalion, Lon was able to follow the fight more closely than he could just by looking over the lip of his trench. The wedge of the Belletiener attack expanded slowly to either side as the point got closer to the defensive perimeter. More troops moved into the wedge, increasing the pace of the assault as their weapons made it harder for the Dirigenters to provide a sufficient volume of accurate gunfire. But as the size of the wedge increased, Lon's men had better targets.

We're never going to hold them, Lon decided fifteen minutes after the assault had started. *They keep coming the way they are, they'll cut right through the line.* "Tebba, Weil," Lon said, switching to their channel. "Slide one or two men back from each platoon to where we've got the extra ammo. If we have to pull back in a hurry, I don't want to leave any of it behind."

"We got as much of it distributed before as we could, Lieutenant," Weil said.

Tebba added, "We got all of the grenades. I think two men can carry all the rifle ammo still back there."

"Well, get it. But carefully. I don't want to lose anyone in the process. The Belletieners are taking more interest in us now. And it's only likely to get worse."

Time twisted around on itself, as it always did for Lon when he was in combat, when fear and adrenaline flowed. At the same time, it seemed to speed up and slow to a crawl. His senses seemed preternaturally acute, his mind running at peak speed. That made external time drag. With the near flank of the Belletiener wedge getting closer, Lon started taking a few shots, when he had a clear target. Each time, he squeezed off a short burst. The goal was to fire three bullets at a time; Lon was rarely more than one off in either direction.

The attacking troops were taking heavy casualties. That was inescapable. But they kept coming. When the platoons at the point lost too many men to remain effective, they went flat and waited until new troops could be sent forward to reinforce them, and then they started moving again, leap-frogging each other—often by no more than one or two yards at a time.

Two men in Lon's fourth platoon were wounded within seconds of each other. A medical orderly crawled toward the nearest, and was himself hit. He managed to crawl on until he could slide into the trench with the first of the men he had been going to, but he could do little more; his own wound was too serious. By the time another medic could reach him, the first medic was dead. The second went on to treat the two wounded men.

A tree almost directly behind Lon seemed to explode—struck by a rocket. The missile hit five feet up, and the trunk snapped, adding wooden shrapnel to the metallic variety from the rocket. The tree seemed to stand suspended over the break for an instant, then the weight of its branches dropped it—toward Lon. He had lowered his head inside his trench, and brought his arms in close to his body at the sound of the explosion. He felt the sharp pricks of small projectiles hitting his back, and the stings of several injuries. Then the tree came down on top of him. Branches snapped as they absorbed much of the energy of the falling tree, cushioning its impact. The trunk did not land directly across Lon's slit trench, but there were branches pressing against him, not *quite* pinning him where he was.

The air was knocked out of Lon. He needed a moment to recover from that before he even became aware of the pain of the shrapnel hits. Those stung, and burned.

"Lieutenant?" Lon recognized Tebba's voice, but was slow to respond.

"I'm okay, I think," Lon said, the words separated from each other as if they were only distant dictionary entries. "I took a couple of hits, either wood slivers or shrapnel. Then the tree came down on top of me."

"Can you move?" Tebba asked. "Or do we have to pry the tree off of you first?"

"I'll let you know as soon as I find out," Lon said, blinking several times. There was an edge of—almost—

shock slowing his mind. It was difficult to draw a full breath.

He moved cautiously, experimenting to discover if movement would bring increased pain. When it did not, he tried pushing himself back toward the rear end of his trench, then tried sliding left, farther away from the tree trunk. The branches covering him pressed down, and caught in his clothing and gear.

"I could move if it wasn't for this tree," Lon said. "I'll have to cut my way free. You pay attention to what's going on. Don't try to come in for me. I'll get out on my own."

It took ten minutes for Lon to cut his way out. He used his bayonet, thankful for the time he had spent stropping the blade until it was razor sharp. The fallen tree would have provided excellent cover, but Lon could not see what was going on from under the tangle. The branches and leaves were impenetrable on the end nearest the enemy. And Lon feared not being able to see what was going on more than he feared the loss of protection.

By the time he did get out and was able to see the progress of the battle again, the tip of the enemy wedge had reached the ninety-yard gap in the defensive perimeter.

23

"All hell's breaking loose,'' Captain Orlis said, talking to both of his lieutenants by radio. Carl Hoper's platoons had moved back until they were with Lon's, facing the Belletieners on two sides, and the captain had moved his command post at the same time. ''If we can't shut off this breakthrough in a hurry, we're going to have the biggest mess you ever dreamed of.''

''We getting any help?'' Carl asked.

''There'll be two fighters down in six minutes, four more eight minutes later,'' Orlis said. ''But on the ground, we're it for now. It's going to take time to move troops up from the west side of the perimeter. They're already moving, and Calypso is moving some of its people around from the east. But for at least the next ninety minutes, we're pretty much on our own.''

''Whichever way they turn, they've got the numbers to roll us up,'' Lon observed. His wounds, all minor, had been treated. Slivers of wood had been pulled from his back and thighs and med-patches applied over the wounds. The anesthetic had already numbed the pain, but Lon's legs felt stiff.

''If they bother,'' Orlis said. ''So far, it looks as if their only goal is to push through to Government House.''

''That doesn't make any sense!'' Hoper protested. ''They can't ignore us. What the hell good would it do to take a building four miles away and leave us all to close back in on them?''

''You're asking the wrong man,'' Orlis said. ''Our orders are to hold as best we can, make the breakthrough as expensive for the enemy as we can, buy time for Colonel Gaffney and the locals to move more men into position.''

The only way we have to slow them down is to make them take the time to kill us, Lon thought. He swallowed hard. *And I thought the Corps didn't believe in 'last stands.'*

Two minutes later, even harder orders came from Lieutenant Colonel Flowers. ''We're to counterattack, try to pinch the gap closed again, minimize the penetration,'' Captain Orlis told his lieutenants. ''Bravo Company will attack simultaneously from the other side. Charlie and Delta are moving in to take care of the ones still to the north. We'll worry about the soldiers who've already pushed through the gap later.'' Lon thought that he could hear anger in the captain's voice.

''Nolan, we'll pivot on your fourth platoon, use the other three platoons to try to push our half of the gap closed. Hoper, your platoons will be on the wide end. We go in three minutes.''

Automatically, Lon checked the timeline on his visor display. He passed the orders on to Tebba and Weil.

''Pivot on us?'' Weil asked. ''Hell, it's all we can do to hold with everyone here. They'll step on us like we were bugs.''

''Sting hard then, Weil,'' Lon said. ''We do what we're told.''

The first two Shrikes hit the Belletieners in the gap while Alpha and Bravo companies were marshaling for their counterattack. The planes came from the south, diving straight into the advancing enemy, as if they were trying to stick fingers in a leaking dike. They strafed with rapid-fire cannon and fired rockets. The ferocity of the attack had to stop the Belletiener advance, if only for a few seconds. Before they could start to move again, the mercenaries on the ground started toward them.

Lon moved with third platoon, staying close—almost too close—to Tebba and his second squad. They all crawled, one squad moving forward a few feet while the other three squads provided covering fire. Then the next squad edged forward.

The first pair of aircraft came back for a second pass, then peeled off to the east, climbing for orbit. Until the next fighters came in, the men on the ground would be alone again.

During the first moments of the advance, the enemy did not seem to be aware that a counterattack had started on the ground. The Belletieners in the wedge resumed firing at them, but much of that fire went well overhead, as if it were still aimed at the positions that Lon's men had abandoned.

The attack from the air left them dazed, Lon guessed. It would not last long. "Let's push it a little before they get their wits back," he told Tebba. Then he called Captain Orlis and said the same thing, making it a suggestion this time.

"Do what you can," Orlis told both lieutenants. Like them, Orlis was moving forward, with his headquarters squad, only a few yards behind the line.

Dirigenters did not go into combat wearing body armor. That had proved to be a vain quest generations before. Whenever better body armor was invented, someone else came along with bullets that would penetrate it, until the necessary level of protection could only be had at a cost—in weight—that was too much to allow an infantryman to carry an effective load of anything else. Only their helmets provided any real protection against small arms fire and shrapnel—as much for the benefit of the electronics as for the soldier—and even that was not one hundred percent effective.

Lon felt one bullet ricochet off his helmet. The force of the slug slammed his face into the dirt, dazed him, and started a ringing in his ears that shut out any other sound. When he did start to hear voices on his radio again, they seemed hollow, faint. He shook his head, trying to clear it, and ran the helmet's diagnostics to make certain that the electronics were still functioning.

He slid forward another six inches, firing a couple of

short bursts as he moved. The enemy was so close that they were almost impossible to miss if they got any higher off the ground than Lon was. He moved behind the trunk of a tree about eighteen inches thick. That could cover him from only some of the enemy.

A deep breath. Lon squeezed his eyes shut for just an instant. They had been watering freely. He blinked several times to clear his vision. The radio chatter was louder, almost normal.

"Flatten out and stay put!" Lon recognized Captain Orlis's voice, then noted that he was on the company all-hands channel. Lon went motionless. No more than five seconds passed before he heard incoming fighters and their streams of cannon rounds and rockets. The two Shrikes went south to north, through the Belletieners who were part of the breakthrough and across the open field to spray the enemy troops who were covering the assault. One fighter peeled left and the other right.

Orlis changed channels to talk to his lieutenants and noncoms. "There'll be four passes altogether, two by this pair of fighters and two by the next. As soon as the fourth pass ends, we go, and we keep going until we link up with Bravo."

That'll help, Lon thought, his faceplate in the dirt. *It takes time to recover from that sort of hell.* Aerial strafing could be deadly when the targets were in the open with no cover . . . and the Belletieners in the gap between Alpha and Bravo had very little. Much of what foliage there had been had already been shredded, and each aerial assault pruned it back even more. Lon turned his head to the side, so that he could see a little of what was going on. The Shrikes came back for their second pass. The cannons opened up earlier this time, targeting the enemy troops who had taken the tip of the Belletiener wedge past the defensive line on the ground.

Lon watched the strobing muzzle blasts of one Shrike's cannon, saw the trail of fire and smoke behind a missile. Then the aircraft was past, out of sight, but the sounds of guns and rockets continued, marching north through the enemy troops.

Don't give them time to start moving again, Lon thought. *Keep hitting them until they're too shocked to do anything.* He could not think of the enemy as humans now, not men like him, obeying orders and trying to do their duty. The worse they were hurt now—the more killed and wounded— the easier it would be for Lon and *his* men. Fewer friends and comrades would die.

The next pair of Shrikes made their first run. The return of the cacophony shut out the cries of wounded and dying Belletieners, some of them no more than thirty yards from where Lon lay. The strip of forest itself continued to suffer mightily from the airborne assault. Bullets ripped through foliage and snapped small branches, wounded larger branches and even trunks. Rockets blew trees, some of them a century or more old, into kindling. Lon could smell burning wood, a new tincture added to the odors of com- bat—predominantly the smell of gunpowder and other ex- plosives. Lon tried to assure himself that there was too much moisture in the trees and grass for the fires to spread far. The wood was not dry enough for the fires to burgeon into a major conflagration that might be more dangerous than the Belletieners.

Another pass. For a few seconds, Lon squeezed his eyes shut, focusing inside. Soon, he would have to get up with his men. Once the last pass of the fighters ended, Lon and his men would be up and moving across the river of blood and death that the Shrikes were leaving.

''Tebba, Weil. When the time comes, get everyone mov- ing in a hurry,'' Lon said. ''The quicker we make this link up, the fewer casualties we'll take. Get the hole plugged, then worry about the enemy inside our perimeter later.''

''It's like a slaughterhouse out there, Lieutenant,'' Tebba said. ''I can see a couple of men who were chopped up so bad it's hard to tell they were human.''

I wish you hadn't said that, Lon thought, feeling a spasm in his stomach.

The fifth pass went through. In the few seconds of quiet

following it, Lon thought that he heard fewer wounded Bel-letieners moaning or crying for help. He tried not to think about men who had already been seriously wounded being killed, but the more he tried to steer his thoughts elsewhere, the more they concentrated on that image. *Better them than us* did not help as much as Lon thought it would.

"Get ready," Captain Orlis ordered. "As soon as the Shrikes move past us again, we move."

Lon passed those orders to his noncoms, then replaced the magazine in his rifle, putting a full one in and sticking the not quite empty one in a pouch on his belt. He checked to make certain that there was a round in the chamber, and that the safety was off. Then the Shrikes returned.

Lon shifted his weight, ready to get up and move forward as quickly as possible when Captain Orlis gave the order. He was expecting the order, but when it came, it still startled him.

"Go!" Lon said on the channel that connected him to everyone in his platoons. He was pushing himself up as he spoke, getting his knees under him, then springing to his feet, his rifle moving into firing position.

The scene in front of him had changed since the last time he had looked. It was as if a tornado had swept a forty-yard-wide channel through the arc of trees that cut Ocean-view off from the rest of Calypso. Two dozen air-to-surface missiles and more than twenty-five thousand rounds of 25-millimeter cannon shot had turned the forest into a macabre salad. Tree trunks and branches were scattered like forgotten toys. A bluish haze hung over the ground. Here and there Lon could see fallen enemy soldiers . . . or remnants of them. Even in infrared there was a haze across his vision, hot spots from small fires, charred bits of wood and flesh, and the bodies of both live and dead Belletieners. Lon's gag reflex came and went so quickly that he scarcely noticed it. There were more important things to concentrate on.

Lon moved forward with third platoon's second squad. He looked for targets, for threats, but saw nothing in front or to either side. There did not seem to be anyone firing toward his men. He had gone forward four or five steps before he heard the sound of the Shrikes' weapons cease as they completed their pass, swinging along the enemy lines to the north.

He almost tripped over a leg. Just a leg, in boot and camouflage battledress. Lon stopped for an instant, then kicked the disembodied leg to the side, under the fallen branch of one of the many destroyed trees. *Right leg,* he realized after it was out of sight—not that it made any difference.

"Okay, Tebba, start peeling off the squads to form the new defensive line," Lon said a moment later. "Keep the line close. We've only got eighty yards of front to cover with three platoons." The original gap between Alpha and Bravo had been ninety yards. The Belletiener wedge had rolled back the lines another seventy yards before the Dirigenters stopped them.

One by one, third platoon's squads were pulled out of the advance across the gap and directed to establish new positions to close the breach. Carl Hoper's platoons went on; then they too started moving into defensive positions. They could see the men coming from the other side, from Bravo Company, before there was any indication of renewed enemy activity. Scattered rifle fire started coming from the north again. The line was complete across the breach before there was any heavier enemy action.

"They're coming again," Captain Orlis announced, biting off each word without inflection.

Lon looked over the tree trunk he had taken shelter behind, just enough to see. The Belletieners were coming forward again in another wedge, starting almost from scratch, picking up survivors as they moved along. It took Lon a moment to realize that they were not coming directly toward the spot where they had made the first breakthrough, but off to his right, where Bravo Company was, and maybe a little beyond.

What's driving them? Lon wondered. *What keeps them going?* He did not try to answer the question. He turned to the business of directing the fire of his men into the point and flank of the new enemy advance.

Then a second wedge started, to the left, picking up more of the survivors of the first attack.

"They break through on both sides, we're going to be left hanging with our butts in the breeze," Weil told Lon. "And I don't see how the hell we can stop them again, unless we've got more Shrikes coming down in the next few minutes."

Thirty yards away from fourth platoon's sergeant, Lon shook his head. It was unlikely that they would get more close air support that quickly. It took too long for the turn-around, the trip up to the fleet for rearming and refueling and the trip back down. It would be a miracle if there were Shrikes on the spot in anything under an hour.

"We do what we can, Weil," Lon said. "Don't forget to have someone keeping a watch on our backsides. There might be a couple of hundred of the enemy inside the perimeter."

"I got one man in each squad looking south," Weil said. Lon nodded to himself. That was the same arrangement Tebba had set up for third platoon.

For the next thirty minutes, the fighting was intense along the entire section of front that Lon could monitor. The new Belletiener wedges stalled, unable to get past the middle of the open killing zone between the two armies. More Dirigenters arrived from the western part of the perimeter around Oceanview, adding their weapons to the fight. Then the wedge on the east started forward again. Belletiene pushed more men into that. Just before they reached the line of Dirigenters, the invaders were hit by another pair of Shrikes.

This time, the Belletieners were ready, and they hit back. Lon was certain that at least two dozen antiaircraft missiles were launched at the Shrikes. The lead aircraft exploded before it got to the line. The second corkscrewed to the ground, almost in the middle of the protruding wedge of enemy soldiers.

Lon felt bile rise in his throat. He was certain that he

heard enemy soldiers cheering the downing of the two planes. *We're in for it now,* he thought as the Dirigenters surged forward again. Within minutes, the perimeter was again breached. More Belletieners charged across the field, into the gap. No matter how many casualties they took, they kept coming.

And kept going. They did not stop to continue the fight, except long enough to allow the rest of their force to cross the gap and move through the open hole. They broke through and headed on, into Calypso's capital, leaving behind their dead and anyone who was too seriously wounded to keep up.

24

"Battalion's estimate is that two thousand Belletieners made it through our line," Captain Orlis told his lieutenants after he had taken part in a briefing for all of the Dirigenter company commanders in the Oceanview sector. "Calypso has pulled its troops from the lines around the city to hit them as quickly as possible, to try to stop them . . . or slow them down until we can get back into the act. Except for Second Battalion, the rest of our people on the perimeter will be moving within the next fifteen minutes. Only a few platoons will be left to mount patrols."

"When does our turn come?" Lon asked.

"Soon," Orlis replied. "We deal with our casualties and those the enemy left. We do a little scouting to find out how many Belletieners were killed in the breakthrough. Then we get our asses moving, trail the Belletieners, stay behind them while everyone else tries to get in front of them. We take care of any strong points they establish between here and there, wherever 'there' is, and block any attempt they make to retreat. Tentatively, we move in two hours."

"We make our plans based on that assumption?" Carl Hoper asked. It was always better to get orders spelled out in detail.

"We plan on that basis until we know differently," the captain confirmed. "In part, it depends on how long it takes to care for our wounded." He paused. "A large part. I haven't heard the count yet, except for the rough numbers I got from you and Nolan. I'm waiting for the medics to give me something firmer."

"Who does the scouting?" Lon asked.

"Charlie and Delta, since they're the ones who didn't take the brunt of the attacks. They've already got men out starting the count and looking to make sure there aren't more of the enemy lurking around to play hell with us."

Lon's platoons were becoming seriously depleted. Three men had died in the Belletiener breakthrough, two from fourth platoon and one from third. Five men were wounded seriously enough to need time in trauma tubes, and two of those might have to be sent up to the fleet for rehab before they could return to duty. There were another nine less seriously wounded men who, like Lon, were able to continue.

It was too soon for Lon to feel anything emotionally about the loss of more men. His mind was too numb to deal with it. Even his own aches were unable to make much impression. He did those things that were immediately necessary, talking to his squad leaders and to groups of men. He listened to them. He gave necessary orders. But he was little more than an automaton, going through the motions. He did not think to take a few sips of water or eat a meal until Tebba suggested it, with some force.

The water did little to temper the dryness of Lon's mouth and throat. The food went down with difficulty. After he had forced half of it down, Lon went to where Carl Hoper was sitting, likewise eating. Hoper seemed glad for an excuse to set his meal pack aside. The two men talked for several minutes, exchanging details of the losses in their platoons. Then Lon went back to his own men. The two hours were nearly over.

Dawn. A light rain was falling on Oceanview, just enough to add to the misery Lon had started to feel. Second Battalion was on the move, following the trail left by the Belletieners. Charlie and Delta companies were leading the way, on parallel streets, with flanking squads farther away. Alpha and Bravo came behind, keeping three to four hundred yards of separation between them and the leading units, putting out their own flankers and the rearguard. Wil Nace's squad was on the left flank. Carl Hoper was taking care of the right flank and, for now, the rear.

Lon plodded along the left side of the street, between his platoons, only three men from Dav Grott's squad right with him, his unofficial security detail. As usual, that consisted of Phip, Janno, and Dean. The battalion's advance had been maddeningly slow, never as much as a mile in an hour, because the leading companies checked each building they passed to make certain that no Belletieners were lurking inside to ambush the rear of the formation. Colonel Flowers did not force the pace. He gave his men frequent breaks, a less than satisfactory relief for men who had had too little sleep and too much danger.

Despite aerial harassment and the arrival of ground troops to block their way, the Belletieners continued to press toward the governmental district of Oceanview. Neither the Calypsans nor Colonel Gaffney had been able to get enough troops in position to stop the enemy for more than a few minutes at a time. The Belletieners chose to go around blockades when they could, and when they could not, they went straight ahead, forcing their way through, leaving their dead and seriously wounded behind.

Attrition will stop them if nothing else does, Lon told himself. Each engagement cost the enemy. Already, this Belletiener force had a thousand fewer men than they had landed with. *What good will it do them to take Government House if they don't have the men to defend it?* Lon had no answer to the question. Little about the invasion made sense to him. He did not see how the government of Belletiene could hope to conquer Calypso now. It was sometime later before a random thought gave him what might have been at least a partial answer. *Gold lust has made men do crazy things for thousands of years.* And gold was one commodity that Calypso had in abundance.

Much of the time, Lon was unable to recall the talk he heard on the radio about troop movements, the variety of small engagements, and enemy casualties—both in the capital and in The Cliffs—seconds after he heard it. The fighting in The Cliffs had moved deep into the city, block by block through residential and commercial neighborhoods. A large part of Calypso's largest city was on fire. The Belletieners were burning buildings to deprive the defenders of cover.

It was all Lon could do to concentrate on the data he really needed, reports from his squads, information passed back from Delta and Charlie companies, and so forth. He walked with a leaden slowness and a glassy-eyed stare. Lon tried to force himself to be more alert, to pay more attention to his surroundings and to what he was hearing, but his efforts were never fully successful and did not last for long, despite his self-nagging and guilt. *I can't slack off; I'd give any of my men hell if I even thought they were being so negligent.*

Finally, there was a longer break. Word came back from Colonel Flowers to move into the nearest buildings, set watches, and take two hours. The colonel had recognized that his men needed more than ten minutes at a time, that they were getting to the point where they would be unable to function coherently, or cohesively, if a firefight did start.

Lon got his men situated, saw to the posting of guards, and then collapsed in a corner of the nearest room. There could be no walking around to talk to each of the squads to show the men how much he was concerned with the welfare. Lon's exhaustion was near total. He gave his mind over to the void that had been trying to claim it for hours. He was asleep before he could even complete a sigh of relief at being off his feet.

The two hours had nearly passed before Lon was wakened by a call from Captain Orlis. "The enemy has been stopped," Orlis announced. He paused, giving Lon a little time to force himself to some semblance of alertness. "There's a big fight going on, a few blocks west of Government House. For the time being, our orders are to stay put."

"How long?" Lon asked, forcing the words out past a yawn.

"I don't know. Figure at least another two hours."

• • •   •

Lon even managed one more hour of sleep for himself after taking a few minutes to check with each of his squad leaders, and with Tebba and Weil. It was only minutes short of noon when the respite finally ended.

"We're on the move again," Orlis told his lieutenants and their platoon sergeants. "The Belletieners are making a stand just west of where they were stopped, partly in government buildings and partly in the nearest civilian office buildings. The government wants them out. We move in five minutes."

Lon noticed that his men got up and ready to start hiking without protest, without much noise at all. It was not just sound discipline; they were *too* quiet. *A bad sign when they're too beat or discouraged to even grouse,* he thought. Lon looked around. It would do no good to say anything, but he knew that he would have to keep his eyes open, look for ways to bring his men out of their doldrums.

"Captain, any word on what's going on in The Cliffs?" Lon asked once the company was on the move.

"Nothing recent," Orlis replied. "The last word was that they're facing the same sort of problem we are. The Belletieners moved into the city, found a place to hold out, and started destroying buildings around them to provide wider zones of fire." Orlis paused, then said, "I know, none of this makes sense, unless they're expecting more troops from their homeworld, and there's no sign of that. Yet."

"They get more people in, we're going to be seriously overmatched," Lon said. "We're having enough trouble as it is." *And it'll still be weeks before we can expect any reinforcements,* Lon thought when Orlis did not respond.

Lon listened as the battle grew louder. Alpha was moving directly toward the noise. During the early part of their hike, they saw a few civilians, people daring to look out from whatever refuge they had found before—faces in doorways, behind windows, in the shadows. People looked, then faded back into the shadows, and into whatever safety they thought they had.

There was one extremely loud explosion, so massive that Lon felt the dying edge of the blast wave. A large cloud of black smoke rose above the buildings to the southeast. On the periphery, Lon saw two civilians drop to the ground inside a house, behind a large window that rattled but did not break.

Alpha Company stopped momentarily while Captain Orlis tried to find out what had happened. "The Belletieners had time to booby-trap a building facing the section where they've established their lines, enough explosives to collapse the structure," Orlis told his lieutenants and platoon sergeants. "Apparently it caught quite a few people inside, a platoon or more. I don't know if they were Dirigenters or Calypsans."

Lon felt a tightness in his throat and swallowed. Fifty or more men lost at once? If the building had collapsed, there seemed little chance that many would come out alive.

"If they rigged one building, they might have done others," Lon said. Captain Orlis did not bother to reply.

Alpha came under enemy fire three hundred yards from the Belletiener redoubt. At first, it was only from snipers with beamers, silent killers. Two men from fourth platoon went down before anyone knew that they were being shot at. Everyone scrambled for cover, moving to one side or the other. Since the columns had been close to buildings on either side of the street, cover was not far away. Lon followed Phip Steesen and Dav Grott through a doorway into the nearest structure. As he did, he thought of the building that had been blown up. It was that destruction that had apparently given the enemy snipers a clear shot at Alpha. The remains of the structure had been directly in front of them.

"Get men looking for explosives, quick," Lon told Tebba. "Check everything." Tebba nodded and started giving orders to squad leaders and individual soldiers.

Lon moved with the platoon's second squad, looking around himself. He lifted the faceplate of his helmet enough to let him breathe the air in the building without filtration.

The smell of spent explosives was thick, not quite a visible haze—the odor of gunpowder and grenades, the most familiar scent in the galaxy to a professional soldier. But there was no way a human nose could sniff out unexploded munitions, and those were the ones that could kill.

"Nothing in here, Lieutenant," Tebba said. "Nothing we can spot." The search had taken less than three minutes. If explosives had been concealed beyond where a quick inspection could look, there might still be danger.

"Okay. Keep two or three men looking, Tebba. We might be here for a bit. Captain says dig in and find whatever vantage we can for firing on the enemy. That means the east end of the building. The upstairs windows give us a clear field of fire?"

"Not much, Lieutenant. The windows and doors on the front and back of the building are better for that. There is an access ladder to the roof. I've already got fourth squad up there. Three-foot plascrete parapet around the roof gives them some cover. They've got clear fields of fire over the next building, into where the enemy's holed up."

"How much room is there on the roof?"

"I wouldn't want to risk more than one squad, Lieutenant," Tebba said. "It would crowd them together too much."

Lon nodded. "Weil's people are in that next building, between us and the enemy," he said. "Once we get settled in here, I'm going over there to have a look."

"Might be tricky," Tebba said. "No doors on that end, either building. You'd have to go out either one side or the other, then around. That might put you in somebody's sights."

Lon laughed, a short bark. "I can climb out a window if I have to, Tebba. And have somebody from fourth platoon open a window in the other building."

Tebba shrugged. "When you're ready to go, maybe I should send a couple of men with you."

"Not *with* me, Tebba. I don't need minders. If there's room for more of us in that next building, I'll call and have you send some of them across, get us closer to the enemy."

Lon moved toward the east end of the building, anxious to see for himself just what kind of fields of fire his men had. Captain Orlis talked to him briefly, to repeat that they would be staying put for the time being and to get where they could inflict damage on any enemy soldiers who showed themselves. "There's some kind of big powwow going on," Orlis said. "Trying to figure out what the hell we're going to do." Lon thought that he heard disgust in the captain's voice, but it was not clear enough for certainty.

We've got them bottled up, that's enough for now, Lon thought. *As long as there's not another Belletiener fleet coming our way, all we have to do is sit on them until they run out of food or ammunition. Wait them out. They'll have to surrender sooner or later.*

It sounded inescapably logical to Lon. But the thought gave him no comfort. The Calypsans seemed as incapable of logic in this fight as the Belletieners did.

25

The fight continued through the afternoon, mostly the exchange of rifle fire across two hundred yards of no man's land. The range was extreme for accurate RPG fire, and the Belletieners appeared to be short of rockets. Lon's guess was that they were saving any that they still had for use against Dirigenter Shrikes. The Belletieners had occupied an area that was about nine hundred yards square with some twenty large buildings in it. They had thrown up barricades across streets and between buildings, and—when any activity could be seen behind those barriers—it looked as if they were continuing to strengthen their defenses.

In response, the Calypsans and Dirigenters did what they could to fortify their own lines, putting a complete ring around the section of Oceanview that the enemy controlled. Where possible, men were moved forward into the buildings closest to the enemy, and behind new barricades between buildings. More sophisticated equipment was brought in to insure that no explosives had been planted in any of those buildings.

Lon's platoons moved a little closer to the enemy. There was one intact building beyond the one where fourth platoon had taken shelter when the sniping started. Both of Lon's platoons moved into that, and to either side of it, behind makeshift ramparts—two disabled ground-effect trucks, stacks of office furniture, and such stones and dirt as they could move into position. Trenches were dug behind the improvised barricades and extended to either side.

When sunset came, there was still no new plan from regiment.

"I think that's encouraging," Lon said. He was sitting with Tebba Girana. They were eating. "It means they haven't decided on anything foolish yet, like a frontal attack. We can just sit here and wait the Belletieners out."

"You don't sound very confident that we'll keep doing that," Tebba observed.

"I'm not counting on it," Lon said, very softly.

"I can't see Colonel Gaffney agreeing to risk us on something like that, not even after all the men we've lost." They had learned that the platoon lost in the destroyed building had been Dirigenter. Forty men from 1st Battalion were missing, presumed dead because no one had been able to get into the ruins to search for survivors.

A half hour later, there was an officers' call, on radio, for 2nd Battalion. "We have a new plan of operations," Colonel Flowers started. "I'm not happy with it, and none of you will be either, but we will carry out our orders, as always."

Here it comes, Lon thought. He closed his eyes as Flowers continued.

"Our contract calls for us to provide support for any Calypsan military action," Flowers said, "and they intend to attack the enemy troops in their capital city, requiring us to also attack. They will move first, on the east side of the enemy. Once their assault has begun, the rest of us are to move forward as well. We're to go in and clean out any enemy opposition remaining."

Colonel Gaffney should have been able to prevent this, Lon thought. *There's always a way.*

"We will make every effort to minimize our exposure and casualties," Flowers said. "Since this is to be a broad advance, all the way around, we'll set the fire and maneuver at company level, one platoon advancing while the other three provide maximum covering fire. We will also have close air support. Colonel Gaffney has ordered all of the Shrikes in to provide that, in three rotating shifts. It won't be constant cover, but it will be the best we can manage. As I understand the situation, the Calypsans have dropped their insistence that we defeat the enemy without damaging any of their precious buildings.'' There was no mistaking the bitterness in Flowers' voice as he said that.

''The Calypsans are scheduled to launch their assault in forty-five minutes. Our jumping-off time is five minutes after that happens, whether it's on schedule or not.''

''I don't like this, Lieutenant,'' Weil Jorgen said on a private channel. ''I'll carry out orders, but I want you to know I don't like it. There's no call for this.''

''Until we're promoted to the Council of Regiments, that's all any of us can do, Weil, carry out orders,'' Lon replied, keeping his voice as neutral as possible. That Jorgen spoke at all was a clear sign just how upset he was at the plan of staging a direct assault against the Belletiener enclave. ''Let's just do what we can to keep this from getting too costly.''

''One man dead from this cockamamie scheme is too costly.''

Truth, Lon thought, but—for the sake of discipline— could not say *I still can't believe the colonel is going along with this.* Anyone in the Corps could make suggestions, but the DMC was not a democracy. Once the orders were given, they would be obeyed. No army could function without that surety.

''Just have the men ready to go when the order comes,'' Lon said. Tebba had said much the same as Weil, but in more diplomatic words.

Lon watched his timeline carefully. He expected that he would hear the Calypsan assault before anything else, and perhaps see evidence of a sudden increase in the intensity of the fighting. The sniping back and forth had slowed. On both sides, men seemed to be doing what they could to conserve ammunition, firing only when there was a visible target.

If we don't move until five minutes after the Calypsans attack, there's still some hope, Lon thought, without really believing it. *There's always a chance they'll change their minds and not attack. Maybe Colonel Gaffney is still work-*

ing on their leaders, trying to convince them that this is stupid.

There might be times when a frontal attack on enemy positions would be the preferred tactic, but it was gospel in the Corps that those instances would be vanishingly rare. "There's almost always a more cost-effective alternative," one of the instructors in boot camp had told Lon's leadership class. "The challenge is to find it and not waste men. In the Corps, wasting men—spending them needlessly—is one of the worst sins."

Lon heard the sudden increase in gunfire. Distant though it was, it was quite noticeable. He checked the time, so that he would be ready for the order to attack. Five minutes. He mentioned the increase in gunfire to Tebba and Weil, along with his supposition that it marked the start of the Calypsan assault. He had scarcely finished that when Captain Orlis called to tell him that the five minutes was running.

Lieutenant Colonel Flowers had provided his company commanders with detailed instructions for their part of the attack. Beyond the beginning, though, Flowers conceded that the rest would have to be improvised. "We'll take advantage of whatever weaknesses we find," he had told his commanders. "Push as hard as we can without acting like lemmings."

Lon talked to each of his squad leaders, doing what he could to ease the tensions he knew they had to be feeling—because he was also feeling them. When there was just a minute left of the five, he stopped talking, waiting for the order to start forward. Alpha's first platoon would be the first to advance from the company, with the rest providing covering fire. Then second platoon. After that, it would be the turn of Lon's men, third and then fourth. Lon would move with third, as usual.

"The first four Shrikes are on the way," Captain Orlis informed his lieutenants. "They should start their attack runs in about ninety seconds. As soon as they hit, we start moving. On my order."

Where will they hit? Lon wondered. The men going in directly behind the air attack would have the best odds of getting through intact. The rockets and cannon of four Shrikes would disorganize anyone in the line of fire. *Maybe they'll spread it out, hit as much of the enemy line as possible.* He heard the fighters coming in, two pairs on separate vectors. Lon could not see the Shrikes. It was dark, and the aircraft would be nearly invisible to human or electronic eyes.

The rockets came first. Their trails were visible as their fiery exhaust streaked the night. Then the planes started to strafe the buildings on the Belletiener perimeter, pulling to right or left to cover as much of the front as possible.

"First platoon, go!" Captain Orlis ordered over his command channel. "The rest of you, covering fire."

Lon repeated the orders for his men, aiming at a second-floor window on the enemy line and squeezing off a first burst while he was talking, as first platoon started to advance. He moved his point of aim from window to window, looking for any movement, any sign of an enemy weapon.

Second platoon moved, covered by first already out in front and by third and fourth behind. The Shrikes made another pass at the enemy buildings, hitting different sections this time, spreading their munitions around as much as possible.

Then it was third platoon's turn.

Lon was the first man forward, with Janno Belzer, Dean Ericks, and Phip Steesen close to him—Phip to his right, the others to his left. The arrangement was not Lon's doing. His friends had set themselves their usual task of staying with Lon in danger. They moved forward on hands and knees, then went down on their stomachs, rifles carried over their forearms, held by the slings. They had twenty yards to cover, to the curbing on the east side of the street. The few inches of plascrete marking the edge of the avenue would be their only cover.

The Belletieners were shooting only sporadically, never in great volume. Lon did not know if that was because the suppressive fire by the rest of the company was so successful or if the Belletieners were simply not organized yet . . .

or if they were too short on ammunition to deal with even a direct assault of this nature.

As soon as the platoon reached the curb, the men moved their rifles into firing position and started targeting the windows and doorways that might harbor Belletieners. Along part of the line, Lon's people could only aim at the upper stories of the nearest enemy-held building. The collapsed ruins of the building that had been demolished with Dirigenters inside was in the way.

Next time, we'll be going through that, Lon thought. "Tebba, when we get to that building, I want squad leaders and assistants listening for any sounds that might indicate survivors under the rubble," he said.

"Right, Lieutenant."

Fourth platoon was on its way. They would go to the edge of the destroyed building. Lon divided his attention between providing his share of the covering fire and watching the progress of his other platoon. Enemy fire was beginning to get more organized. Lon saw one man in fourth platoon struck by a slug. The bullet hit the man's leg, just above the boot. The leg jerked. The man stopped for an instant, then started pulling himself forward again, favoring the wounded leg, leaving a thin trail of blood. Cover was ten yards away. He would attend to the wound then.

There was only a minimal pause before the platoons started the next rotation, moving forward. Two Shrikes made a run across the front, at an angle, rockets opening up holes in two of the buildings along the Belletiener perimeter. The gaps were high, though, one on the second floor, the other near the top of the third floor of the second building. *Nothing that will give us ways in,* Lon thought, shaking his head.

"We won't be close enough to use RPGs until we get to the far side of the ruins," Lon told Tebba and Weil. "I want the grenadiers ready then."

First platoon had pushed forward only five yards past fourth. Second started past them, each man flat on his stomach, head down, barely able to see three or four feet in front of him.

Lon felt a tug at his right foot, as if someone were trying to yank the boot from it. He turned and looked. Part of the boot's heel had been ripped free, obviously by a bullet. Lon felt no pain, and he was able to wiggle his toes and flex the foot without discomfort. *Close,* he thought, letting out a breath and drawing the foot in nearer his body. *Too close.*

Second platoon stopped ten feet in front of first. Lon ordered third platoon forward again. "We're going all the way to the rubble this side of the building," he said on the platoon channel. "Just keep going. We'll have better cover there. I want the men out on the side to slide in so the whole platoon's behind decent cover." Fourth would also be coming up to the razed building, to Lon's left, overlapping on the far side. He would give them the same instructions when their turn came.

Lon pushed forward, crawling as rapidly as he could on his stomach, elbows and feet digging into the turf for leverage once he was off the paved street. The ruins provided more cover than the curbing, but—at least along the west frontage—nothing stood above three feet high. Two men in Ben Frehr's squad had been wounded in this last push. One injury was slight, the other required another man to administer first aid after dragging the casualty to the cover of the wall.

Fourth platoon started forward again. Lon turned his attention to the enemy, spending ammunition more freely this time. He was up on one knee, exposing little of himself past the side of one of the higher portions of the ruins. His concentration was so intense that he was scarcely aware of the talk on the command channel, commentary on the firefight from a dozen voices, officers and platoon sergeants talking about what they were facing.

When third platoon started forward again, they were in the debris of the building. Blocks of plascrete, beams, and bits of furniture blocked their way. The footing was treacherous. Things tipped or slid underfoot. Lon fell to the side, going limp and bringing his arms in close to his body to minimize the possibility of serious injury, taking the impact on his shoulder and helmet. Other than a moment of vertigo, he was uninjured—except for aches that would soon fade into insignificance.

Fourth platoon was already moving into the ruins as well, past Lon. His platoons were soon the most advanced part of 2nd Battalion's share of the assault. The rest of Alpha moved sideways, taking cover behind the western edge of the debris. It broke the symmetry of the attack, but gave the battalion a solid core, a thumb almost in the eye of the enemy, and the 150 men still fit for action were able to give much more effective covering fire for the companies to either side.

Rocket-propelled grenades started arcing from the ruins toward the enemy buildings that were now within range. Some of the grenadiers were extremely accurate, able to put a grenade through a window at their weapons' maximum effective range.

"Lieutenant, there's no way we can tell if there's anyone alive under this rubble," Tebba said after third platoon had been in it for five minutes. "With all the racket, we might miss ten men screaming for help at the top of their lungs."

"We've got to make the effort, Tebba," Lon replied. *There wouldn't be any of them screaming anyway. If anyone was conscious, he'd have used his helmet radio to call for help . . . if he still had a working radio.*

The attack was finally showing results. Gunfire from within the Belletiener defenses slackened, and did not pick up when the other companies of 2nd Battalion continued their advance.

"Our turn again," Orlis told Lon. "Same rotation as before." The captain had moved close to Lon a couple of minutes earlier, but they were still communicating by radio.

"Too close in for crawling now, isn't it, Captain?" Lon asked. "Aren't we to the point where it's better to get there as fast as possible?"

"Just about," Orlis said, "but not yet. At least not until the last platoon leaves the cover of this . . . building. Colonel Flowers will give the order."

At the eastern edge of the debris, Lon found himself hesitating behind the last vestige of cover. Briefly, Lon felt fear grabbing at him, tugging; he did not want to abandon that final illusion of safety. He felt his hands trembling, recognized his fear and forced himself over the slab of wall in defiance of it. He dropped to the ground on the other side and crawled away, far enough to dispel any fancy of going back. Then he looked left and right, checking on the positions of his men. Third platoon moved forward then.

Fourth platoon was moving past when Captain Orlis passed along the order to fix bayonets. Lon pulled his bayonet from its sheath and attached it to the muzzle of his rifle. The operation took little more than a second.

The nearest enemy-held positions were still a hundred yards away. There was some rifle fire coming from the buildings and from the makeshift ramparts between them, but too little to stop the battalion, and too ineffective to cause the extreme casualties that a stalwart defense would have inflicted.

Let's get it over with! Lon thought, glancing in the general direction of Captain Orlis. *Get up and get in.*

"The Calypsans have broken through on the east side," Orlis said a few seconds later. "They're reporting a complete breach, but with heavy fighting continuing."

It was another minute, another round of crawling forward for third platoon, before Orlis returned with the order that Lon had been anticipating. "On your feet! Let's go. At the double."

Lon was on his feet almost before the order was out, glancing to either side to make certain that his men were getting up. Then Alpha moved forward at a jog, a disciplined, slow run. The pace was designed to let a man fire his weapon with *some* effectiveness at targets within a hundred yards, and the enemy was within that range now. As soon as the Dirigenters were on their feet, the volume of fire from the enemy compound increased dramatically. It was not just that the same men started firing more rapidly. Lon was certain that there were more of the enemy shooting than before. *They've been waiting for this,* he thought, feeling his face flush, as if he had embarrassed himself. *Waiting for us to give them easy targets.*

But the enemy had to present a target in order to go after one. Lon shot at each hint of a Belletiener, spraying freely, no longer holding to the discipline of a three-shot burst. He changed magazines on his rifle; he was fifty yards from the enemy.

There was a doorway in front of Lon. The double doors had been blown out earlier. Pieces of them were visible. Lon aimed directly for that opening, ready to charge in and face whatever he might find. For the moment, he had forgotten the demands of leadership. All he could think of was getting out of the open and closing with the enemy as quickly as possible. His pace increased. He did a lot of running in garrison. As a teenager on Earth, he had thought that he might have championship talent. He very nearly broke into an all-out sprint over the last forty yards.

At the last moment, Phip veered just enough to make Lon break step and slow down. Janno and Dean moved ahead of them, going through the doorway first. One man turned to each side. Lon saw the flaring of muzzle blasts as they scoured the entryway, shooting first. There would be no need to ask questions later.

It was no more than an entryway, sixteen feet wide and twenty long, with doors to either side and a narrow corridor extending to the other side of the building. There were stairs and elevators near the rear. Janno and Dean moved toward the stairs as the rest of their squad came in the doorway behind Lon. They had only a fraction of a second's warning as a hand grenade bounced down the stairway from the second floor.

"Grenade!" Janno shouted as he and Dean both dived to the side. The rest of the Dirigenters in the foyer also went down—the only recourse any of them had.

The grenade exploded as it hit the fourth step, and that was perhaps all that let anyone in the foyer survive. Most of the shrapnel went up or straight out to the side. The men on the floor were below most of it.

Most of it.

Lon felt hot metal lance his back, through his pack or burrowing under it from the side. The burning sensation was all he felt at first. When debris stopped raining down on him after the blast, he looked around, already starting to get to his feet. A few of his men were quicker, firing rifles up toward the landing on the second floor.

Not everyone was able to get up. Janno remained down. So did Dean. Dav Grott, the acting squad leader, got to his knees, then fell forward again, barely catching himself before his face could hit the floor.

"Phip, take the rest of the squad. Get whoever's up there," Lon said. "I'll be with you as soon as I check on the others."

Only six men were able to follow Phip up the stairway to the second floor. Lon called the other squad leaders, to check on their situations, and to find one squad to come in immediately to help second. "This is where access to the upper stories is," he said. "This is where we've got to go up."

There was hand-to-hand combat in the rooms on the first floor that Lon's men had broken into. A few Belletieners had turned and run when it was clear that their line was about to be overrun. But more stayed and continued to fight.

In the foyer, Lon was amazed that none of his men had been killed by the grenade. Three men—Dav, Janno, and Dean—would need time in a trauma tube—*soon*. Everyone else had minor wounds. As soon as Lon had helped staunch the bleeding on the seriously wounded, he went on up the stairs. Phip and the rest of the squad were fighting on the second floor.

Lon called the other squad leaders again and told them to hurry. There were enemy soldiers on the upper floors of the building, and second squad needed help.

The squad had not managed to get off the landing on the second floor. One man stood at the stairwell, making certain that no one could drop a grenade from the top story of the building. The others were at doors. They had thrown their own grenades into the adjoining rooms, but there were Belletieners waiting, returning fire—and coming out, ready to engage.

Bayonets and fists. Lon moved into the fray. A few seconds later, part of first squad came up the stairs, and the fight moved from the foyer into a large room at the side. Lon faced off against one soldier—a faceless figure behind a tinted faceplate. The maneuvering was too quick to be thought out in advance. This was where training, and scores of hours drilling the standard tactics of bayonet fighting, paid off. The adversaries thrust and parried, working for the advantage that would mean survival. Lon gritted his teeth and pressed his foe as hard as he could, his goal being to kill, and kill quickly.

The fight ended when Lon's opponent, taking a step backward, slid on blood and went off balance. Lon reacted instantly, parrying the man's rifle up and out of line, then thrusting forward, burying his own bayonet in the man's chest. Lon twisted his rifle as the blade went in, and kept twisting as he pulled it back. He had to drop the man to the floor and put his foot on him to free the bayonet. The man was dead by then.

Another Belletiener moved toward Lon, lowering his rifle as if to fire. But he did not get a shot off. Lon brought his rifle up and pulled the trigger, stopping the enemy soldier and dropping him with at least four hits.

Lon looked around. Phip was still fighting. Lon clicked to Steesen's radio channel and said, "Drop!" Phip collapsed immediately, and Lon shot his opponent. One shot was all that took, which was fortunate for Phip, because Lon's magazine was now empty.

The fight on the second floor was over. Lon went out to the hallway. Third and fourth squads had moved to the top floor. They reported that the fighting was over there as well.

For Lon and his men, the second Battle of Oceanview had ended.

26

By noon the fighting was over in both Oceanview and
The Cliffs. More than four thousand Belletiener prisoners
were taken to a location northwest of the Calypsan capital
and forced to build their own POW camp under heavily
armed supervision. The Calypsans and Belletieners buried
their dead. The mercenaries who had died were taken up
to their ships to be returned home for burial. The wounded
were treated. The remaining soldiers of the 7th Regiment
rested.

Four days later, after the government of Belletiene continued to refuse to acknowledge any radio transmissions
from Calypso, Colonel Arnold Gaffney took the Dirigenter
fleet to Belletiene's territorial space and put the ships in a
parking orbit over the world's major population centers.

From three hundred miles directly above the capital of
Belletiene, Gaffney broadcast his ultimatums. Key to forcing a response was his threat to bombard that city and destroy any Belletiener spacecraft in the system. Gaffney's
message required the Belletiener government to send del-
egates with plenipotentiary authority to conclude a treaty
of peace with Calypso. Gaffney went beyond his authority
when he threatened Belletiene with the unlimited use of the
Dirigent Mercenary Corps to force compliance and insure
that Belletiene adhered to the treaty that he was ready to
dictate.

"I was beyond caring about such delicacies," Gaffney
said in his final report on the Calypso contract. "Seventh
Regiment had suffered a total of more than four hundred
men killed on Calypso, with an additional one hundred and

twenty-seven men injured severely enough to require lengthy regeneration and rehabilitation periods. While I accept my share of responsibility for the extent of our casualties, my state of mind at the time was such that I could think of little beyond the fact that it was the worst casualty count that any regiment of the Corps has suffered since the Wellman debacle—and the unmistakable necessity of insuring that Belletiene would not attempt a third invasion of Calypso while my men were still on that world.''

By the time 2nd Regiment arrived to reinforce 7th, the treaty between Calypso and Belletiene had been signed, all prisoners had been repatriated, and Belletiene had made the first installment on a staggering reparations bill that Colonel Gaffney had insisted upon. That payment included the funds to pay off Calypso's full contract with the Corps—which Gaffney promptly accepted and transferred to his ship.

Three days after the arrival of 2nd Regiment, Gaffney and his men returned to their transports and started for home. Before they left, Gaffney sent an MR ahead, informing the Council of Regiments of their expected date of arrival . . . and included his resignation from the Corps—to avoid the embarrassment of being forced to resign when a court of inquiry or court-martial finished examining his decisions on Calypso.